(1179)

W9-BZF-546

Wrong Man in the Mirror

Books by Philip Loraine

And to My Beloved Husband
The Break in the Circle
The Angel of Death
Day of the Arrow
W. I. L. One to Curtis
The Dead Men of Sestos
A Mafia Kiss
Photographs Have Been Sent to Your Wife
Voices in an Empty Room
Wrong Man in the Mirror

Wrong Man in the Mirror

Philip Loraine

Random House: New York

Copyright © 1975 by Philip Loraine

All rights reserved under International
and Pan-American Copyright Conventions.
Published in the United States by Random House, Inc., New York
Originally published in Great Britain as *Ask the Rattlesnake*
by William Collins Sons & Company, Ltd., London.

Library of Congress Cataloging in Publication Data
Loraine, Philip, pseud.
Wrong man in the mirror.
I.   Title.
PZ3.L8838Wr3 [PR6062.067]   823'.9'14   75-12701
ISBN 0-394-49810-0

Manufactured in the United States of America

9 8 7 6 5 4 3 2

First American Edition

Part I

The Waiting Man

One

The small girl was now sure that the man was following her. A chill north wind had sprung up suddenly, as it often does on the beaches of Southern California; like a stiff broom it was sweeping Malibu clean. Surfers still in their dream, hastily reassembled families, clinched lovers, paddling ladies with veined legs—all were skittering away towards Santa Monica, leaving the small girl alone, sand cold between her toes, alone with the man who followed her.

The emptying beach made him conspicuous, so he had gone up onto the highway and was moving along it parallel with her; she glimpsed him out of the corner of her eye every now and again as he appeared between seaward-facing houses or apartment buildings.

She was eleven years old; her name was Joanne Christina Kenny, and only the discerning could recognize that one day she might well become beautiful. She had certainly worked hard to disguise the possibility, and when Joanne Christina worked hard at a thing, she invariably achieved her aim. The jeans were too baggy; the loose shirt hanging outside them successfully hid any suggestion of hips or waist; the face was still a childish oval egg waiting to hatch into distinctive personality; but the eyes were extraordinary, a brilliant piercing blue, snapping on everything and retaining it. Not wanting any old person to look directly into her soul (she agreed one hundred percent that the eyes were the mirror of it), and not wanting to be extraordinary in any way, she always wore large round tinted glasses. Her grand-mother, with whom she lived, began each admonition or serious conversation with the words "For God's sake, take those dreadful things off your nose!"

She paused to examine an uninteresting piece of seaweed, wondering whether she was scared at the idea of being followed by a man with a beard. On the whole, no—but it was a pity about the beard, underneath it he might be handsome. Without him, the beach would be more boring than usual; she had wanted to spend the day out in the desert, but nobody had seemed at all willing to take her there. That was one of the terrible things about being eleven: you were entirely reliant on adults when it came to getting from A to B; though as a matter of fact, and without the adults realizing it, Joanne Christina was a great deal less reliant than most other children of her age. There were ways; oh yes, if you worked hard at it, there were certainly ways.

Where was the man now? She caught a glimpse of him half hidden behind a group of surfers who were packing their gear into a Volkswagen camper.

Was there . . . could there possibly be some plot against her regarding the desert? Adults could be very sneaky in certain respects, and never thought twice about adopting tactics for which they would instantly bawl you out if you used them yourself. Her grandmother was not above a little quiet snooping when it suited her; was it conceivable that she had discovered the big glass pickle jar, its tin lid pierced with holes—discovered it and guessed its purpose, which was to contain the rattlesnake when and if Joanne Christina succeeded in capturing it?

Impossible! The jar could just as well be intended for . . . butterflies; her grandmother was remarkably quick on the uptake, but she wasn't psychic, for God's sake!

Well, they could stonewall her any way they liked; she intended to get to the desert and she intended to bag a rattler, and that was that.

A thought flashed through her mind, banishing the desert altogether: she had seen the man with the beard before. Yes, it was true, she had. Now where?

She stood for a time gazing at the waves, searching her

memory, fascinated by the idea that she was the object of continued, not just casual, scrutiny. Was it . . . ? Yes it was: at Maisie's on Sunset, last Tuesday, just as she was about to buy herself a Special Nut-Crunch Fudge Sundae with hot chocolate sauce. (Oh, how she longed to get fat, with all the grownups in sight going on and on and on about their boring *neurotic* diets, but maddeningly, not an ounce could she gain.)

The man had disappeared. Perhaps she was imagining the whole thing, anyway. He was going to kidnap her and demand a million dollars from Grandmother Virginia, who would refuse to pay—natch! So then he'd cut off one of her ears and send it to 234 Upper Canyon Circle, and Old Virginnypants would have the screaming hysterics and faint into the arms of every good-looking man who happened to be within screaming distance (at her age!), and still she'd refuse to pay, even though peeling off a million would hurt her rather less than peeling off an Estée Lauder beauty mask. So then the Beard would cut off her other ear, or maybe one of her boobs . . .

She paused, looking down doubtfully at her flat chest; then she jumped up and down a couple of times. Only when she jumped up and down was there any indication at all that she might at some future date sprout a pair of breasts: she could feel something jiggling about under her shirt, but when she took the shirt off and looked at herself in the mirror, there was nothing there. Not that *she* cared, it was old Virginia who showed such intense interest. As far as she was concerned, she didn't care if she *never* sprouted them; she'd have her hair cut and dress like a man and that would be the end of that. She wouldn't even have to alter her name, since she was known as Chris, anyway, having long ago dumped Joanne Christina, and having been defeated in the matter of Jo, or even Joe, by her grandmother, who occasionally drew a line somewhere: "You can't walk about all your life sounding like a hamburger joint!"

She bent right over, looking between her legs towards the highway, and saw, in spite of a tangle of hair and falling glasses, that the man was still watching her. As she straightened up he disappeared again.

So she hadn't imagined him. Was she scared? No, not exactly. It wasn't even the first time that a man had followed her, but this

5

one was sober and young and showed no inclination to open his fly and wave anything at her. She jumped up and down again a few times, and came to the conclusion that cutting off a boob and sending it to 234 Upper Canyon Circle was right out of the question. He was probably just a nutso, in any case—nothing really *interesting* ever happened to her.

"That's it," she said aloud to the Pacific, which was assuming one of its mean and steely moods, "he's nuts. Just my luck!"

A very wet and rangy and worried-looking dog that had been nosing about in a tangle of seaweed looked up at her doubtfully, unsure of whether he had been addressed or not; he wagged a raggedy plume of tail politely. Chris said "Hi!" The dog, who could recognize another loner when he saw one, picked up a piece of driftwood and brought it to her, laying it neatly at her feet. The small girl took it and flung it hard at the Pacific Ocean; the dog sped after it, meeting a spiteful wave head-on and plunging through it with practiced ease.

Turning, Chris saw a man-made depression in the sand, with a sandy headrest at one end of it; she recognized this: here, some hours before, she had left Leo basting himself in hot sun. Leo was Grandmother Virginia's latest male attachment, no better and not much worse than any of the others. ("Now, dahling, why don't you jump into that *nice* new car of yours and whisk little Chrissy down to the beach?" Leo, who could have basted the body almost-beautiful just as successfully by the pool, had given little Chrissy a dark look but had all the same bundled her into his Mercedes. He had no option, Chris guessed, since old Virginia must have had a hand in transforming his beat-up Mustang into this glittering white status symbol.) Anyway, he at least had the sense to accept Chris's hostility and contempt at their face value; some of his predecessors had tried a kind of Jolly Uncle approach, with disastrous results.

She raised her eyes from Leo's tanning-nest to the Golden Marlin, where they had arranged to meet. Although it was only a few minutes after five, she could see that the chill north wind had filled the place to capacity with a gaggle of already intoxicated adults. It was a sight and a sound to which she was well accustomed. Her grandmother was remorselessly sociable; even when she wasn't entertaining officially, the pre-dinner martini trip was seldom shared by less than six casual guests, chuntering on and on about the movies they'd been in and the people they'd known, who were invariably dipso or dead. Joanne Christina was too young to care that she was mixing with the *crème de la crème* of Hollywood's grand old, great old days when God was in his heaven (where? at Metro?) and stars were stars. As far as she was concerned, they had to be nuts, every one of them, since the movies they were forever talking about could be seen any night on the Late or Late-Late Show, and boy, were they *terrible!*

The dog had reappeared, laying the piece of driftwood neatly at her feet again; the man with the beard was nowhere to be seen, but she had a feeling that he was in the parking lot of the Golden Marlin. The dog shook himself violently, drenching her, which was okay, since it could only improve the quality of her entry into that bar full of freaked-out adults. She picked up the driftwood and flung it as far as she could along the beach; the dog streaked away after it, scattering sandpipers that were busy pursuing the lacy and retreating edge of each wave before being repulsed by the advance of its successor.

Chris ran quickly up the wooden steps leading to the bar and restaurant. The shriek of alcohol-maddened humans surged over her as she opened the door. A few of them gave her distracted glances, but looked away quickly, as if fearing that she presented some kind of a problem which they themselves might be called upon to solve.

The small girl had made a bet with herself that she would find Leo with at least one busty, and probably well-heeled, broad draped around him, and she wasn't disappointed. If he had disengaged himself any more swiftly, the lady in question would surely have fallen flat on the floor. Chris understood that he hadn't yet grasped the fact that she was no carrier of tales, even though her grandmother's antics vis-à-vis men were a constant source of fascination. She was also feminine enough to take pleasure from the fact that scruffy old Joanne Christina, aged eleven, was in the process of abducting the only remotely attractive man in the whole bar.

"Kid doesn't like friend Leo. Why? Leo's quite high, feels like being buddies. Kid walks ahead of him, gets into Merc, slams door—but *hard*. Leo's mad, pulls open his door, looks as if he's going to tell her go screw. No—thinks better of it.

"Jesus, she's some kid! Gives him a look like he's shit, which he probably is. The kid may be a danger. Note this, the kid may be a danger.

"Leo gets in beside her. Makes a zing-zang takeoff to impress a couple of passing birds. Must be forty at least, but behaves like a dumb teenager. Leo's weak. Check this: is Leo weak? Or acting? Check Leo."

The bearded man, sitting in the dilapidated Chevrolet pickup, switched off the small cassette recorder and watched the white Mercedes recede swiftly along the Pacific Coast Highway towards its junction with Sunset Boulevard. Even if she had been close to him, Chris would have been unable to say whether or not he was good-looking; he wore both his beard and hair long: dark gold streaked a little with grey. A full mustache hid the lines of the mouth. That left the eyes and the nose. The nose was straight, even aristocratic; the eyes were brown under strong brows, and they were watering.

Damnable contact lenses—would he never get used to them? Were they, in fact, the best that money could buy, or had that bum in Portland screwed him? He took their case from his pocket, and bending low so that no passer-by should see, slipped them expertly out of his eyes, which were revealed as being, in fact, a hard grey, as steely as the ocean confronting him.

He mopped the eyes with a tissue; then sat for a time in deep thought; then activated the little recorder once again: "I let the kid see me. Stupid—needn't have done so. Does this matter? Check carefully: *does it matter that the kid became aware of me?* Range, never less than a hundred yards in failing sun. Are her eyeglasses a gimmick or corrective? Check this."

The question now was whether it was necessary to go bird-watching again? This was beach weather. Only a few miles inland the sun might be shining on Coldwater Canyon; Los Angeles was like that. Yes, he knew L.A. At least that was one thing he didn't have to research. He knew it and he hated it, but he felt at ease in the dump; if he had been forced to go to work in, say, Chicago, Phoenix, Philadelphia . . . No good. There was something about knowing a place; the minds of the people in that place operated in a certain way. He had never set foot in a house remotely resembling 234 Upper Canyon Circle, yet he knew it instinctively because he could feel his way instinctively into the minds of the people who lived there.

Yes. If the sun had begun to show by the time he reached the freeway, he would spend an hour bird-watching.

As he drove he examined himself: this new fear which had erupted the night before, fear that he would never actually move, never bring himself to the moment of truth, the point of no return. He had spent so long in research, preparation—years! That seemed incredible, but it was true; he had spent *years* in preparation. And now . . . now, the longer he put off the moment of truth, the more it seemed to him that he would never arrive at it.

He said aloud, "Maybe I'm an eternal student." Oh yes, he'd read Chekhov. That was one for the book! He'd read Dostoevsky too. Somehow or other, they'd appeared among the Marx and the Mao. Why not? Whatever else the Vietcong had been, they were certainly not stupid; they probably reckoned that Chekhov and Dostoevsky had as much to say as Karl Marx about revolution in Russia, and they were probably right. No, he was not the eternal student, but it was a real fear that had haunted him last night and, perhaps, a real danger. He could not afford to delay much longer; he must act, he must cancel out the years of preparation by that one moment of action.

But even as he thought of it, his stomach contracted in anticipatory fear. All those years, all that obsession (yes, it was an obsession now; he could not turn his back on so vital a fact), all this work, risk, sleepless nights, all depending on one appalling moment of truth.

His headache was coming back; the pain seemed to creep up from his wounded jaw into the back of his skull. Was he a sick man still? Was he even insane? The thought made him lift first one hand, then the other, from the steering wheel. The fingertips looked almost normal again, except that the new skin was smooth, unmarked; but the memory of that agony, joining the pain in his skull, did not answer the question, they only underlined it: Was he even insane?

No, he was obsessed. There was a difference. Or was there?

He needed to act, once and for all, decisively. He must begin the countdown. Soon. Once the countdown started, there would be no drawing back. He must reach that point from which there could be no return. Beyond it . . . Oh God, he felt sick, physically sick, but that was the price of obsession; also, his own personal price for that goddam war which never existed: the war which never began and never ended and never achieved anything.

He parked on Mulholland in the usual place. He removed the cassette from the recorder and put it inside the headband of his bush hat; he rammed the hat on the back of his head and hid the recorder under the driving seat. From beneath the passenger seat he dragged the dirty old canvas bag containing his binoculars, reference books and sketchpad. He got out of the pickup and went to the edge of the road where a few feet of scrubby sun-blasted grass separated it from the drop below, and he sat down in his usual place.

The police car might or might not come by around six-fifteen. In case it did, he turned a new page of the sketchpad, opened *Birds of Western America* and made a quick but adequate copy of Gilmore's hawk, ". . . at one time almost extinct, but now making a welcome reappearance in the foothills of the Sierra Nevada."

The cops had stopped a couple of times. He had shown them his hospital card and Dr. Kallman's letter; he had also shown them his amateurish drawings and, as luck would have it, a pair of jays at their mating games. The cops had become quite interested ("You mean they fuck in the *air!*"), and in any case, they were Los Angeles men operating in their own area, who probably didn't care if this amiable freak *was* planning to rob one of the plush joints down the canyon in Beverly Hills. Not that they suspected him of any ulterior motive, as far as he could tell; and he was pretty good at telling what was on the minds of Authority after those weary years in a Vietcong POW camp outside Hanoi.

It was a good position in any case, overlooking a vast tract of still-undeveloped hillside. There were few houses in sight, and none directly below him; yet, by raising the binoculars only a few inches, he could see, over the hill which hid most of Coldwater Canyon, the top end of Upper Canyon Circle and the whole garden face of Number 234, including the walkway from the garages, though not what was inside them, the pool and a stretch of the drive.

This evening there were three women and two men on the terrace (it was really a little too grand to be called a patio), but no sign of Leo, who was doubtless beautifying himself indoors, nor of Chris, who was usually absent anyway. Her grandmother, Virginia Kenny, lay back on a white chaise facing the binoculars directly. The man with the beard recommenced his study of her, hunched in concentration.

As far as he could tell, she looked particularly good tonight, a woman in her early forties rather than the middle fifties. She was talking, telling some amusing story. The others laughed but she did not even smile; she had this habit of turning away when other people laughed at what she had said, turning away almost as if impatient with herself. Still turned, she spoke again. He ached, with a sickening physical ache, to know what she was saying.

She was saying, "Cass forgave him; I never did."

One of the men said, "Cass forgave everybody, God bless him."

Virginia Kenny stayed with her head turned away. She was thinking that it would be pleasant to say to these men and women, "Yes, Cass forgave everybody. He even forgave you bitches when you never raised a finger to help him. A bit part would have done, *any* part, and each of you could have gotten one for him with a nod of the head, you were all big then. But did you? Did you—hell!"

She looked back at them, smiling softly, examining the famous faces. While Leo and her granddaughter had been at the beach she had spent her day in the beauty salon; all that pummeling and smoothing and cleansing and polishing had invested her with a new lease on life. She felt as good as she looked: a tall, leggy American blonde who had once been miserable because she wasn't pretty; now she thanked God for it; prettiness faded fast, as two of the once-worshipped female faces sitting opposite her demonstrated all too plainly. Good bones, imagination and the right clothes could still create, in her, an illusion of beauty, though in fact she had never been beautiful either. Experience was what mattered—experience, as much happiness as you could wrest from life, and she had wrested her share, and love.

Smiling, she would like to have said to these defunct dinosaurs, "Well, my darlings, Cass showed you in the end, didn't he? Suddenly the whole shebang slipped away from under you, and here you sat in your palaces wondering what had hit you, while my Cass was still making a fortune in Europe. Serves you right!" But still smiling, all she said was, "Yes, God bless him."

As always, the thought of that husband whom she had loved made everyone else seem small and dull. And, oh Jesus, Peter was going to tell them *again* about the latest addition to his family! Would he never stop this rabbitlike breeding? Hadn't he proved his point *yet*? And Janey, poor slob, was pretending that the latest young Roman candle of a director from New York wanted her to play the mother in his new picture, when everybody knew that everybody in show business would rather have Medusa on the set.

Why had she ever come back? Why had she bought this goddam barn of a house? Why hadn't she stayed in Europe, where everybody had loved her because they had loved Cass? Because she hadn't had the courage, that's why. So many corners, so many faces, so many bars, towers, vistas, smells would have pecked and picked at her grief.

That had been ten . . . no, twelve years ago. In those twelve years she had lost her husband and her son. Was she an unnatural mother? Why did the loss of Cass pain her more, still, than the loss of their only child? Could it mean that still, after so long, something deep inside her refused to believe that he was really dead? She shook her head at this thought, and Jerry, the idiot, said, "You don't agree? I think it was the best performance he ever gave."

"I liked him better in *Secret Games*." She could carry on these conversations in her sleep, let alone when her thoughts were elsewhere. If only the official notification of her son's death had read "Killed in action" and not "Missing, believed killed in action." And then there had been that letter . . .

No! She wrenched herself away from the subject with an effort. Cass was dead, and Jeff was dead, and she was unable to make contact with the only living person she really cared about, her granddaughter, who spent most of her time on the other side of a chasm over which there seemed to be no bridge.

She could hear Leo coming across the drawing room. She wondered glumly why men were still necessary to her, or indeed, *if* they were still necessary. Really, she must throw off this mood at once, or the evening would end up wrecked on it. She smiled at him and said, "You all know Leo."

The others paused in their incestuous talk for a moment and gave Leo, each according to judgment, the look or greeting which best balanced their private opinion of him with decent respect for their hostess. Yes, they all knew Leo. A shadow of weariness passed over the terrace like a breath of wind. They had all known so many Leos on so many terraces over so many years.

The talk resumed: ". . . but of course we'll tour it before Broadway . . . Bought a couple of options . . . Heard she's living in London now, God knows who with . . . Listen, I said, who's *not* interested in TV these days?"

They bored her, they bored her to death. Then why ask them? Where was Chris? Where was reality, with its piercing eyes and its shapeless clothes covering some fear of womanhood? Probably sitting up in her room, near the window, listening to all this garbage and despising it, despising her because she seemed to be a part of it.

Well, Chris, we all do the best we can. If you can do better, good luck to you!

She seized on Leo, because . . . Why? Because in his own way he at least was honest. He wasn't very much and he didn't pretend to be very much; he had charm, he was expert in bed and he adored the good things of life which he was unable to afford. She could afford them, and so they took each other at face value. They were the only honest people on her terrace tonight.

"Darling." She turned, holding out a hand to him. He took it with relief and sat down next to her. "Tell me about your day on the beach? Did Chris do anything terrible?"

Darkness was falling now. The bearded man could no longer maintain his watch through the binoculars; the strain on his eyes was too great. The prowl car had passed by over an hour ago. One of the cops had raised a hand in greeting; he had waved back. He'd become part of the scenery—that was how he wanted it.

Activity on the terrace, which was now a soft glow of light, made him raise the binoculars again. They were all moving, standing up. The small girl had appeared, wearing the clothes she had worn on the beach; among so much casual but expensive elegance she looked like a beetle among butterflies; she was shaking her head with determination.

Leo appeared with a white shawl, which he put around Virginia's shoulders.

Now—which restaurant would it be? He must guess and the guess must be correct. It mattered, it was vital. Friday was a busy night in L.A., so they'd choose somewhere exclusive; not totally exclusive, like Riccardo's where you only got in if Riccardo himself knew and liked you; that was kept for Saturdays when everywhere else was quite impossible. Somewhere like La Bonne Table or Scotty's. No, she wasn't dressed for Scotty's.

He told himself that it didn't really matter whether he guessed where they were going or not; it would matter on one night only, and that night was not yet. But the obsessed part of his mind continued to enumerate the restaurants he knew she visited, picking and discarding like some complex machine, which was in effect what he had made of it.

La Cappella? Far too noisy on a Friday. Young's? A possibility. No, *Angelique!* It clicked into place with a sense of total rightness.

Now, if he had the nerve, he would get into the pickup and drive like a bat out of hell down Benedict Canyon, arriving at Angelique before they could possibly hope to do so. He jumped to his feet excitedly, but came to an abrupt halt, not merely because he felt dizzy (jumping to his feet always made him dizzy—something to do with the wound), but because he was transfixed by a fearful doubt. He could not risk going to Angelique, only to find that they didn't appear there; it would destroy him.

Balls, he told himself, it makes no difference if you get it wrong!

But it does make a difference. I have to be right.

The endless, exhausting interior dialogue began all over again, one voice saying, "Don't you dig, this is the test? If you're right on this, you can move, you can begin the countdown," and the other voice saying, "But if I'm wrong, it will be the end of me."

So that terrible fear came back to engulf him as it had engulfed him in the middle of last night: he would never act, he had lost the will to act; all he could do was to watch and plan—and that was insanity.

He stood on the edge of Mulholland Drive, trembling, unable to move. After a time he walked unsteadily to the pickup, hauled himself into it and drove slowly to the junction with Coldwater Canyon, turning down it. He knew that in the grip of that fear he could no more have gambled on their going to Angelique than he could have cut off his right hand.

He loitered until the car—the Rolls tonight—swayed out of the steep drive and set off down the canyon, and he followed them meekly, like a lamb led to the slaughter. For indeed they were not going to Angelique at all, but to Young's.

He told himself that it didn't matter. So he'd picked the wrong restaurant! As far as he was concerned they could go eat in the nearest pig-bin, it meant nothing to him.

But it *did* mean something to him; he'd been wrong, he couldn't afford to be wrong, ever, about any single detail.

He told himself to act, now; but he also told himself that it was impossible for him to act now. Why? Because . . . Because the kid had seen him following her on the beach; she was a bright kid, she might put two and two together. But this was only an excuse; even as he consoled himself with it he knew that it was an excuse.

Act! Now!

No, not yet.

What was he waiting for? What in the name of God did he think he was waiting for? A sign from heaven?

Two

At first, for the first three months, he had lived in a small cheap apartment; but an apartment, however small and cheap, is a kind of home: homes have neighbors; neighbors are curious, or genuinely helpful, or lonely, or in need of a bedmate; suddenly you are part of a human nucleus, and that was the last thing he could afford to be. So now he lived in motels; there is nothing so unneighborly as a cheap Los Angeles motel, nothing less curious or less genuinely helpful. He stayed a night or a week, according to atmosphere or whim; he reckoned that there were so many motels to choose from, he could live to be eighty and never stay in the same one twice.

Five weeks after the defeat of Angelique he was at the Valley View Motor Hotel.

It had been a good day. Wearing some of his new smart gear—a rather cool number in leather with which he had armed himself against certain contingencies—he had dropped into the real estate agency which had, he knew, sold 234 Upper Canyon Circle to Virginia Kenny some eight years before. He also knew that Mrs. Rhinehart, who had made the deal, was still a very active partner, possibly the most go-ahead of the many go-ahead ladies engaged in Los Angeles real estate—which is saying something.

His name, he told Mrs. Rhinehart, was Frank McNair, and he wanted to buy a small house somewhere up in the hills. He indicated, in a shy and offhand manner which he had lately perfected, that money was no object, thus ensuring that Mrs. Rhinehart didn't hand him over to some ignorant junior.

An hour and three house-viewings later he and Mrs. Rhinehart were taking coffee together and chatting of this and that. Two hours later, when they returned to the office and parted company, with a promise on his part to return tomorrow when he'd made up his mind, he found himself in possession of a great many hitherto unknown facts; for not only had Mrs. Rhinehart sold 234 Upper Canyon Circle to Virginia Kenny, she had, many years before when a mere girl, sold *for* Mrs. Kenny and her husband, Cass, the even larger house in Bel Air which had been the proper stable for the up-and-coming young star that Cass certainly was at the time. This was before the couple's penniless retreat from Hollywood in 1950.

Now, pacing about his shabby room at the Valley View Motor Hotel, he was aware of the fact that Mrs. Olga Rhinehart had in some imprecise way represented a milestone. A sure instinct told him that he had now turned a corner and was facing in a new direction; he even *felt* different. He felt confident suddenly. Is confidence an instinct? Perhaps. Perhaps, all along, he had been doing the right thing in relying on some inner balance which would not let him move until everything was in the right conjunction: his knowledge acting as exact counterweight to this confidence.

He came to a stop and stood for a time in deep thought, testing his feelings; then he went to a built-in closet and unlocked it. He took from the closet a cheap new suitcase, placed it on the bed and unlocked it; from the suitcase he took a black tin box and placed it on the only solid table in the room; he unlocked it and took from it a medallion on a chain. The disc was gold, and at the center of it was not the expected Saint with Child but a secretive oriental-looking eye. The pupil had once been made by a stone of some kind, but the stone had dropped out and the claws which had held it had worn away or been filed away.

The man with the beard looked hard at this eye, as if demanding that it should give him some sign—a wink perhaps. Evidently it did so, because he nodded to himself, a grave preoccupied nod.

17

He then took from the box an exercise book: good quality, fine paper, but much thumbed; he placed it on the table, pulled forward a chair, switched on the lamp and began to read. He read very intently, not skipping a sentence, not even a word, though he must have known it all by heart, having reread it God knew how many times. Every now and again he added a line or two in distinct and meticulous handwriting: new data by courtesy of Mrs. Olga Rhinehart.

It seemed that Cass Kenny, poised on the brink of stardom, had met Virginia May Werner at the Burly Burger Beanhouse, where she was then working as a waitress. The year was 1939. He was thirty-four, she twenty.

Nobody had ever claimed that Cass Kenny was one of the great actors of his generation; in the Hollywood of that time talent mattered less than looks and personality—"star quality" as it is still, somewhat wistfully, called. Cass had possessed the looks and the personality, but . . . The "but" was never put to the test, perhaps luckily for Mr. Kenny. Europe was up to its old tricks again; plunged itself into war. The United States was still standing undecided on the diving board, and Cass Kenny was busy making something called *Rancho Desperado*, when Japan fell on Pearl Harbor.

The studio had not been altogether happy about their boy's new girl friend; but his first marriage, blessed by them, had been such a disaster that they were not in much of a position to protest. Moreover, there was a new feeling abroad in the land, and the publicity department suddenly saw that "star marries mere waitress" was not such a bad angle, after all. It might have been better if she'd been a *pretty* mere waitress, but presumably the make-up department could do something about that; at least she wasn't interested in getting into movies, which would have been a disaster.

At this point Cass compounded the situation by volunteering for the Air Force. Moreover, he did so without telling the publicity department, who thereby failed to get a picture of him doing it. (Somebody was sacked for this.)

In any case, "heroic star marries mere waitress" was something you could get your teeth into, and since Cass was the first well-known name to offer his services to God and Country, the publicity department bared its fangs and set to work.

It was generally agreed that they made a terrific job of the wedding. Neither his colleagues nor the glittering superstars of the time had to be coerced into attending; Cass was popular, he was a regular guy, and his gesture of enlistment touched a genuine emotional response. In fact, if the publicity boys had not been so busy congratulating each other on their know-how, they might have noticed that "genuine" was the key word of the proceedings. The wedding was really a success in spite of them, not because of them; for Cass and Virginia were genuinely in love, and the ordinary people who turned out in their thousands to cheer the happy couple were genuinely moved because a heroic star in uniform was marrying a mere waitress who wasn't even pretty. Moreover, as everybody soon found, to their irritation and inconvenience, Cass Kenny had joined the Air Force in order to fight his country's enemies, not to provide pre-publicity for a string of action movies in which Cass Kenny avenged Pearl Harbor single-handed before coming home to a hero's welcome and June Allyson, who had been singing songs at the Stage Door Canteen (for light relief) throughout.

Of course he should have known better; if he had any intention of continuing his career at a future date, he should have known that the big studios of that almost legendary era were like elephants; they never forgot. To make matters worse, he did indeed star in a single epic, *Suicide Squadron*, which made a small fortune and served to taunt the studio bosses, every time the receipts came in, with a reminder of the money which Cass Kenny was losing for them by default.

Photographs of the time showed Kenny and Virginia as two tall, loose-jointed, almost gangling young Americans. Very *typically* American, they look, these two, with their clear clean smiles and their healthy tans and their uninhibited adoration of one another. All over the battle zones of the world, people would have been able to recognize in him the decent, quiet, polite boy (for he looked much younger than his thirty-five years) whom their daughter might bring home for a meal and who, next day, would disappear into the slaughter fields, silently, cloaked in security.

And Virginia? Yes, in those days she could have stood for all the young wives who stayed behind with their kids (young Jeff had been born in 1940 by Caesarean—she would never be able to have another) and their war work.

The man with the beard had collected sixteen photographs of this family. He examined the first few of them with minute attention.

1943. Cass on leave, a major now. Thirty-eight years old and suddenly looking it, strain and fatigue showing in the lines around his eyes and at the corners of his mouth. This was a face of character and strength, yet with that boyishness which is so charming in American men when they don't pursue it and capitalize on it. Virginia, at twenty-four, seems unchanged. Young Jeff is staggering about in the inebriation of his third year.

1945. Cass has been wounded. His leg is still in plaster. He will walk with a slight limp for the rest of his life. He is forty, lean and hard. A man who has seen death and lived through a lot of pain. Virginia, at twenty-six, has still not changed physically, but it is a woman who is looking up at her husband, not a girl. Behind the smile is assessment; perhaps she already knows how the studio bosses are going to greet him. Young Jeff, in foreground, is a five-year-old Indian chief complete with war paint. Behind them all, like a grandiloquent memorial to all that Cass Kenny has given up, can be seen almost the whole of the house in Bel Air: twelve bedrooms, Spanish-style, two pools, two tennis courts, water garden and orange grove.

1948. The photograph tells the story of three years. Cass is still lean and hard, but now he is bitter as well. The lines have deepened; booze as well as bitterness has had a hand in that. Virginia, fifteen years younger and no drinker, has shown more physical resilience, but the smooth planes of young womanhood have gone forever, and that joker, Time, has wrought one of his paradoxes—for Virginia Kenny is now almost beautiful; she is guarding her embittered husband and her eight-year-old son like a lioness. So they've hit hard times! So the beach house behind them is on loan from a friend! So what!

20

The bearded man studied this picture for a long time, then laid it aside and returned to his notes.

They told him, in arid little sentences, of how Cass Kenny, his wounds finally healed, had presented himself for duty, only to be told . . . No, he was *told* nothing; that would have been much too straightforward. Only to find out gradually, over a long time, by a process of moral erosion, that nobody intended to give him a part ever again. He had broken the Golden Rule. Nothing, but nothing, and certainly not God and Country, must ever be allowed to come between the hireling and his studio.

Those were rough days in the dear old town, anyway; a lot of bright young faces had appeared from nowhere during the war years, and the bright old faces were fighting for survival. The fact that there were a dozen parts for this older, harder Cass Kenny was neither here nor there. He was down for the count; all he had to do now was get out of the ring.

He couldn't do it. He, who had known so many other worlds in time of war, knew only this world in time of peace; he was stricken with paralysis. Virginia realized that they were beaten, that they must accept the fact and move. But Cass couldn't move; he sat where he was and he drank bourbon, and his expression grew more bitter, the lines became ever deeper; the eyes were the eyes of a beaten dog, and grey peppered his brown hair all over; as for that boyishness, it faded away altogether except on the rare occasions when he smiled.

So here he was, a tough, dogged, beaten loser with a smile like that of a puzzled child. And over there, on the other side of the Atlantic, were millions of people waiting for a certain kind of man; the man they were waiting for was a tough, dogged, beaten loser with the smile of a puzzled child. They didn't know it, and Cass didn't know it, and Virginia didn't know it, and Old Hollywood, still perched on its worm-eaten past, certainly didn't know it. But Piero Gaetano Larosso knew it the first time he saw that face; he knew it, not in his wily Milanese brain, and certainly not in his bankbook, and perhaps not even in his heart, which was not very large, but in his gut. He knew it at once and absolutely, and because he was young and determined and full of a kind of ratty charm when he cared to turn it on, he managed to make Virginia see it too.

And that was how, after many scenes and silences and many bottles of bourbon, Cass Kenny was dragged protesting to Rome, through the portals of Cine Città studios and into the spotlight of show-business history.

It is now largely forgotten that Kenny and Piero Larosso ever made anything together but inexpensive and wildly successful "Italian Westerns." Their first effort, *Goodbye, Naples, Hello*, though certainly inexpensive and certainly successful beyond anybody's wildest dreams, was the rather touching story of an American soldier's return to that city in search of a girl and the black-market profits he had been forced to leave with her. Within a few weeks Cass Kenny became a bigger name in Italy, France and Germany than he had ever been in the United States. Five years and eight movies later, when Cass and Piero parted company by mutual consent (they had never been able to stand the sight of each other from the start), they were both millionaires in anybody's currency, and there wasn't a producer in Europe who didn't want Cass in his next picture.

The Kennys had by now acquired a house in Switzerland, a palazzo apartment in Rome and a hideaway in Ibiza, which was at that time unspoiled and unpretentious, and still awaiting the invasion which was later to spoil it utterly. Cass was fifty-two, but having given up the bourbon, looked several years younger. Virginia was thirty-seven; she had found to her intense interest that in Europe it was not necessary to be pretty or even beautiful as long as you had style. It seemed that style was something she had possessed all along, and since her looks were improving yearly, and since she also had the money to be dressed by whomsoever she might choose, her every public appearance began to be greeted by the click of lenses; she was voted one of Europe's most interesting women.

Jeff, on the other hand, was now a problem. After bouts of lackadaisical education at various "American schools" he was found to be almost completely uneducated. Worse, because he had no ear for languages, he had picked up nothing to speak of during his parents' travels. At fifteen, rather too late by any standards, he was packed off to a special school in England—a country which he hated but which his parents, like so many Americans, loved. It was the kind of school that is populated by the displaced young of all nations; there was hardly a boy there who didn't have ten, fifteen, fifty, a hundred times too much pocket money: the sons of oil sheiks, of Greek shipping magnates, of junta-deposed South American entrepreneurs . . . as well as of film stars. None of these young gentlemen showed much desire for work, since most of them considered, rightly, that their parents had made ample provision for them never to have to engage in anything so distasteful. They simply went on with the tedious business of growing up, exchanging tall but perfectly true stories of their past and chasing the girls in the local town. They also, because they were young, absorbed a certain amount of the information which was smoothly handed out to them by the teaching staff. Nobody worried very much about exams, but some of the more retentive brains scored reasonable marks, Jeff Kenny among them. From here he would move without undue worry into the calm atmosphere of the University of Southern California in Los Angeles—not, it will be noticed, U.C.L.A.

Meanwhile, his father had given up "spaghetti Westerns" forever, and was working with a highly commercial but ingeniously intellectual young Frenchman. Hollywood had been able to laugh at the Larosso epics; it was quite unable to laugh at this conjunction of Cass Kenny and Jean-Paul Revel. Monsieur Revel knew exactly what Cass could and could not do on the screen, so he surrounded him with the finest actors he could find, particularly feminine ones. The second of these films hit the box office dead center in the United States.

And so, for Cass, the wheel turned full circle. A whole new generation of Hollywood producers went down on their knees to him, while the old men who had thrown him out (those that were left) formed a satisfyingly obeisant chorus in the background; after all, the bright new young men were their investment, using their money. However, the old studio bosses were not the only ones with elephantine memories; not one man who had turned Cass Kenny down in his time of need ever made a penny out of him now; they had to sit by and watch others doing so.

Though both Cass and Virginia enjoyed their return to the town where they had met and fallen in love, they were also human enough to enjoy the show they staged when they got there: refusing to rent a house or give any other sign of putting down the smallest root, but settling somewhat restlessly in a hotel, with trunks not fully unpacked, as if at any moment they might decide to go somewhere else.

Their real friends could come and go as they pleased, but other "friends" were granted very limited access. The stability of their marriage, which many people in the old hometown had been sure was a façade, was now seen to be a solid fact. Amid so much chopping and changing and coupling and recoupling, this solidity seemed somehow chic and interesting; they had even managed to make a virtue of virtue, which, as ever, made a lot of unvirtuous people very angry indeed.

Of course, the bored Beverly Hills gossips were not the only ones to be troubled by this phenomenon. Producers and publicity men all over Europe had stubbed their toes again and again on the apparent happiness of Cass Kenny's marriage; they had made a few half-hearted attempts to cook up little adventures for him here and there, but without success. There were not even any frantic denials, not even any lawsuits, from the Kennys, who remained obstinately and publicly loving towards each other. Cass, it was true, broke several *paparazzi* cameras and one *paparazzi* jaw, but there was nothing very unusual about that, it happened all the time. The producers and the publicity men, as well as the bored gossips of Beverly Hills, sighed and resigned themselves to the fact that they were confronted by a happy marriage, whatever that might mean. It meant, as indeed it always should, that if there were rows and frictions and fleeting infidelities, Mr. and Mrs. Kenny were old-fashioned and sensible enough to keep them to themselves. The reason for their marital success was as plain as daylight to them, and if others were too stupid to understand it, that was no concern of theirs, for the answer *was* very simple. Cass had the career and Virginia didn't; she was abundantly happy to be his wife; no conflict of interest and no reason for absence (which does not make the heart grow fonder) except when they both knew they needed a rest from each other.

On the second of these return visits to California they settled young Jeff into U.S.C., where he was to continue his pattern of education by happenstance; unfortunately, he now had a good reason for his lack of interest, in common with the other male members of his generation. The dreary, purposeless entanglement in Vietnam already had its web cast around him; university could only postpone the moment—long enough for it all to end, the Kennys hoped—when he too would receive his draft papers.

They none of them knew it, but a shadow was stealthily creeping out towards them all. The decade of success and sunlight was over (it was almost exactly ten years since Cass had been dragged to Rome), and the sixties, that decade of violence, was not going to leave them untouched.

The man with the beard suddenly stood up, impatient with his notebook and his photographs; he was suddenly bored to distraction with all these facts which he had read and reread so many hundreds of times. Confidence and certainty seemed to have been building up inside him with every word, so that now they were quite unbearable.

He went into the shabby bathroom and switched on the overbright lights, staring at himself intently in the mirror.

So the moment had come, unbidden, as he had hoped it would. The waiting and the prevarication and the fear of prevarication had all been necessary, had all led irrevocably to this moment when confidence and certainty would come surging into him without warning.

He looked deeply into his own steely grey eyes; then ran a finger over the strong brows (a little *too* strong in fact) and then through the thick hair of his brownish-golden beard. His fingers ran along the line of the concealed wound and out of the hair over his lips. As usual, he was aware of the fact that the fingers did not relay texture and sensation as efficiently as they had done before the burning, but presumably that was natural.

Yes, it was time for the countdown. Now he could break the glass seal and throw the switch that locked him into countdown. From this moment, this here and this now, there would be no turning back.

Countdown!

He turned from the mirror, crossed the worn room and went out, locking the door behind him. As usual, there was nobody in the motel office, but the old man was brewing up his interminable coffee in the small, cluttered room beyond it. He came wavering out, looking as though he expected trouble, and was false-toothedly amiable when he found there was to be none. No, Mr. Grainger's slate was clean, he owed them for nothing. The old man was sorry to hear that Mr. Grainger would be leaving in the morning early, he'd been a nice customer, clean and quiet and well-mannered, not like some of that trash . . .

The man with the beard got into the pickup and drove a couple of blocks to the gas station on the corner where there was a telephone booth. (The old man could hear every word that was said in the one next to his office.) He called United Airlines and booked onto their nine-fifteen flight to Denver, Colorado, using the name Petersen. Then he called American and booked onto their flight, Denver–Los Angeles, at seven forty-five the following morning, using the name White, James White.

Next he drove to the nearest market and bought half a cooked chicken, some tomatoes, bread, butter, cheese, apples and beer. He went back to the Valley View Motor Hotel and locked himself in his room.

From the closet he took a second suitcase, a good one, and placed it beside its humble relation on the bed. Then he divided all his possessions into two piles, so that after a while it began to look as though two men were occupying the room: one, a raggedy, rootless individual, given to worn jeans, fringed jackets, bush hats; the other, some kind of minor executive type who might of an evening care to go to a smart disco wearing something impressively casual. This schizophrenic division of himself was very thorough; nothing, not even a toothbrush, made its way from one man's possessions to the other's . . . until he came to the well-thumbed notebook, the photographs and the gold medallion on its chain. These, and only these, crossed the great divide. They had been prepared for. A neat cavity had been made for them under what appeared to be the bottom of the leather case in which the young executive type kept his shaving gear, cologne, et cetera.

All this, done slowly and methodically, took time. Darkness had fallen at some point during the proceedings, and he was hungry. He ate the food he had bought at the market and drank some of the beer. Then, still sitting at the table, he counted his money; he reckoned that by the time he returned from Denver he would have only $1,875 left. It wasn't enough; it would not buy him very much time. (He agreed with the man who had said "Time is money," but not quite in the way that the man had intended.) Somehow he would have to make it enough; he would have to move swiftly and surely. A lot would depend on how quickly he could pick up the right kind of girl. Or perhaps he should change that plan . . . ? No, the plan was good, stick to it.

He put his money away and went into the bathroom. He had bought himself one of those do-it-yourself haircutting combs, but was not sure how successfully he could use it. In fact, because he had allowed his hair to grow so long, in keeping with the beard, he found that he could achieve a reasonable longish cut which would certainly not seem out of place; if it looked as though he could do with a visit to a barber, so much the better.

Now he must deal with the beard itself.

He stood for quite a long time, razor in hand, looking at his reflection. His heart had begun to beat very hard. This made his jaw ache, and this in turn sent those well-known tendrils of pain curling up into the back of his head. It meant nothing; it meant only that he was facing the fact that the removal of the beard was his Rubicon. If he wanted to, he could, still, turn back.

The indecision lasted only a few seconds. His heart steadied; the jaw relaxed; the tendrils of pain withered and died.

Without the beard his whole face was changed; it looked younger and stronger. The mustache would go too, but not yet; this transformation had been planned with care, obsessive care. Gazing at his reflection, he wondered again about the obsessiveness of it all. The trip to Denver, for instance, was it really necessary? Possibly not, but it was a part of the ritual, and as such, it had to be performed; the obsession told him that any part of the ritual left unperformed might constitute a fatal flaw.

He touched the scar; it ran from just under his left ear across the cheek. Women found it attractive. He felt pretty sure that he'd be able to get the girl, the right girl, without too much trouble.

Long ago he had steeled himself against the temptations and

fears which now attacked him. He could ignore them. He cleared up the mess of hair and flushed it down the toilet, drank a little more beer, cleaned his teeth, took two sleeping pills, set his alarm for six and went to bed.

Virginia Kenny watched Leo get back into his Mercedes. She liked the way his jacket molded itself to waist and buttocks as he did so; he really was a very desirable man, and for a moment she was annoyed with herself for having pleaded that most boring of feminine late-night complaints, a headache, when of course she had no such thing. Also, she wasn't at all sure that he hadn't received the news with faint relief. The idea that he might now go to a bar and pick up a girl, something twenty, thirty years her junior, struck her with aggravation.

Watching him drive away, she sighed. "But I do ask for it." And again she wondered, as she had wondered so often recently, whether she needed a man any more. Cass had been dead for more than twelve years. It was odd that for the first three or four, wrapped in loss, she hadn't even been lonely. Loneliness had come later, after her son's death, after the battle for his child, sudden devastating loneliness.

She wandered through to the terrace and stood staring across it at the pool, at the garden that looked like everybody else's garden for miles around, as if the set-dressers had just finished with it in preparation for next day's shooting. It was beautiful, but it bored her; every place that she had not shared with Cass bored her. Then why not go back to Europe? Take Chris and go? Chris would like Europe. Or would she?

Glancing up, she saw that the light was still on in her granddaughter's bedroom. She sighed. Who knew what Chris liked or disliked? Nobody, including Chris probably.

"I think," she said to herself as she crossed the vast drawing room and the vast hall, and went up the vast staircase, "that I must stop having men around the place, I'm getting too old. And yet . . ."

She stood at the top of the stairs, looking at herself in a gilt Italian mirror that had once hung in the Rome apartment; she saw a very elegant lady in a long honey-colored dress of silk jersey which accentuated an elegant figure. It was the same color as her hair; her arms and face were a few shades darker; an elegant lady aged . . . Mm! Say . . . forty-seven. She was in her fifty-sixth year. Not bad.

The thing was that she liked men and she liked sex, now and again. Was that wrong? "Is that wrong, Cass?" She would often ask him these things. "I'd forgotten about loneliness—or perhaps it's a different thing in a war; and I had my baby then. I *detest* loneliness, Cass, it scares the hell out of me. Am I wrong?"

There was no answer. Once, long ago, she had toyed with the idea of spiritualism; she had needed him back that badly. Thank God, she had never done anything about it.

Leo wasn't a bad man; he had a decent job, something to do with the Stock Exchange. He could get by quite comfortably. "But I'll tell you a secret," he had said, lying beside her on that first night. "I'll tell you a lousy secret about Leo N. Faber, shall I?" He had been a little drunk that night. "He loves luxury. He adores luxury. Look!" And he'd touched her exquisite sheet with a sensual hairy-backed hand; pointed to the bottle of fine red wine which they'd brought up to her room with them (they both liked red wine), leaned over and sniffed her perfume. "I like nice expensive things," he had said, smiling like a naughty boy over the confession. She, for her part, had liked his honesty. The understanding was a comfortable one.

Joanne Christina was sitting up in bed, reading. At five minutes to twelve! Caught out, she looked up over her book and said "Hi!" brightly.

"Hi!" Virginia knew that it would be worse than useless to draw attention to the hour. More was achieved by ignoring it.

Chris said, "You look pretty."

"Thank you, darling." Sometimes, at odd moments like this, there seemed to be no chasm between them; they were good and close friends.

"I thought you were out with Leo."

"I was." She looked at the book, *Famous Ghosts and Hauntings.* "That'll keep you awake all night."

"I don't think so." She laid the book aside. "It's mostly in Europe. We don't seem to have so many ghosts."

It seemed like a cue line. "Would you like to go to Europe, Chris? To stay for a while, I mean?"

The child had a curious and unchildish way of considering carefully before she answered. Where had it come from? Certainly not from Jeff, who had never considered before he *acted*, let alone before he spoke. And not from that emotionally unstable slut of a mother.

Chris was wondering whether there was some subtle ulterior motive behind this Europe business. Guilt being what it is, she thought immediately of Friday afternoons. Could her grandmother possibly know? Had she been followed? No—the reaction would have been much more violent and perfectly straightforward. In any case, her comings and goings were so arbitrary and often so unlikely that it would take the C.I.A. to disentangle the ingenuous motives from the ingenious ones. And thanks to an amalgam of lifts, buses and cabs, Friday transport presented no problems.

Virginia was thinking that this child never behaved in the way that most children behaved, in order to please grownups. She was completely herself; an admirable trait but a slightly alarming one.

Chris was now thinking of the desert. It wasn't likely that they would depart for Europe at once, if they ever departed at all, and so she would have plenty of time to achieve her aims in that direction. She therefore said, "Yes, I'd like to go to Europe. There's a fabulous dollhouse at Windsor Castle, did you know? Even the plumbing works, and famous painters did all the tiny pictures, and famous writers wrote all the books in the library, and they're no bigger than your thumbnail, and I'd like to see the leaning tower of Pisa too, before it falls down clunk."

Virginia frowned over this willingness now that it had been put into words. "You ought to have more friends here."

"I have Tony"—Tony was the Filipino manservant—"and Leona"—Leona was the black cook—"and Mr. Liang"—Chinese gardener, who often taxied her about in his little truck—"and Sally Gombowl"—black help of the Garston house next door—"and Pete"—who cleaned the swimming pool, and who also gave her lifts to strange and sometimes unknown destinations—"and . . ."

"Friends your own age."

"They're all so dumb."

"You like Jane," said Virginia doubtfully, naming the only child whom Chris had ever brought home from Miss Mannering's, where she was at the moment being schooled.

"Jane lives right down by the marina. And anyway, her parents are dia-bo."

"Are what?"

"Diabolical. They fight. Her mother's a bitch."

"You could have her to stay if you like." The idea of Jane, who was square and silent, squatting about the house like some large uncommunicative cat was not pleasing to Virginia, but her granddaughter's aloneness, so foreign to her own personality, worried her. It hadn't been easy for either of them, this childhood without father or mother. Virginia felt that she had truly and honestly done her best, and yet . . .

"I'm quite happy, you know," said Chris, following her line of thought as usual. "What I mean is, I guess I'm a funny kind of a person anyway—they all say I am at school."

"You don't care?"

"Why should I? *They're* the ones with the troubles. Boys, and parents who drink martinis and fight, and always wanting some stupid thing because everybody else has one. Honestly I think they're . . . dumb."

Virginia was thinking, as she often did, that this self-made ugly duckling was going to be pretty. Well, Cass had been a gorgeous man, and Jeff had been very attractive, and Holly . . . Yes, she had to admit that the mother who was never mentioned now, who had mercifully disappeared altogether, had been an extremely pretty girl; the blue eyes came from her too.

She yawned and said, "Wow, I'm bushed! Let's go to sleep now. We can think about Europe and having Jane to stay, things like that, in the morning."

Obediently—for this was the kind of remark that secured obedience from her—the small girl put down her book and banged her pillows into their sleeping position. As she lay down she said, "I was horrid to Leo that day at the beach. Will you tell him sorry for me?"

Her grandmother paused at the door, looking back. "Don't you like him?"

"He's okay, I guess. Does he want to marry you?"

"Good God, *no!*"

"Harry did."

"I know." She hadn't known. She was, in fact, shocked by the information as well as by its source. "How did *you* know?"

"Oh, he told me. He was weirdo, he thought I could help him or something. Me! I told him what you did was nothing to *do* with me, but he had this weird idea. Honestly, he was too much, he kept buying me nut-crunch sundaes, I was glad when he . . . went away."

"Goodnight, darling."

" 'Night, honeypot." And as the door was closing: "If we went to Europe, like you said, would Leo come too?"

"No."

"Oh."

She lay awake for a time after Virginia had gone. Was it possible that somebody had followed her one Friday afternoon? No, there'd have been words. More than words, an explosion. Anyway, she'd better change the day. It was a pity, because Friday was pool day, and Pete the pool man gave her a hitch nearly all the way.

Maybe she could have a word with Pete; maybe *he* could change pool day. But of course, if anyone *had* followed her, they'd know about Pete anyway, so that was no good. Perhaps Sally Gombowl would think of something, quite a few black people lived in that area . . . Super about that haunting in England, where pots and pans and you-name-it flew about the house making ghastly noises, wham-bang-clunk!

No, they couldn't know; all that Europe business must have been pure coincidence. If they actually went, maybe they could *visit* that house where things flew around and got smashed . . .

He awoke a few minutes before his alarm clock was due to go off, as usual. He got out of bed, shaved, washed and dressed with care in some of his good new casual clothes; the reflection which looked back at him was the right one: well-to-do, trendy, interesting.

He left the motel at six twenty-five. This gave him nearly two and a half hours before he needed to be at the airport. It was five miles to the dump, and at that hour in the morning, with the freeway almost empty, he made it in good time. Nothing stirred among the piled debris of junked and rusting automobiles, not even a cat. This was one reason he had picked the place—this, and the proximity of the coffee shop around the corner on Ventura Boulevard.

He drove the pickup into its prearranged position behind a sagging truck. He opened the hood, took out the plugs and threw them away; then he unscrewed the registration plates, wrapped them in paper and put them in his suitcase. After this he jacked up the vehicle and removed the offside rear wheel, which he sent rolling down the hill into a pile of rubbish. Without it, the pickup settled back at an abandoned angle. He guessed that within hours somebody would have stripped it of everything else worth taking.

As he walked back to the main road he could not help feeling rather conspicuous in his smart clothes, carrying his smart suitcase, but it was only three hundred yards to the coffee shop. He got there at a few minutes to eight, ordered a large breakfast and took his time over eating it. Then he called a cab to take him to the airport, arriving there twenty-five minutes before takeoff.

As he settled into his seat he felt confident and secure; he had successfully "lost" the pickup; as soon as he returned to Los Angeles he would lose his Missouri license and get himself a new California one, which would be different in several important respects. James White would no longer be described as blond with grey eyes.

He was sure now that this trip to Denver was right. Too many people in L.A. knew too much about actors; it would be plain stupid to take any risks at this point, simply to save one day and an air fare.

The seat next to him was empty, so he took out the notebook and continued to study that endlessly restudied history. The sixties, the violent decade, had come into the ring stealthily, as far as the Kennys were concerned. It wasn't until September of 1961 that Jeff met a girl called Holly Loring; at some point in the relationship they had evidently shacked up together; in July of '62 she announced that he had made her pregnant. Cass and Virginia were in Spain, where he was filming a World War II epic. They were not informed until August, after the wedding, of what had been going on in California. Virginia flew there right away; she was obviously expecting the worst, and the worst was what she got. As far as she was concerned, Holly was a vulgar, ill-mannered, ignorant little slut; at the time of their first meeting she had been reasonably high on marijuana, so that her beauty, her one asset, had been as slurred as her speech and manners . . .

He looked up from the notebook, staring down at the desert far below, as dry and as dead-looking as the wrinkled sloughed-off skin of some huge reptile. He was frowning because there were certain things about this period of the Kennys' life which didn't quite seem to add up, however you looked at them; he had researched it as carefully as he had researched any other period, yet it remained indistinct. Of course, rich people whose sons made grave errors had the wherewithal at their disposal to hush up whatever displeased them, but in that case, the very hushing-up would itself leave traces; he could detect none; he merely had this uncomfortable feeling that there was, there had to be, more to it all than met the eye.

He slipped a photograph of Holly out of the back of the notebook and studied it: a very pretty girl with bright blue eyes; not a strong face certainly, perhaps a weak one, but it looked . . . nice. That was a wet word, but it was what she looked, a nice pretty girl. So why did Mrs. Kenny take such exception to her? She could have been so much, much worse.

He sighed and returned to the notes. It seemed that Virginia had gone back to Spain in a state of resigned bad temper. Joanne Christina was born in the middle of the following February, 1963.

The year of John F. Kennedy's assassination was a year of disaster in all respects. Cass, Virginia and Jeff were not to escape it. The boy finished his time at the university and received his draft card without delay; like his father before him, he opted for the Air Force. Holly was left alone with her baby, whom she adored but whose screaming drove her crazy. She wasn't the kind of girl, evidently, who could bear to be alone for very long; she soon found company, male company.

In Italy, at dusk on the Autostrada del Sol in a blinding

November rainstorm, Cass Kenny drove his Maserati into the back of a broken-down truck that was showing no lights. He had been going well over a hundred miles an hour. The car blew up, but Cass was certainly dead long before that.

Virginia might as well have been in the car with him, for when they brought the news to her she suddenly ceased to live. Her son was granted leave, and flew over to be with her; she was presumably glad of his presence and his help with the formalities, but as soon as she could get away she went alone to Ibiza, where the storm-racked winter nights and the deserted beaches helped her to feel her way back to the threshold of reality again. In 1964 she went about Europe like an automaton, tidying up her husband's affairs, selling property, and shocking more than one lawyer with her grasp of financial affairs. When all this was settled she went back to the troubled United States.

Here she was faced by more legal problems, since it had become obvious, even to her son, that Holly was no fit mother for Joanne Christina. By this time Jeff was on active service in Vietnam, so it was left to Grandmother to start proceedings on his behalf. Holly offered little opposition, and in May of that year the baby, aged one year and three months, was installed in the plush nursery which had been prepared for her at 234 Upper Canyon Circle, where the decorators were still at work in most of the other rooms.

In September, one impossible day when the Sant' Ana was blowing, that burning belch of desert wind which periodically reminds Los Angeles of where it is situated, the last blow fell. Jeff Kenny was reported missing, believed killed.

An exhausted calm fell on the big house. Cass was gone, Jeff was gone, even the decorators had gone. The forty-six-year-old woman, whom time had in some subtle way made beautiful, played with her granddaughter or sat alone by the pool, with needlepoint or a book lying disregarded on her lap. Tony, the Filipino manservant, and Leona, the black cook, and Mary, the nice young English nurse, all wished that she would go out and have a little fun. But Virginia Kenny never went out. Time had stopped.

He took a cab from the airport to a motel far removed from

the din of jets, told the driver to wait while he checked in and was then driven into downtown Denver.

He knew that it might take him a little while to find exactly what he was looking for, but time would now prove less expensive than a mistake; with $1,875 in the kitty, he could afford no mistakes.

He visited seven hairdressers before returning to the third of them. This seemed to him to combine all the right elements: an elegant exterior promised tolerable know-how, there were private booths and, as far as he could see, none of the barbers were faggots. A selection of photographed men's heads in a showcase near the door indicated that this establishment could also handle the kind of thing he required of it.

He paused for a few moments, out of view of the windows, collected his thoughts and then went in very quickly, as if in a great hurry.

It seemed that he was an actor, back home here in Denver to visit his folks, and a girl he knew had called him from Albuquerque, where she was on location with a Western. Apparently this guy, who had a good small part, had hurt his foot and couldn't walk, so they needed someone else. The girl had spoken to the director (who knew him anyway, they'd worked together before), and the director had said okay, if he could get his ass on a plane right away, he could have the part. But the thing was, they could use quite a few long and medium shots of this actor who'd hurt his foot as long as whoever took over for him could match up—and the guy's hair was brown with grey streaks in it. So how long would it take to give him a tint with some grey streaks?

The owner of the place was helpful, but pointed out that the process he was asking for took time, a good three hours; also, would the treatment include the mustache? His would-be customer guessed he'd better have the mustache done as well. The girl hadn't mentioned it, and he'd forgotten to ask.

(He didn't like this business of the hair, but it was essential, the only physical detail apart from the eyes which had to be changed completely. He'd checked with various girls, and it seemed that at the least he could rely on the treatment lasting six weeks, possibly as long as ten. He reckoned that by the end of

36

six weeks he'd either be in jail or in a position where a further visit to some distant barber would be simplicity itself.)

The owner, having consulted his appointment book, said that the lunch hour was never a good time, they were always booked solid, but with a little juggling they could start him at two, which meant that the whole thing should be over by four-thirty or five; he knew it seemed a long time, but those grey streaks had to be bleached out; with some guys it didn't work at all, but since Mr. McNair was darkish blond it should prove no problem. Of course, if Mr. McNair had a *picture* of this other man . . . ?

No, Mr. McNair had no picture.

But of course, he had two pictures, two pictures of two other men. They were in his suitcase at the motel.

When he got back there at five-thirty he was trembling; at the barber's, in the mirror, it had seemed good—better than he had dared expect. But there were still things to do before he would know for certain.

This was the first test, perhaps the most important; everything hung on this; in a few moments he would know whether all that time, all that planning, had been well spent or utterly wasted. He could barely keep his hands under control as he unpacked his razor; and of course, the wound was up to its old tricks again.

It was a pity about the mustache— all that wasted tinting and bleaching, all that extra expense; but the mustache, he knew, was the last vital link with the past, the final shred of the old mask. It changed his face even more than the beard had done, and if they recognized anybody at that barber's shop, if anything leaked out to make them suspicious, it would be the man with the mustache that they would remember. Tomorrow, when he got back to L.A., he would even have the hair recut, differently styled, shorter. And he must remember to thin out his eyebrows.

The mustache had gone. He looked good; better, he looked completely different.

But that in itself was not enough. He paused for a moment, steadying himself against the bathroom door, while those tongues of agony, like tongues of fire, leapt up from the broken jawbone into the back of his skull. Then he went into the bedroom and felt inside his suitcase for the box that held his cuff links; this was where he kept the contact lenses; he slipped them into his eyes with care. Then, and only then, he picked up the two photographs. He went back into the bright light of the bathroom. He looked at the photographs very intently: first at the one of Cass Kenny, taken on his wedding day when he had been thirty-five, and then at the one of his son, Jeff, taken in Vietnam shortly before his last mission; he had been twenty-four at the time.

Only when he had studied them both for what seemed to him like a long time did he dare to raise his head and look at the reflection confronting him.

The likeness was so uncanny that his heart leapt inside him. Of course, he'd known all along that he looked a lot like Kenny, though the realization had been slow to strike him, and the other men in the hut had found it more remarkable than he had. ("Hey, Jeff, here's your brother come to join you.") But this . . .

Turning his head to and fro as he studied the reflection critically and with care, he came to the conclusion that this was clever: this was a projection of Kenny as he might have been if he had suffered a serious face wound, if he had lived on through another seven years as a prisoner of war.

Yes, it was clever, but was it clever enough? That was a question which could only be answered by Jeff Kenny's mother.

Three

"Hi, baby, how are ya?" Murray had reappeared; his voice over the phone was totally unmistakable, a Bronx-sharpened and California-slightly-blunted hacksaw.

Virginia sighed and said, "Fine, Murray, just fine. How are you?"

"Richer. We sold every apartment of that goddam building in Nice, how do you like that?"

"Great, Murray."

"Can I come up and see you sometime, like now?"

"Of course. When did you get in?"

"Five minutes ago."

"Sure, come on up." She replaced the receiver, remembering how she herself used to feel after that thirteen-hour flight: incapacitated for about a week. But Murray Forde was Murray Forde. A shave, a quick shower, a change of clothing, and there he'd be.

There he was, a square rock of a man, grizzled hair cut short, ugly engaging face showing no more and no less sign of strain than it ever did. Sortilège and a fabulous beige crocodile handbag from Hermès for her, and for Chris . . . It had to be admitted that this seemingly unimaginative individual was endowed with a perfect, a profound understanding of that seemingly intractable child. Who else, who else in the entire world, would have thought to bring her a miniature and original caftan from Morocco, coffee-colored, embroidered with gold thread around neck, front, sleeves and hem? He must have had it specially made.

Seeing it, Virginia's heart contracted at the devastating unsuitability; seeing Chris's face as *she* saw it, she realized that he had been extravagantly, uniquely right all over again. In fact, he had been more than right; he had been perceptive in an extremely subtle way. The gift proved that he, too, had realized that eleven is a terrible age, that the baggy jeans and the owlish sunglasses were a protection against inevitable womanhood; he had realized that even if Joanne Christina never wore the caftan in public, and she probably never would, she would try it out in front of her long mirror, and perhaps—who knew?—see herself as the attractive girl she must sometime make up her mind to become.

Cursing Murray, for he often moved her when she had no wish to be moved by him, Virginia turned away to fix him a drink. How on earth could so profoundly blunt, often infuriating, a man be so profoundly subtle?

The subtlety alarmed her. One day, if she wasn't careful, she might find that it had undermined her; she might find herself married to him; he had asked her enough times.

He was telling them that the Europeans had gone crazy. In spite of every kind of economic trouble, they were still buying property; but he personally was pulling out. If they could finish selling the complex in Mallorca, complete La Terrasse du Soleil at Ajaccio and get rid of the remaining properties on the Algarve, that would suit Murray J. Forde just fine. He had enough stashed away to see himself dead in luxury, and his goddam son and daughter, with all their fancy pretensions (based on whose money, he might ask?), as far as he was concerned they could go screw; if there was anything left, he'd leave it to an old folks' home.

Chris, clutching the caftan to her stomach, feeling the odd foreignness of it with sensitive fingers, gazed at this man through her huge glasses with complete attention; he was virtually the only one of her grandmother's friends who ever engaged her complete attention. It always seemed to her that in comparison to everyone else, nature had left him unfinished; he reminded her of something in her sculpture book that somebody, Michelangelo or someone like that, had abandoned in mid-creation. There were times when, comparing these half-finished things with the final perfection, she thought they were more exciting; there seemed to be a kind of force in them, like the force of the stone itself. Murray affected her in the same way; she could almost see the energy crackling around him like something in a comic strip—Zing! Whang! Crunch!

With another part of her mind she was wondering how Murray was going to get along with Leo, and vice versa.

Virginia was wondering the same thing. Leo was due to put in an appearance in about an hour's time; it would probably be better if he didn't put it in alone. She excused herself and went to a distant phone, called Mary Thorensen, who could always be relied upon to fill an awkward gap (and, alas, tell everybody all about it later, but that couldn't be helped), and asked her for cocktails, adding that Leo would pick her up and drive her to the house. She then called Leo at his office and asked him to do this.

When she got back to the terrace, Murray was telling an enraptured Chris about the Ouled Nails, the North African tribe which trains its women to become whores in the dissolute coastal cities.

The man whose identity documents claimed that he was called James Robert White, and whom chance and careful planning had transformed into a clever likeness of Jeff Kenny, missing and believed killed in Vietnam, got back to Los Angeles at ten o'clock next morning as planned. He checked into the Sunset Plaza Apartment Hotel, where he had made a booking; it was a friendly place, much used by visiting actors, musicians, advertising men. He told them at the desk that the weather in the Middle West had been terrible, and that what he wanted most in the world was a little of that good old California sunshine. (As a result of losing the mustache and beard, he looked peaked, sallow, and this was not at all the image he wanted to project.) However, the sun would wait. First things first. He needed a new driver's license displaying a photograph of the new James White—hair, brown; eyes, brown. Once that was procured, he could feel that he had covered his tracks; the old James White—hair, blond; eyes, grey—would have been disposed of officially.

He changed out of his smart clothes into jeans and a shirt, and went to the offices of the Department of Motor Vehicles. He presented the necessary forms, already filled in, and his papers from the Aldington Institute. The usual bureaucratic face examined them with the usual bureaucratic suspicion.

"A new license?"

"Sure. Why not?"

"You never held one before?"

"Nope."

"How come?"

He had suffered a good deal from bureaucracy during his rootless youth. "Look," he said, with controlled savagery, "I was a kid when they sent me to Vietnam to fight your lousy goddam war for you, and I was a P.O.W. for ten years. Why would I need a car?"

Evidently bureaucracy, like everyone else, didn't want to be reminded of that war. James White was tested, photographed, processed, issued with a California driver's license in record time.

After that he rented himself a car; drove it to a good barbershop, where he had his hair cut and restyled; drove it back to the Sunset Plaza Apartment Hotel, where he parked it in the underground lot before offering himself to the sun for the rest of the day. He knew that with care and caution and the right kind of cream he would be looking very different by late afternoon, even if he would be feeling rather overheated.

At five o'clock he reeled back to his apartment, lay down and slept for a couple of hours—the sun always demanded that of him. He awoke feeling and looking good. As he showered, dressed, went out, drank four Scotches and ate a steak, he considered the next part of his plan, the girl-hunt.

It was a tricky operation for many reasons, not the least of them being that the girl would be the first human being other than himself on whom he would have to rely. Primarily he needed a nice girl, an intelligent girl whose reflexes and responses were in the right places. Of course, she must find him attractive, and if she wanted to go to bed with him, so much the better, but the vitally important thing was that he should *appeal* to her, to the woman in her; and that hoary old cliché, when all the pretenses had been stripped away from it, meant the mother in her. This was vital; nothing else mattered very much. He wanted a nice girl with motherly instincts and a big heart.

He washed his hands in the men's room of the restaurant where he'd been eating, and combed his hair. Yes, he looked good. Hi, Jeff Kenny!

But just as he was turning away he suddenly caught a glimpse of that reflection from a completely different angle, and it made him turn back to the mirror, examining the face more closely. Hi, Jeff Kenny! I killed you, didn't I, you poor son-of-a-bitch?

The thought didn't trouble him unduly—it never had. What troubled him was the idea that it was himself, his own reflection, that he had killed.

Rose Maddox would have scoffed at the suggestion that she was a nice girl. No actress could afford to be "nice," everybody knew that. She would have denied any motherly instincts, since nothing plays havoc with a career as sharply and as irrevocably as kids. She was, however, beginning to suspect that she did have a big heart. Too big. Anybody who made, and continued to make, such a fool of herself over men had to have too big a heart.

In that case, what the hell was she doing propping up the bar at the Intermission, all on her own, like a hooker?

Well, in spite of the looks that cow Liz Ellis was giving her, secure among a bevy of other people as usual, she was not on the lookout for a man. A man was the last thing she was on the lookout for, so thank God for Terry, who had appeared like a fat and friendly puppy at her elbow. No one could accuse Terry of being a man. And if only she wasn't feeling so damn low, she would really be enjoying his description of this audition he went to where he hadn't realized that they were looking for a black actor. She liked Terry; she knew that he had joined her because he was sorry for her in her loneliness, and recognized that she was not the kind of girl who liked propping up bars on her own—even at the Intermission, which was almost entirely patronized by actors. He probably knew all about Paul, too; the

Terrys of the world seemed to know all about everything to do with other people's love affairs, particularly the disastrous ones.

He was saying, "Honey, don't look now, but there's something really rather lovely down the end of the bar who is de*vouring* you with bedroom eyes."

Rose sighed. "Dark hair with grey glints and a two-hundred-dollar leather coat?"

"Trust you to know. Could be a director, darling."

"In here! Could be a waiter from Hamburger Hamlet."

"Well . . . he can pop *me* into a bun and douse me with mustard any time he likes."

"Looks that way to me."

"Uh-*huh!*" He shook his head decisively. Rose hadn't really thought that. As soon as she saw the man she had thought, Watch it, dear! because he was a type she had tripped over before; she definitely didn't intend to trip over that type ever again, measuring her length on the floor, or worse, the bed. No, no, never again! That type or any other.

"He approaches!" said Terry, sotto voce. "By the pricking of my thumbs, something groovy this way comes." And, loudly, for effect: ". . . it wasn't really your *part,* darling, but you were super. I sat through it twice."

Rose could feel that the good-looking man in the leather coat was now just behind her; he was asking the bartender for another drink; he had a nice voice. Terry (he must have heard about her bust-up with Paul, he was behaving like a matchmaking aunt), speaking across her, said to this total stranger, "Your name isn't Bill Smith, is it? Somebody was asking for a Bill Smith on the phone just now."

"No. I'm James White."

There was nothing unusual about this. Actors were always being called at the Intermission; jobs often arose from these calls, so they were important.

"Hi, James White, I'm Terry. This is Rose."

Rose made a face at him, and then turned. "Rose Maddox."

"You're English."

"Bloody Limey," said Terry cheerfully. "Take it or leave it, you know what they're like."

When he smiled she noticed for the first time that he had a

scar down the left side of his face, there was something sad about the smile, something a little wistful, which moved her in spite of herself.

"On the whole," he said, still smiling (turning on the charm a bit, she knew that), "I guess I'd be inclined to take it."

His drink arrived. He offered Rose and Terry one. Since her glass was empty, she could hardly refuse. Terry had managed to sidle away; he had other fish to fry. The man with the scarred face said, "Why so blue, Rose Maddox?"

"That's my habitual expression."

"And that's a lie."

She had no intention of telling him one single thing about herself. On the other hand, that bitch Liz Ellis was looking at them with fury—as well she might, since all the men she was with were long- and greasy-haired slobs, and the only one who was good-looking was a fairy. So Rose smiled and said, "I was turned down for a part today, and I'm far from home."

"Don't you like it here?"

"I'm a pro. I like anywhere I'm getting jobs and making bread. And yes, I like it a hell of a lot better than bloody London."

She had no intention of telling him one single thing about herself. But she did. He took her to Romy's, where there was music, and he gave her quite a lot to drink. He made no secret of the fact that he found her attractive, but he wasn't pushy. And since every other tune they played was a painful link with Paul (there was nothing like pop music for turning that particular screw), she suddenly found she'd told him everything. He had the nicest brown eyes, and he listened so attentively. About one man in a hundred ever listened to a woman at all.

He listened and he assessed; and she had no way of knowing that behind the mask of the contact lenses, which were beginning to irritate him again, his eyes were as cold and bleak a grey as any she had ever seen.

This wasn't the girl he'd envisaged, not at all; but it was beginning to seem possible that she was right. There was a kind of . . . what was it? . . . a directness about English girls, which would be very effective when it came to the crunch. And it would be unexpected. The unexpectedness of her being English would probably confuse the issue to his own advantage. As for her looks, nobody could have called her pretty, but she was very attractive, with that tawny hair and slightly tip-tilted nose; her figure was superb; she was intelligent (too intelligent?) and she had that air of finish, of being at home anywhere, which he had noticed before in actresses. And why not? They were used to being a hundred different people. Of course, she was an idiot about men . . .

Obviously, as any other man could tell right away, this Paul was an utter louse. They had been on tour together with some play; the contract had lasted as far as L.A., but there was a chance of going on because the play was a success: Phoenix, Dallas, points southeast. But this Paul had fancied his chances in Hollywood, and rather than lose him, she had left the company too. So then it had become the usual story of unsuccess, and to compound matters, she had been the one to get any work that was going; so gorgeous Paul sat around and sulked, and, inevitably, packed up and disappeared three days ago while she was auditioning for this part she had failed to get. Had he known anything about show business, he might have heard this story a dozen times.

But it was amusing to see Los Angeles through her eyes: its devastating ugliness, which he never noticed; the odd arid beauty of the hills surrounding it; the enormous disappointment of Malibu, which had always sounded to her so glamorous but which had turned out to be any old stretch of sand, overbuilt for its entire length with mostly horrible houses—and the Pacific so icy cold! Sometimes in the mornings she would wake up and look out over the city, flat under that kind of *sodden* sunlight, with smog hovering like a dirty yellow veil to the east, and she wanted to sit down and cry. She would trudge along Hollywood Boulevard, unable to believe its particular brand of poverty-stricken yet brash squalor, and then suddenly it would be night, and there were things happening, fun places to go, smart places like Romy's, grotty places like Barney's Beanery (as opposed to London, where there was nowhere, but *nowhere*, to go), and suddenly you were with the right people or person—she squeezed his hand gratefully—and everything was wonderful and exciting.

And then, even if it was all ugly and blank sometimes under the overhead sun, it all *worked.* Oh my God, he had no idea what it was like to live in a city like London where nothing worked. You dialed a number, and it was the wrong one. You went out to replace a bra, and the shop you'd bought it at not only didn't have one, but denied that they'd ever stocked it. You sent your best dress to a cleaner and it came back dirtier than when it had gone, and with a tear on the hem.

Soon, he knew, he would be unable to bear the contact lenses a moment longer. He wasn't sure about this girl, and he had no intention of making snap judgments at such a late stage of the proceedings; her part in his plans was not a big one but it was vital. Anyway, just in case he decided to use her, there was no harm in planting one of the seeds which, if he *did* use her, would have to be planted anyway.

He passed a hand over his face and grimaced a little, artfully. She got it in one. "Does it hurt you? The scar, I mean?"

"Sometimes. I get these headaches."

"How did it happen? Jesus, I've done nothing but talk about myself."

"You needed to." With a wan smile.

"Vietnam?"

He nodded. He was putting her to the test, the first test. He had an idea that she'd pass it with flying colors. She did: "Come on, take me home. You ought to have told me it hurt you, you ought to be in bed."

He managed a rueful grin. "Whose bed?"

"Your own, darling."

He kissed her with a good deal of warmth before letting her go. She responded instinctively, but then pulled away. He knew that she liked him, maybe quite a lot, but that Paul had slid between them. On the whole, he wasn't altogether sorry about Paul. But he continued to hold her.

"Please," she said, "I must go."

"On one condition."

She peered at him in the shifting light of streetlamps through trees.

"You have dinner with me tomorrow night."

"Okay. What time?"

Yes, he liked that directness; no itsy-bitsy prevarications, pretending she had another date. "Seven-thirty? Here?"

He watched her let herself into the small apartment building. North Hayworth, it seemed exactly the right place for her to live. Everything about her seemed right, though not at all in the way he had foreseen. Well, that was life; but life had to be watched, it could come up with some very unexpected twists, particularly as regards the human element. He must play it cool, cool and thorough, the way he'd played everything else. So far.

At 234 Upper Canyon Circle, Chris lay in bed savoring her evening. It had been a *smash* evening, with all the adults in sight behaving in their goofiest manner. And, boy, could they be goofy!

If it came to giving out marks, and Joanne Christina often gave out marks to her elders and (doubtful) betters, the special prize, pretty nearly ten out of ten, had gone to guess who? Leo!

Of course, he and Murray had disliked each other on sight. Natch! Bulldog and Tomcat. Dear little old Grandma, in her bonnet and knitted mittens, had for once been at a loss, not knowing how to cope. Her dreadful friend Mary Thorensen, a really *grisly* lady in her mid-forties, once uneasily married to some director who had steered Grandfather Cass through a couple of long-dead Westerns, had taken about six cocktails too many. When this happened she tended to resent the fact that she had long ago wasted all her departed husband's dough, so instead of smoothing things over, which was obviously what Virginnypants had planned, she had decided to take out her biggest wooden spoon and *mix*.

By dinnertime (obviously Virginia had decided that whatever was going to happen had much better happen at home rather than in some crowded hashhouse) Mary Thorensen had mixed to such effect that Murray, who drank very little as a general rule, had hit the bourbon bottle, but good!

At the table, under the impassive eye of Tony the manservant, the only adult around to behave like a human being, Mary had finally gone as far as she could go, by saying, "Well, I don't know, I *really* don't know why you and Murray haven't got

48

hitched years ago, darling. It would be such a rest for you, darling, to know he wasn't after your money." (Three out of ten. She could have done it much better sober.)

Murray (seven out of ten) had said, "Oh, for Christ's sake, Mary, keep quiet."

Virginia (nought out of ten) had laughed very unsteadily and said, "Darling, I thought Dr. Nelson had laid you off the vodka for good."

Leo (seven out of ten at this moment, now she came to think of it) had asked Tony if he could have a little more bread. He was biding his time.

The rest of dinner was given over to a monologue from Murray about "old times," designed to show Leo that he had known Virginia for very, very many years, during which more than one Leo had come and gone unmourned; this was punctuated by hiccups from Mary, who, it was perfectly true, had been warned by her doctor on pain of death to cut down on hard liquor.

Leo (eight out of ten) had noticed that Virginia was not all that fascinated by Murray's list of dates, some of which were antediluvian, and had capitalized by saying in an offhand manner, "That one *has* to be wrong, Murray; Virginia can only have been a kid."

This, of course, made clumsy old Murray aware of what he had been doing agewise during the entire monologue, so he lapsed into bourbon-bemused silence while Tony tried to get Mary to gulp down a little neat vinegar. The hiccups had got that bad.

But prime time came after dinner when Leo had put down his coffee cup and had stood up, ignoring both drunks and saying to Virginia, "Well, honey, I'd better be going now; I seem to be the worker of this little party." Nine out of ten! And Chris had admired him so much that she had emerged from her usual position in semidarkness at the edge of the circle (fearing that she might be sent to bed and so miss a punch-up) in order to be included in his goodnights. If it had been possible, she would have congratulated him out loud.

Virginia had been completely taken aback, and her "Oh no, Leo, don't go yet" had held genuine surprise, even shock. Leo

49

had said goodnight to Chris, nodded to the other two, and had set off across the terrace towards his car. Virginia, still pleading with him to stay, had gone too.

Chris had no way of telling what occurred out of earshot, but it was the result that gave Leo Special Prize and ten out of ten; for presently there was the sound of the Mercedes driving away. The small girl and the two adults looked towards the drive for Virginia's return, but . . .

And here Joanne Christina actually hugged herself in bed, so deliciously zany had the grownups become.

But Virginia did not come back. Somehow or other, Leo had whisked her away in his car. And oh, the ecstasy of awkward conversation between Murray and drunken old Mary Thorensen that then followed! It had to be heard to be believed. Mary, who had sobered up a bit and had probably realized that she had gone further than too far, would have liked to go home, but could hardly do so without saying goodnight and thank you to her hostess. Besides, unless she sent for Tony (who was obviously giving Leona a rundown on the whole thing in the kitchen), she had to rely on Murray or a taxi to get her there. Murray, of course, could not budge one half-inch until Virginia reappeared.

This she eventually did, looking discomposed and perhaps even a little younger than usual. She refused to give any explanation (seven out of ten) and recaptured control of the entire situation (nine out of ten) by coming out fair and square on Leo's side, scolding her two old friends for their shocking behavior. "If I didn't love you both so much, I swear I'd never ask either of you to this house again."

Oh yes, a *super* evening, proving beyond doubt that Lewis Carroll had always written about adults exactly as they were, and that the only people who thought he'd been writing fantasy were adults themselves, like crazy people who know that everyone else is crazy and that they are sane.

Moreover, as penance, Murray had promised to take her to Disneyland tomorrow; it was Friday, which was a pity, but she'd have to give that a miss for one week. He had even agreed, in theory, to making an expedition to the desert at a later date. She hadn't mentioned the rattlesnake project, correctly believing that where Murray was concerned, it was better to take one step at a time; but she took her rattler jar out of the back of the closet and punched a few more airholes in the lid—for luck.

Chris had given Leo a Special Prize and ten out of ten. Leo, who knew himself better than she did, might have come up with a doubtful three. He recognized the face that gazed back at him from the gold-marbled mirror in this dreary bar as the face of failure. Carrying off Virginia like that, leaving those two slobs to marinate alone on the terrace, was in fact a meaningless gambit; he knew that he had neither the self-assertion nor the cunning to stand up to a man like Murray Forde if a man like Murray Forde wanted him out. The moment of braggadocio, which Chris had admired so much, had left him feeling flat, deflated; he didn't for one instant suppose that Forde or that appalling woman had been impressed by the action (he was constitutionally incapable of believing that he could impress anybody— apart from a certain kind of woman, given the right circumstances), and as for Virginia, he guessed, correctly, that she had probably forgotten the whole episode already.

Leo Faber's father had been a stunt man in the good old, grand old days, and his mother had been a stand-in. One had fallen off horses and crashed cars to save other people the risk and trouble; the other had stood for hours while cameramen fiddled about with lights which, in the end, would illuminate some much more famous face for a few minutes; they were both non-people; it had never surprised their son to find that he, too, was a non-person. Even his (very minor) job with Dalton, Schlock and Humboldt, stockbrokers, was liable to slip away from under him at any moment; he had only held onto it for so long, he guessed, because of an incident involving Mrs. Humboldt at a Christmas party last winter.

He ordered another Scotch, drank it quickly and ordered yet another, his fifth. Scotch was a help; and there was a passable blond lady of about forty at the other end of the bar who was giving him the eye, though she didn't *look* as if she had any more money than he did.

He hadn't been lying when he'd confessed to Virginia Kenny that he loved luxurious things; it was one of the few honest remarks he had ever made to her, but it had not, in fact, gone quite as far as the truth. The truth, which he now acknowledged gloomily as he gazed at his cracked reflection in the marbled mirror, was that he *worshipped* luxury.

No, even that was not quite the truth. When he had first set foot in 234 Upper Canyon Circle it was like taking an enormous gulp of some exotic and instant aphrodisiac. Luxury actually made him . . . yes it did, horny.

Oh come on, he thought, you're getting loaded!

This was the way he usually dodged his own infrequent attacks of honesty, but it didn't seem to work this evening. He looked it in the face and admitted it. Mrs. Virginia Kenny thought he was a pretty good lover, and she was obviously pleased that she excited him so much; but the fact was that she didn't excite him at all, and that when he made love to her he was making love to all the beautiful and expensive things surrounding her. It had been the same with many other ladies—even Mrs. Humboldt during that brief scuffle among the satin (satin!) sheets in her guest room while Mr. Humboldt was singing "Oh, come all ye faithful" with other inebriated members of the office staff downstairs.

Leo sighed, turning his elegant back on the passable but unluxurious blonde at the end of the bar, and ordered yet another Scotch.

Four

He could not sleep. He had taken the usual pills but they were not doing their job. There was this continual desire to get up and look at himself in the mirror. Could there be some doubt buried deep inside him? On the surface he didn't feel doubtful at all; he felt confident and strong.

It was partly to do with the girl. First of all, he could not get over the ease with which he had found her. Not that she was by any means the first he had tried out during the course of the evening in a dozen different night-spots of various kinds; he hadn't really expected to hit on anything remotely suitable on the first night's hunting anyway. Well, that was good; it meant that luck was on his side, still. But now that the girl had emerged as an actual person called Rose Maddox, with a whole being of her own and a personality, a strong one, to go with it, she had ceased to be a single cog in his carefully designed machine; she posed all kinds of questions, as human beings always did.

Also, the time factor was wrong. He needed to know her for two or three weeks before bringing her into play, but this was right out of the question for two reasons. The first was money; he couldn't afford to live this way for long. The Sunset Plaza Apartment hotel and the car rental were digging great gaping holes in his remaining capital. Romy's had proved to be shockingly expensive. Dinner tomorrow (no, tonight, because it was already three A.M.) had to be expensive too. The second reason was more vital still. He now looked remarkably like Jeff Kenny, and Jeff Kenny had spent several years in this town;

therefore, he couldn't possibly risk exposing himself around the place for the two or three weeks that he really needed to prepare the girl. The whole plan could blow up in his face if he was recognized just casually, by anyone. It was the kind of story that might even hit the newspapers, TV . . .

This appalling thought heaved him out of the bed yet again, a cold sweat in the small of his back.

Once long ago, before he had thought this thing through really carefully, he had contemplated just such a meeting, just such publicity following it; but only a little reflection had shown him the pitfalls. There must be no publicity of any kind; he would find himself surrounded by prying eyes and Pandora's boxes. Therefore, the plan he had decided upon was the right one and must be made to work. In four days, five at the most, he must act and the girl must be ready.

But Rose Maddox, and whatever complications she might pose by being a real live person and not a blueprint, was not the root of the trouble that kept him awake and pacing. The root, he realized as he stood looking at his reflection yet again, was the reflection itself. It was Jeff Kenny who stood between himself and sleep . . .

. . . None of it seemed real to him. The doctors, to whom he'd naturally been lying anyway, said that this was due partly to the wound and partly to a syndrome often found in returned prisoners-of-war. It was like looking back at one of those dreams which seem very vivid and real at the moment of waking, but which become more and more disjointed and absurd the longer you consider them. Parts of this near-waking dream have a habit of escaping altogether, yet, disconcertingly, the absurdity and the fragmentation seem to be capable of touching real fears and emotions.

A miasma of hash and booze, black-market everything, little kids (ten? eleven?) asking if you wanted a fuck, thousands of hopeless, homeless people piled up with their possessions along the roadside like garbage, watching you, the conquering hero, the liberator, as you selected your girl on Tu Do Street, or reeled out of the Caravelle, having spent what you knew was enough money to keep one of their families for a whole year.

He could *feel* the obscenity of it, even though there were so few actual details that he could really remember. The obscenity, hopeless, purposeless, joyless, would occupy the marrow of his bones forever. All wars were probably hopeless and purposeless to the poor dumb soldiers who were instructed to fight them; but *that* war . . . ! Oh Jesus Christ! Even furlough, even the longed-for moments of respite were obscene; more so, in many ways, than the actual fighting. He could taste, now, as he gazed into his own eyes in Jeff Kenny's face, the vomit of those drunken, hash-haunted furloughs. Sensual gratification without pleasure, joyless merrymaking, always watched by the piles of rotting yet living humanity along the roadside.

He had led a rough youth; it wasn't possible that Saigon should sicken him more than other men, yet some had professed to be untouched by it. Could that have been true? Could it be that his own youth, so violent and so sickening, had found an echo . . . ?

He tore his mind away from this, and thought of combat. "Combat!" What a typically military word! How those shaven-headed automatons, marked up as majors or colonels or whatever, had gloried in that word, *combat*. What the hell had they been thinking of in their brainwashed little crew-cut heads? Custer's Last Stand, maybe. Or Hannibal crossing the Alps. Whereas combat was rain and bugs and bad feet, and huddling under a rag of canvas with Perry, who was always so high that he could have done the Indian rope trick as efficiently as he could fire an automatic weapon. Perry had a habit of singing "Michelle, ma belle" every time he was sent out on patrol, so it wasn't very long before a small yellow man in a big tree shot *him* through the head. Plop, he went, disappearing into the muddy yellow water of some paddy. Plop, plop—that was Ed and Johnny. You had to fish for them, which made you a sitting target, in order to find out if they were dead or well enough to be patched up for an eventual repeat performance.

Arthur made "combat" possible because he was Jewish New York, and his folks had seen so much trouble in Russia and thereafter that he found almost anything funny. Plop. Poor old Pete this time. "They'll never get me," said Arthur, "they don't like kosher meat."

Perhaps he was right; he'd certainly been absent, doing his term of joyless furlough when *it* had happened.

It was, to any but a crew-cut brainwashed major, a foregone conclusion; at least that was the opinion of his know-nothing, bombed-out, militarily ignorant slaves. "I'm here to tell you men that there's been a big breakthrough." After a while you could follow their language, kind of. The "big breakthrough" simply meant that a few billion dollars' worth of merchandise had been fired, dropped, rocketed northwards, and the little yellow men, possibly a couple of hundred of them, had come down out of their trees and tippy-toed away in the night, leaving behind them a mild-looking bunch of peasants, any one of whom might whip out a small gun and shoot you in the back before returning to the propagation of his rice.

"We," the major continued ("we" always meant "you"), "are going to exploit this situation to the full . . ."

No need to go further. The only people to exploit the situation were the little yellow men who had taken up advantageous positions some twenty-five miles further north.

For some reason he was overcome by a desperate urge to get the contact lenses and slip them over those grey avid pupils. Yes, he did indeed look very like Jeff Kenny: not the Jeff Kenny whom he himself had last seen, a young man wasted by fever and sickness, staring up at him in surprise as he had placed a piece of sacking over his face, pressing gently in order to stifle him; not that Jeff Kenny, but a metamorphosis of that Jeff Kenny, an act of the imagination.

It would be eleven years since Jeff's mother, or anyone else outside the service, had last seen him. That would ordinarily be rather a short time as far as faces were concerned, but the circumstances were not ordinary; there was nothing ordinary about war, and wounds, and internment in a Vietcong P.O.W. camp.

Would it work? Would she, they, accept him? This was where, in the last resort, he was being really clever. For he was not going to say, "I am Jeff Kenny." He was going to say, "Am I Jeff Kenny?"

It was odd: he could not even remember all the details of that inglorious patrol. Why had he been chosen, anyway? Perhaps the major had a grudge against him; perhaps he was one of the few men in the company who wasn't bombed-out; perhaps by keeping his mouth shut he had earned the reputation of being a reliable soldier.

Slosh slosh through the paddies, swish swish through those goddam bamboos with leaves like razor blades, crunch crunch over stubble, clatter clatter up a slippery hillside . . . The little yellow men in their nests must have been plotting their approach for hours.

The actual engagement was unspectacular: a rattle of automatic fire, a few rounds of well-aimed sniping, a few grenades throwing up cocoa-colored dust—and silence.

"I'm here to tell you men that there's been a big breakthrough, and we are going to exploit this situation to the full."

Obviously, he was unconscious for quite a long time. When he came to, it felt as though he had a huge hole where the bottom of his face had been. He didn't know that only two of his companions had survived to beat a hasty retreat, and if he had, he would never have blamed them for leaving him among the dead. He would probably have concluded that they'd done him a good turn, since it must have been the fact that he was the only living survivor which had kept him a living survivor. The little yellow men expected him to give them information; it must have been touch-and-go when they realized that he was not going to be able to speak a word for weeks. Or perhaps that doctor who looked young enough to be in high school (but he was never able to tell their ages) had a special interest in jaw surgery; if so, this was his first case, because the darned thing mended crooked, hence the headaches. Anyway, at least it did mend, and at least he stayed alive to appreciate the fact.

First of all, the smiling kid doctor got him into what must have been a field hospital, though it looked like the result of an Indian massacre that hadn't yet been tidied up. He had no idea how long he was there—no idea how long he was anywhere. What did time matter, anyway?

Eventually they put him in a truck and drove him northward; then dumped him out and made him walk; then put him in another truck; then made him walk again. Occasionally various people would ask him questions about movement of units and positions of landing strips. Perhaps they couldn't understand what he was talking about; his tongue kept getting in the way of his teeth, and of course he knew nothing about units or airstrips, but he gave them complicated answers, and they were too polite to show how much he bored them.

One day he arrived at a village around which they had thrown up a wire fence; it was the first camp, a forward one which was eventually to be abandoned. And here there were majors and captains and the rest of them, doing their thing, like elderly ladies in reduced circumstances, trying to pretend that some ratty old boarding house was the grand hotel to which they had once been accustomed. The enlisted men paid as little attention to them as was possible.

And here, as he entered the hut allocated to him, one of the guys already there uttered the magic words that were to change the whole course of his life: "Well, I'll be darned! Hey, Jeff, here's your brother come to join you!"

At first he couldn't see it at all. The young airman lying in the corner had brown hair, whereas his was blond, bleached a little by sun; he had dark-brown eyes, whereas his own were sharply grey; he had no ugly red-raw scar disfiguring his left cheek. But gradually, as time went on, the similarity began to strike him as possible. They were almost exactly the same height and possessed of roughly the same facial bone structure, though that would never be clear now because of the older man's wound. (He was, in fact, a year and nine months older than Jeff Kenny.) In the end he had to agree that there was a kind of likeness, but he didn't find it very interesting. Neither of them did.

But then, in the boredom of those endless hot damp days, he began to realize that his fellow prisoner in the corner was the son of a famous film star. He himself had been quite a Cass Kenny fan; a loner himself, he had been attracted by the loner that Cass had always played: a glamorized loner, catalyst in the lives of more ordinary, involved people, who would like him or need him or love him or come to rely on him for the requisite number of reels, before he went away alone, lost in the sunset (if it was that kind of Western) or in the city's teeming streets (if it was that kind of private-eye concoction) or simply disappearing through French windows, leaving the curtains billowing gently in the wind machine (if it was that kind of love story).

Then he found that, born in poverty and disaster himself, with a mother who had disappeared during his sixth year, unremembered, he was fascinated by Kenny's background, so utterly different: the money and the constant movement—Rome, Gstaad, Paris, Madrid, Munich, Ibiza, England, New York, Venice, Dubrovnik, Rome . . . And as he watched and listened, something about their similarity came to him slowly; they were not superficially alike at all, they were deeply alike. The surface of each of them was very different, but it was this deep resemblance which had been recognized instantly by the man, not a very bright man either, who had called out, "Hey, Jeff, here's your brother."

This was food for thought during the restless nights when each of them was trapped in his own self, alone in the very special way that all prisoners are alone.

He had no idea just when the idea, the fantasy idea, slipped quietly into the back of his mind; often, during those nights, he would imagine how it might have been to experience a childhood, a young-manhood like that. He was quite sure that the idea had ceased to be fantasy long before Kenny had fallen ill; it must have been prior to the illness that he had surreptitiously studied the other man's body, while they took their turn at the makeshift shower, to see whether there were any physical dissimilarities—birthmarks, moles, anything really noticeable—that would distinguish them utterly one from the other. He found nothing, and from this moment, possibly without his knowing it, the course was set.

There was no American doctor in that camp. A couple of medics did what they could with whatever the Vietcong could let them have in the way of drugs, they readily admitted their absolute ignorance of the disease which had seized on Jeff Kenny, and aspirin was all they could prescribe.

He had no idea of exactly when the plan stepped out from the back of his mind, ready for total action. Suddenly one day, crouching by Kenny's mattress, watching his uneasy breathing, the sweat that stained his smelly shirt, he knew that he could become this man—that he *would* become this man. Why not? If he ever got back to the States, what awaited him? He had nothing to look forward to, not even a home. He had little education, no money, no friends, and by the time all this was over, he'd have no strength either, so that the rough manual jobs which had kept him solvent before the war would be closed to him.

But what would Jeff Kenny go back to, if he survived? A rich house in Beverly Hills, a rich mother to supply everything the returning hero might need, an income of his own no doubt, a marriage which the said rich mother had tidied up so efficiently that it was now no marriage at all—except for a kid who hadn't even seen him, and a wife who, by all accounts, had been banished by mother to the outer limits of Antarctica.

Oh God, what the hell was he thinking about? Half the guys in the place were going nuts, and he was on the brink of joining them. And poor old Kenny wanted more water.

But once born, the idea would not leave him; it grew day by day like a large and rapacious infant, and very soon reached maturity. In maturity it revealed itself as being stronger than the father who had sired it; this was when the idea became an obsession. The obsession said that first of all he must find out everything, yes, everything there was to know about the sick man.

Later he was to look back at those early detective efforts and be appalled by their amateurishness, by the thousand wasted opportunities; but it had taken his brain a long time to get going on the project, and of course, as he now realized, he had been fighting all the time against the effects that imprisonment were having upon himself: debilitating inaction and a diet that barely kept him alive. In the circumstances he had not done too badly, but there had been some terrible moments. He could remember very clearly, more clearly than he could remember the diastrous patrol which was responsible for the whole thing, the night when he had started up from the edge of sleep in a muck-sweat because the thought of blood groups had just popped into his mind.

Agony had followed; an infinity of waiting and prevaricating until he could reasonably bring up the subject, using the remote, indeed unfeasible, possibility that somehow a transfusion might be arranged to help the sick man. If the answer had been anything but "O," he wondered what he would have done. The thing had such a grip on him by then that he probably wouldn't have been able to abandon it even if reason had told him he must.

And so he would sit, day after day, night after night, watching, waiting for Jeff Kenny to emerge from his bouts of fever so that they could talk. Luckily, once a bout had passed, Kenny returned to a normal, though each time weaker, state of mind. What did he think of this soldier with the wounded face, this soldier that some of the men said was so like him, who pried and pried and pried into his past? It was hard to say; his upbringing and background had perhaps made of him a rather spoiled and self-centered young man; he had always only needed to raise a finger to get whatever he wanted from adoring parents—adoring and perhaps guilt-haunted parents, who felt at the back of their minds that their way of life was not giving the boy any of the chances, the education, the friends, that he should really have. Perhaps he, too, felt that his life had been unusually interesting and glamorous, and should, by rights, occasion curiosity and envy in a poor uneducated soldier born on the wrong side of the tracks. Or perhaps, trapped there, he merely found it a comfort to recall happier days; perhaps he merely needed a friend and someone to help him in the weakness and indignity of his sickness.

Every one of these conversations was rewarding to the man who searched, but each was followed by a period which, unknown to Kenny, was even more rewarding, the period when he began to slip back once more into the fever. His voice would become slurred; the pauses between sentences became longer; the pained brown eyes would close in the pale, drawn face, but the voice would go on.

Now the soldier would have to lean closer and closer to hear the words; and the words were like nectar to his obsession, because now the semiconscious, the subconscious, was speaking, and for a few minutes he could almost feel that he was entering the other man's mind. What was going on there was never easy to follow; only occasionally would the words tie in with something that had been said consciously; yet in a strange way, which he would try to define but could not, it was these minutes of semioccult communion which gave him confidence to believe that he could do the thing he planned.

When Kenny at last relapsed into silence he would retire to

his own corner and mull over what had passed between them; he would go over each detail again and again in his head, for these were the only notes that he dared make. To write anything down was impossible; it would be taken away from him and destroyed.

The rough day-to-day, hand-to-mouth life he had always led on the wrong side (which is to say the east side) of Los Angeles, and the company he had kept at that time, had demanded very little of his mind, so that it came to him as something of a shock to find that he not only had one but that it was very cunning and keen and, more important, linked to a retentive memory; it was as if Fate had let his mind lie fallow in preparation for this extraordinary idea, this overbearing Authority, which was one day going to invade it, take it over completely and use it to its utmost limit.

Gazing at himself—some nine years later in a mirror at the Sunset Plaza Apartment Hotel at four in the morning—he realized that this late discovery of his mind and its power, and the subsequent concentrated use of it, had actually changed his face in some indefinable way. Age, of course, had changed it too, but age alone would not have given the boy from East Los Angeles this kind of . . . yes, it was a kind of refinement. Use of his intelligence had given him an intelligent look. He now realized that it was probably this, as much as anything else, that had completed his close resemblance to Jeff Kenny and, to a degree, his father.

There it was. Nature and his imagination had worked together to produce protective coloring.

He remembered that there had been much talk at this time about evacuating the camp, which had in any case been rigged up as a temporary measure. The commandant had asked the senior American officer how many of his men would be able to begin the long journey north on foot. Whatever the answer, Jeff Kenny cannot have been numbered among them; the two medics agreed that it could only be a matter of time, though there was a chance that transport might be provided for the sick, and that Kenny might thus reach a proper doctor in time to save his life.

Of course this was unthinkable; therefore he had to be killed, poor bastard.

It was odd that neither then nor at any time since had this action, the pinching out of Jeff Kenny's wavering flame of life, troubled him at all. He often wondered about it. Did it mean that he had been born with a capacity for murder? Surely not? Did it mean that all men were born with a capacity for murder, and all their preaching and punishing and moralizing were simply belated efforts to hide the ugly truth from themselves? Quite likely. Or did it mean that a compulsion as overwhelming as the one which possessed him was a morality and a law and a god unto itself, for whom there was, quite simply, no wrong?

He didn't know. He only knew that he had moved over to Kenny's mattress one night, as he did five or six times every night, that he had in his hand the gunnysack which he used as a pillow, that Kenny had been awake and had given him a strange look (of recognition? of relief? of surprise?) as he had placed the sack gently over his face, leaning on it with only a little weight. There had not even been a struggle, no struggle of any kind. It was almost as if, all along, Jeff Kenny had known this helpful and curious young soldier to be death in torn denim, and had simply given himself, unprotesting, to the inevitable.

Death had crouched by the bed for a little while afterwards, pouring out some water and whispering as he always did, in case any of the others were awake and watching. During this little while he removed from Kenny's neck the medallion he always wore, a gold disc with an eye engraved on it; he also removed, from a slit in the grass-stuffed mattress, some folded paper that he knew was hidden there: a letter to his mother which the dead boy had written compulsively when he first came to the place, but had despaired of ever posting.

And so another of them died during the night; it had been expected for a long time; he was buried on the hillside above the camp, four days before the move north was due to begin.

The medallion and the folded letter he had hidden in the ragged hem at the bottom of the left leg of his denims.

All great endeavors demand risk. So far he had risked nothing, but he knew that in order to take the first physical step towards becoming Jeff Kenny, he now had to act decisively. He could not afford to move north with these men who knew him, he might never be able to escape from that knowledge. Therefore, he must part company with them; he must disappear, and since recapture was inevitable, he must see to it that he was recaptured in another place at another time. There were a hundred small details to this plan, and the obsessed mind had, it seemed to him, taken care of all of them. The rest was up to chance, time and the bureaucratic muddle in which, as he well knew, the Services conducted most of their affairs.

He planned to bide his time and to make a break for it at some suitable moment on the road north. He could not know that even as he was formulating his plan, one of his own countrymen high overhead on a reconnaissance flight was busy misreading signs and portents with an efficiency which would put paid to the plan and, nearly, to his life; though there would also be a built-in bonus if he could survive to take advantage of it.

"Enemy forces concentrating in area . . ." or whatever militarese the crop-heads were using at that time. Combat! Strike! Wham! No small and inoffensive P.O.W. compound can ever have been the target of such a massive onslaught. Stop, for Christ's sake! Can't you see our faces are white. All faces same color from that height at that speed. Little running figures biting the dust amid a thunder of explosives. Enemy forces concentrating . . . My country 'tis of thee. Enough hardware pounded into that half a square mile of hillside to pay for the building of a fair-sized cancer research hospital back home plus running costs for five years.

When the roof departed from the hut, he had started running, heading for the hills in the wake of the little yellow men who thirty seconds before had been his prison guards. Chance, seeming at this moment to have attained almost divine proportions (as if someone up there thoroughly approved of all that he had done and planned, which could certainly not be the case), had blown him into what was succinctly known in that camp as "the shit-pit." Gasping and retching, he could be forgiven for not appreciating at the time that this horror had actually saved his life, while most of the little yellow men whom he had been following into the trees had been blown to dust—as had the recently interred body of poor old Jeff Kenny.

When the uproar subsided at some later moment (it could have lasted three minutes, it could have lasted three hours, there was no way of telling), he had disentangled himself from the dead body of one of the medics, who had been blown into the shit-pit after him, crawled out of that life-saving hole and lain there spewing helplessly.

A few men were wandering dazedly about the devastated and smoking area where there remained no sign whatever of a camp or of the trees which had given it a little wavering shade. One or two of them fell over as he watched. Of the yellow men, no sign!

He knew that beyond the hillside where they had laid Jeff Kenny to (short) rest, there was water of some kind. His brain appeared to be functioning, though he could hear nothing but a loud and continuous roaring inside his head. He stood up and began to run towards the water, struggling out of his clothing as he did so, but remembering to hold onto his pants because of what was in the hem of the left leg. On the way he passed the more or less intact body of a pilot called Sullivan, who had known Jeff Kenny slightly and had visited him once or twice in his sickness. He knelt down and relieved Sullivan of his pants and his shirt, which still bore Air Force insignia. The obsession, he noted, was still in full control of its faculties and in no mood to be distracted by a few hundred thousand tons of high explosives. It remembered to take Sullivan's boots too.

The water didn't look very clean or refreshing, but it could hardly be worse than the shit-pit; he dropped the clothing and flung himself in, rubbing his body with a fury of loathing. After that he was sick again. Then he dragged himself into the cover of some bamboos and lay down until a little strength should come creeping back into his body. The roaring in his head continued, and every now and again he was attacked by a fit of violent trembling. Later he extracted the gold medallion with the eye on it and the letter to Mrs. Kenny from his stinking pants, and threw the pants as far away from him as his meager strength would allow. Then he dressed himself in Sullivan's clothes, and staying right where he was, lay down again and went to sleep.

It was dark when he awoke. He felt dizzy and sick, but the roaring inside his head had abated a little and the fits of trembling were occurring less frequently. Making as little noise as possible, he left the bamboos and set off uphill, not wanting to flounder about in swampland all night. Then he turned away from the camp, where no light showed and nothing seemed to be moving, and when he judged the distance to be safe, he took what he hoped would be a parallel course to the road on which the camp had been situated. He had expected jungle country, but presumably the hills were higher than he'd thought, for the going was easy, not much different from a walk across country in Griffith Park. He was desperately hungry and about three times as weak as he'd been before the U.S. Air Force had showered its attentions on him.

He needed food, and he needed to keep going north until he was well away from the patch of scarred hillside which had once been the camp, until whatever might remain of his former colleagues had been collected and taken away or shot dead. And at all costs he must somehow avoid being shot dead himself . . .

. . . As to what actually happened to him, he was only able, much later, to patch together a very few details; the rest would remain forever silence. He could dimly remember becoming more and more hungry; he could remember eating various vegetable things that looked reasonably edible, but were probably not; he could remember thirst, and drinking water which he was quite sure was not properly drinkable; and overall he could remember stumbling along through a countryside which became more and more inhospitable. Sometimes he hid from people, but he was never quite sure whether the people he hid from were real, or existed only in what was left of his mind.

He had no idea of the date on which the camp had been erased by B-52's, and he had no proper idea of where the camp had been situated, so that when he eventually came to his senses and found that it was October 17, 1965, and that he was now in another P.O.W. compound not far from Hanoi, it didn't mean a great deal to him.

He was surprised and impressed, however, by the dogged sense of self-preservation which, as soon as it had recognized consciousness returning to his brain, warned him to take his time about advertising the fact. He seemed to be in a hut that had been set aside for sick prisoners, though it didn't look like

66

an actual hospital. An American Army doctor seemed to be in charge. Long before he opened his eyes, let alone before he opened his mouth, he learned with satisfaction that it was generally accepted that he had been in the Air Force, presumably because of the remnants of Sullivan's uniform which still clung to him when he had first been brought to the camp. His name, rank and number were unknown.

On the whole, it looked to him as though things had worked out very much the way he had hoped, even though everything he had planned had gone awry. Perhaps this was an omen for the future, a warning that the quirks of chance must always be used and not denied. (Rose Maddox was not the girl he had envisaged in his mind's eye, but this didn't mean that she might not work out *better* than the girl he'd envisaged.)

As he lay there listening, and occasionally watching, through half-closed lids, the things that went on around him, he realized that the self-preservation had certainly been correct. Nothing could be gained by recovering consciousness yet awhile—if he could fool the doctor.

This again was a first discovery on which he was to capitalize later. Doctors might be able to amputate legs, perform infinitely delicate rearrangements of brain tissue, even juggle with kidneys, lungs and hearts; they could perform these miracles because such things existed under the rough heading of precise science; but when it came to neuroses, mental abnormalities, disorders of the mind . . . Ah, that was a different matter altogether; they were, in fact, and however they might try to evade the admission, stumbling about in the same dream-haunted darkness as their patients.

He realized that when in his own good time he decided to regain consciousness, he would not be the only man in the hut who had suffered a head wound and was a little batty as a consequence. He realized that the doctor, Major Hart, knowing that he could do nothing for these men, wisely concentrated his energies and his meager supply of drugs on such patients as needed actual and assessable help. He also realized that one day he would probably be subjected to the wiles of the trick-cyclists, but sufficient unto that day was the evil, if any, thereof.

So, for a little while longer, he lay in his pretended stupor, until he had thought out the whole of the next step of his plan. Only one thing really worried him, but that was his own fault for making such a cock-up of his journey across country: he had somehow lost the gold medallion with the eye on it, and the letter written to Virginia Kenny by her son.

Finally, when his mind seemed to have regained its balance and its strength of purpose, and when he judged that there was nothing more he could learn in silence about his companions and the little they knew or thought about himself, he allowed himself to return to consciousness with a good deal of muttering and grunting and rolling to and fro.

The major was summoned; he seemed a pleasant enough man; he gave his patient a great deal of information, almost all of which the patient had long ago garnered for himself. This, he knew, was the first of the medical quests which he would have to undergo. How well could he convince Major Hart that his wound and his experiences out in the wilds had affected his memory?

The answer seemed to be "Very well indeed." His confidence rose as the performance continued. His name? His outfit? What type of plane . . . ?

He gazed vacantly into the older man's kindly face and said, "Jesus, I . . . My name? My . . . It was a . . . a bomber, wasn't it? More than one of us. My name? Jesus, Doc, I don't *know*—what does that mean?—I don't know. What's the matter with me, Doc, am I nuts? Jesus, I don't know my own *name!*"

He must have done the mounting hysteria pretty goddam well. The doctor's face was very serious; the faces of other men in the hut, listening with interest, were round-eyed, gape-mouthed.

He didn't have to act the shock, however, when the doctor had put a hand in his pocket and pulled out something that glittered as it swung before his eyes: the medallion, its golden eye flashing at him. He let out a grunt and seized it. "That's mine! My mother . . . ! I was in Europe . . ." He allowed his voice to trail away. He reckoned that the doctor could have seen, as well as he had seen himself, the tiny lettering in French on the back of the disc.

"Europe?"

But the patient, it seemed, was again lost; he took the medallion between shaking fingers, staring at it.

"And this?"

Well, he had been prepared for the letter. If some Viet had not stolen the gold, there was no reason why anyone should steal the few crumpled pages, still smelling from their ordeal in the shit-pit.

He learned that he had been in this camp, semidelirious, for five weeks; that the doctor had not given much for his chances of survival, but that his own natural strength had pulled him through (and of course, the obsession, but none of them could know how strong *that* was). He thought it surprising that in his delirium he had not apparently revealed the fact that he was a mere soldier, not an Air Force man at all. Perhaps no one had bothered to listen to him, as he had once listened so intently to Jeff Kenny, or perhaps the obsession had stood guard over him even then. Whatever the reason, it seemed that he was accepted as what he had always planned to be: an unknown airman who had crashed and been wounded, who had hidden out God knows where until the wound was healed, who had then been captured and brought north, suffering from malnutrition, lack of water and loss of memory.

He put the gold medallion around his neck once more, and, later, he edited the three raggedy pages written to Virginia Kenny by her son, wetting the corner of page one, thus defacing the date, and destroying page three, which was a little too precise about facts. It didn't seem likely that he'd ever be able to post it, but eventually, during one of those recurring periods when the war seemed to be on the verge of stopping, a mailbox made its appearance in the hut. He addressed an envelope in neat capitals, and consigned the letter to whatever chance awaited it; he had no way of telling whether it would ever reach its destination. Sometimes he wondered whether he would have bothered with it at all if he had known that his imprisonment would continue for another seven weary years.

Five

"Seven years!" Rose Maddox, nice (motherly?) girl that she was, echoed it with horror.

He nodded with what he hoped was just the right amount of nonchalance. No good overdoing it; she was far too bright. At the same time he glanced, with equal horror, at the bill which the waiter had just slipped onto the table at his elbow; it was folded (in shame, he hoped), but the total was all too visible.

It was gratifying to know that once again he had planned correctly. After all, it would have been much easier and cheaper not to have changed his persona; Jeff Kenny, since he'd lost his memory, could have reappeared at any level of society; indeed, the fringe of the subculture would have been a reasonable place to find him, wearing a bush hat too. But at that level it would have been impossible to get to know and to attract a girl like Rose; and the subculture girls would have reminded various people all too bitterly of Jeff's one-time wife, the regrettable Holly. So he had to admit that in all fairness the trip to Denver, the change of persona, even this appalling bill, were all worthwhile.

"And you . . . you mean you still don't . . . you don't remember anything?"

"Not a thing. It doesn't matter, not any more."

"But it *does* matter!" The passion in her voice would have made a bill double the price worthwhile to him. He shook his head sadly in order to stoke up her protective anger.

"But, James, you could be . . ."

"A Rockefeller?" He grinned, teasing her. "Like I told you, it all seems so long ago. I'm doing okay, I'm me, I'll make it my way."

"You don't even have a real name."

He looked into her soft greenish eyes—so attractive, so right with the tawny sheen of her hair. "James White will do me."

"But it's not your *real* name. I mean, how . . . ?"

"They gave it to me at the nuthouse, this kind of experimental nuthouse they sent me to when I . . . got back." He shrugged again, because he knew that the more he dismissed it, the more she wanted to prove that he was indeed a missing Rockefeller.

The Aldington Institute had certainly been a different proposition from kindly, bumbling Dr. Hart and the others who had joined or followed him out there in Vietnam. And yet not so very different. He wouldn't have cared to be one of the criminal psychopaths sent there by various jails and judges all over the States. God alone knew what they had to go through, poor bastards, in the way of shock treatment and truth drugs and you name it. But he was one of the returning heroes, and special instructions had been forcefully delivered. Dr. Kallman, to whose care he had been assigned, was a gentle and humane man, in any case; he wasn't about to add an ounce to the weight of suffering which the prisoners-of-war already carried. It was his opinion that if memory returned at all, it would do so in its own time; the important thing was to get this man back into the ordinary world as soon as possible: train him for some job, settle his more obvious fears, give him the money that was his due, and let Life, that extraordinary healer of ills, do what it could or would. "In a way you're lucky," he had said once. "Some of us would give a great deal to be able to start all over again."

Rose was now determined to pursue the subject whether he wanted to or not. He blessed her for the determination. "But surely . . . surely this 'nuthouse' as you call it made *some* kind of effort to find out . . . ?"

"Oh God, yes. They were terrific, they really were." In actual fact, they might even have followed the trail right up to the door of 234 Upper Canyon Circle if he had not misled them so assiduously; he doubted it, but it was possible. They were a very bright bunch of people, the ones who worked in that department, and they had shown a great deal of interest in his case, particularly in the gold medallion with the odd and unusual eye on it. Naturally, this interest had made him very uneasy; he didn't altogether have to feign the acute mental disturbance which the removal of the medallion from his person had caused him. Dr. Kallman had ordered it to be given back at once, and his patient had calmed down like a baby upon the return of its pacifier. By the time they got hold of it again, he had craftily led Dr. Kallman in the opposite direction, towards the Middle West, which he knew reasonably well, having managed to hold down a job or two there in the past.

He had spent three comfortable months at the Institute. Dr. Kallman wanted to observe him during his period of rehabilitation training, and Drs. Morton and McAlistair had wanted to keep tabs on the wound and the blinding headaches which seemed to spring from it, but might, they obviously feared, be caused by some damage to his skull, induced at the same time and thereafter disregarded because of medical conditions, or lack of them.

At least he had managed to convince them that he had once received a reasonable education; during those weary years as a prisoner he had read everything he could lay hands on; his developing brain, triggered into action by The Plan, demanded it. By the time he was released he was by no means the raw and ignorant manual laborer who had been drafted all those years before. If reading matter was scarce, and it usually was, he would seek out the more educated of his colleagues and set to work on their brains, picking away at them like a dedicated vulture at a carcass. On the whole, these remorseless attacks were taken well; most of the men had a degree of pity for a poor bastard who had lost his memory, didn't even know his own name, had no distant hopes of reunion to keep him going. They weren't to know that his hopes for the future vaulted far beyond their own, which were preoccupied solely with a return to wife and children and whatever more or less dreary job they had once held.

Rose Maddox, who had been looking around her at the expensive restaurant and the expensive people at nearby tables, said, "Well, whatever it was they trained you to do, it must have worked out okay for you." She gestured at the room by way of detailed explanation.

"Production analyst!" He grimaced.

"What's that?"

"As far as I was concerned—pies."

She laughed. "I get it. You sit in a corner of the pie factory and every time a pie passes you on the production line, about one every thirty seconds, you have to take a bite out of the corner and analyze it."

Laughing, she really was a very desirable girl. He had not, at first, been able to visualize her as being anything but a slowly declining failure in her chosen profession; she wasn't pretty enough, for a start. But now he was beginning to see that if she could project this desirability, this seductiveness . . . They were both laughing at the idea of him sitting in the corner of the pie factory, munching. He took her hand and was pleased by the soft strength of it; he hated girls with flabby hands. He said, "Much duller, I'm afraid. All to do with the raw materials used in production; how many pounds of apple slush produce how many pies, fascinating things like that."

"I notice," she said, letting her hand lie in his, "that you didn't have any dessert."

"Knowing what I know, never again!"

The job had been good enough, and certainly not difficult to learn. Towards the end of his rehabilitation period they had sent him as a trainee to a local factory. Dr. Kallman had found him reasonably stable, in view of his condition, and reasonably philosophic about his total lack of a past, though there were fits of acute depression (he made sure of that), while Drs. Morton and McAlistair had apparently satisfied themselves that even if the pains in his head were continuing, they were not a sign of worse to come, and certainly not a sign that he might go about the country murdering little old ladies or snatching babies from their cots.

When his stint as a trainee was finished, they found him a job at a small factory in Greenstown, near Springfield, Missouri. The choice of location confirmed his opinion that he had managed to mislead them successfully about his place of origin.

They obviously hoped that some association or some person in Missouri would start up a train of events which might possibly lead to complete recovery.

Returning the slight pressure of his fingers across the table, for she found him very attractive, Rose Maddox said, "Are you pie-nibbling here, then? Are you a Los Angeles pie-nibbler?"

He shook his head. "There's a production manager's job going; I applied for it yesterday."

"How long before you know?" Like any actress, she had experienced all the agonies of that waiting period—that long waiting period after the audition.

"You can't tell. Maybe one of the directors has a nephew, you know how it is."

She knew how it was all too well. She sighed, looking down at her coffee cup. "And to think that last night I went on and on about my dreary love life when you have all these terrible troubles of your own! What a selfish bitch you must think me!"

He shook his head, smiling, stroking the back of her hand with his thumb. It was not a complete lie about the production manager's job, though of course he didn't stand a chance of getting it. But he'd seen the ad in the L.A. *Times* that morning, and had applied right away. Long ago he'd discovered that the less you told outright lies, the better. He had actually stayed with Susan Sackville Inc. of Greenstown for five months; presumably he had done the job adequately, since no one had fired him; but all his energy and all his time away from the factory had been spent in reading, in a continuation of the reading he had begun from the moment he was released. There were a thousand things that Jeff Kenny had experienced which he had not, a hundred places he had visited that must be visited at least in print. When he wasn't reading he was studying behavior; he saved his money, so that he could attend, alone or with some unimportant girl, the places where monied people went.

Now, looking back and feeling perfectly at ease in this restaurant with this far from unimportant girl, he could condense all that he had learned into one word: "bullshit." The rich and the would-be rich were grand masters of that art, and he reckoned that he was better than most of them: he'd been bullshitting his way through situation after situation ever since the moment he had placed the piece of sacking over Jeff Kenny's face in order to kill him. And he didn't think that any of the monied or would-be monied bullshitters that he had seen playing their games in clubs and bars and restaurants would have the know-how and the guts to pass through the mincing machine of the Aldington Institute as he himself had done.

At the end of the five months he had reported to the doctor responsible for Susan Sackville Inc.'s staff, and announced that the headaches had been coming back with increasing frequency. The doctor, who had of course been instructed by the Aldington Institute, suggested that he could probably do with a rest. It would take time, maybe even a long time, before he found himself to be properly rehabilitated, properly armed against the stresses and strains of life in a competitive world. As for finances, the doctor was sure that the Veterans Administration, or even the Institute itself, would arrange to help him.

Here he had to be subtle yet firm. He knew that the time had come for the next stage of his plan, and neither the Veterans nor the Institute played a part in it; so, haltingly, probing his way around the doctor's opinions and emotions, he said that he didn't want to feel any longer that he was a sick person, a different person. "You see, Doc, I guess I've had enough of that; I guess I'd better just accept the fact that I don't have a past. What the hell! It's better than having a lousy one." (Which was exactly what he did have!) "But I think you're right, Doc, I do need a rest; and I have quite a bit saved up—from the job and from my back pay." (In fact, he had not touched his back pay, which after nine years amounted to a handsome figure.) "So I guess what I'll do is this, Doc—I'll travel around a little, see what kind of a world I've come back to."

The doctor had thought that this plan showed character and enterprise. Of course, he had to inform the Institute of his patient's decision, but otherwise he created no complications, posed no problems. Another victory for bullshit and the half-lie!

So he left Susan Sackville Inc., bought himself some jeans, a leather jacket and the bush hat, and stopped shaving. He took his car to the dealers where he'd bought it, and traded it in for a serviceable but somewhat battered pickup. Next morning he set out for California.

He had long ago armed himself emotionally for this return to the City of the Angels, but at the sight of it his stomach turned to lead and a thousand ugly little memories which he could not evade kept darting in and out of the dark corners of his mind. If it had not been for the power of that obsession, he would probably have turned tail there and then; and if it had not been for the power of that obsession, he would certainly have been unable to face what had to be faced regarding the fingertips.

There was no way of knowing how long he would need for this last, most vital period of his research. Three months? Four? As far as the fingers were concerned, it hardly mattered. He'd always known that they'd present a problem; in the first place, he could never hope to imitate Jeff Kenny's erratic handwriting, though the inability might possibly be covered by the loss of other faculties; what could never be covered by anything else, however, was the fact that somewhere, in some bureaucratic labyrinth, the whorls and loops which constituted his finger-prints were on file, along with those of Kenny and every other serviceman. It wasn't until a certain Saturday afternoon, sitting in the reference library at Springfield, Missouri, that he realized just how big the problem was.

"This fingerprint pattern," he read, "is determined by a conjunction of nerve endings and sweat glands. Not only does it remain unchanged throughout the life span, but there is no known means of destroying or changing it. The distinctive pattern will always reappear after burning, even when new skin has been grafted onto the area in question."

He had sat there while the page reeled to and fro under his eyes; he had looked up to find that the whole book-lined room and all the silent people in it were spinning like a giant top. For this was disaster . . . "even when new skin has been grafted onto the area in question."

Then, slowly, his brain took control of itself again, and at some later time, still staring at the page, he was able to grasp just what this information meant to him in practical terms: a change in timing and slightly greater element of risk at zero hour. It was enough, but it was all.

Further research showed that after a burn the telltale pattern could be relied upon to reestablish itself during a period of from six months to two years, possibly longer, depending on the seriousness of the original damage. He reckoned that within six months he would either have succeeded triumphantly or failed so disastrously that it wouldn't matter either way; but obviously, the convenient industrial accident which he had planned at Susan Sackville Inc. was now out of the question. Too early. He must dream up another type of "accident," which would have to occur at least a month after his arrival in Los Angeles.

It took some doing, even with the obsession riding him, whip in hand and spurs dug well into his flanks.

At first the bottle of whiskey didn't seem to help at all. He went into the kitchen five times, and five times the sight of the electric griddle gleaming so cruelly red drove him out again. Eventually, by the time the whiskey bottle was three-fourths empty, he did it violently and impatiently, flicking the TV set up to full volume, because he knew he would scream, and slamming his arched fingers down onto the red-hot plate before there was time even for a drunken thought.

Passing out had not been a part of his plan, or he would have moved the trashcan well out of the way. He came to in agony—and in a welter of onion peelings, the uneaten portion of pork chops and more or less empty beer cans. The ensuing doctor's bills had taken a ravenous bite out of his capital. But it was done, and there even came a day when he no longer felt sick to his stomach when he thought about it.

Rose had little doubt that this attractive and experienced man planned that the evening should end in bed. At first she had even suspected that the wound and the loss of memory might be twin ploys cleverly designed to capture her sympathy and thus ensure eventual capitulation. Now she was ashamed of herself for the thought; it was the kind of gambit that Paul might have made, but this man was not Paul, and the wound had been real enough, as its scar amply proved. Yet there *was* something actorish about him. She couldn't put her finger on it, but she had known a great many actors in her time; they weren't exactly liars, or if they were, one did not quite judge them as such, since an ability to lie and convince an audience of that lie was the most important part of their trade.

Now, this attractive man, whose hard dry hand cradled hers so gently and yet so commandingly, was not an actor; he was a production analyst, a pie-muncher, so that if he was not telling the truth, he was doing so for some ulterior motive which might or might not be an intention of maneuvering her into his bed, or himself into hers. He was charming and he was wily. (Yes, she knew he was wily, but that didn't bother her; better a wily man than a dull one. Was it possible that Paul had been both wily *and* dull? She must consider that thought at some later date.) The point was that a girl had to keep dead level with wily men, if not a step ahead; failure to take this precaution could land you in trouble, particularly if they were also attractive, particularly if they also made a bid to capture your sympathy: a successful bid, she'd better admit that right away.

Rose Maddox was not a loose girl; she did not sleep around with just anybody, and she had never slept with a man to help further her career; indeed, she had never slept with any man who had not become an important part of her life. Sometimes she wished that she was not constructed in this way; sometimes she envied the girls who took a man as easily and with as little fuss as they would take a couple of aspirins; but generally speaking, she would not have changed places with them for all the tea in China. Even Paul—and she could already see, without admitting the fact to herself, what a stupid, preordained mistake he had been—had added something to her stature, to her being as a woman. Whether you receive love or not, it seemed, the giving of it has some virtue of its own. Rose Maddox had a lot of love to give.

Her background, of which she now betrayed not a trace unless she went out of her way to do so, was solid London suburban working class. Her father had driven a van for Selfridge's and her mother was an office cleaner. There was nothing in the least remarkable, in Rose's opinion, about her slow and laborious transformation from a schoolgirl in Balham to an out-of-work actress in Hollywood; it had taken place along the usual lines and had been attended by the usual family rows. She had paid her own way through drama school by becoming a waitress in the evenings and at weekends. It had certainly been slogging hard work, but then, kids between the ages of sixteen and eighteen were designed to work sloggingly hard if it entered into their minds, or their dreams, to do so.

During this period she had left home in order to escape the rows, which were unnecessarily exhausting on top of everything else, and had shared an apartment with five other girls.

After drama school it had been the usual snail's progress, via a few modeling jobs, a few summer seasons in repertory, a few bit parts on television, to the sudden unlooked-for break, which either did or didn't come your way—according to luck rather than talent. There had been nothing positively unusual about the break either; it had happened to dozens of other lucky girls: an infinitesimal part in a play on Shaftsbury Avenue had carried with it the understudying of the juvenile lead. The juvenile lead, probably succumbing to the prayers and imprecations of Rose Maddox, had retired with shingles, and Rose Maddox had walked into a part which she, and almost any other young actress she knew, could play better than the juvenile lead.

Nice notices, leading to a better part in a musical, leading to some way-out photographs in *Vogue*, leading to a really good part, leading to the play setting sail for Broadway with Rose aboard, leading to a nationwide tour, leading to Paul, the fourth in a chain of disastrous men who had somehow linked themselves into her life.

No doubt about it, her determination to be an actress and her career (career?) thereafter were really very ordinary. She guessed that about six out of ten of her colleagues would have roughly the same story to tell when it came down to basic truths, though most of them had long ago prepared, and sometimes come to believe, a more interesting drama of their own invention.

Perhaps it was this honesty about herself, her work and her talent (which was considerable) which made the men in her life so important to her. It seemed that a person had to invent romance one way or the other; since she was unable to romanticize herself as an actress, she presumably tended to get herself into tangled situations with her lovers, and on the whole she was glad that it was this way round. After all, being in love was real, and if it shook you to your foundations, you at least had the satisfaction of knowing that you were being shaken by reality and not by the play-acting at play-acting which seemed to be all that a lot of actresses needed. But . . .

It was a big "but." For here she sat with her hand enclosed in that of yet another male whom she found very attractive and, worse, intriguing. In the interests of honesty, there were questions which needed to be answered. First, she was smarting from Paul's sudden and unkind disappearance; she was lonely and sad. So, was she leaping in relief at the first attractive male to show his head? Secondly, something deep inside her had sensed that he was not all he was pretending to be. (For God's sake, what man ever was?) Something had been warning her, very quietly and very uncertainly, all through dinner that this man was a mistake. Another mistake! Was this because of Paul, not to mention his three predecessors, or was it whatever tiny fragment of reason she possessed regarding men trying to save her bacon?

She was unable to answer either of these questions, and time was running out; because if there was one thing Rose knew about herself for certain, it was this: from the moment she allowed herself to become involved with a man, physically and mentally, that tiny voice of reason retired into its little house, slammed the door and locked it. From that moment, as far as reason was concerned, she was on her own. And the moment— she knew it, she could feel it, she was sure of it—was approaching fast. She was alone, out of a job, lonely; she needed the reassurance of another person, another heart, another body. And she had nothing but scorn for people who thought that they could do without such reassurance. Of course they could do without it, the stupid hunks, if they wanted to do without Life as well!

The man who had now admitted to her that his name was not James White said, "Hey!"

She looked up from her thoughts into the soft brown eyes. They were watering a little, but as he'd told her, the wound often made this happen.

"Come back," he said. "Join me!"

"Have I been that far away?" She knew she had. He said, "You know you have." And, leaning closer: "Tell that lousy

Paul to get the hell out of it, I asked *you* to dinner, not him."

She smiled. He knew that it had not only been Paul who had occupied her mind, it had been himself as well. Okay, he hadn't wanted a dumb girl, and it stood to reason that a smart girl was going to assess him pretty thoroughly. But he needed to know, soon, whether she was going to work out for him or whether he was going to have to look for another. He hoped not; she was right for a hundred different reasons, and he might have to hunt for weeks to find anyone half as suitable.

There had to be something wrong with these fucking contact lenses, they were killing him! How the hell was he going to be able to bear them for another hour, or two or three? He dabbed at them with his napkin.

Fate certainly moves in a mysterious way; for it was this action, which he regretted having to make, that suddenly caused everything to click into place in Rose's mind. In one of those flashes which seem to make all clear to us (but often, in retrospect, are seen to have done no such thing) she understood. Of *course* he would appear to be other than he pretended; of course there would seem to be an actorish quality about him, and of course he might even seem to be a liar. Really, what an idiot she could sometimes be! He *was* other than he pretended, he *was* acting and he *was* lying. Since he had lost his true identity, what else could he possibly do, poor man?

Actors had to create parts, and sometimes that seemed a big enough ordeal, but this man was having to create an entire life! And she, Miss Clever-clever, had been sitting here wondering if there could possibly be something phony about him! What a dumb cow you are, Rose Maddox!

She did not appreciate, in the inspiration of this flash of insight, that neither of her eminently reasonable questions about the man, and herself vis-à-vis the man, had yet been answered; and the tiny gnome of reason who dwelt within her hadn't drawn her attention to the fact. Perhaps he had already stumped into his little house, slamming the door and locking it behind him.

Some hours later, when they were lying at rest, side by side on his bed at the Sunset Plaza Apartment Hotel, it seemed quite

natural for him to say, "You know, it's a funny thing . . ."
Long pause.

"What, darling?" She turned towards him, her head pillowed
on his muscular arm. He was staring at the ceiling, and she
could not see his eyes very well. (He had been forced to remove
the contact lenses and had arranged the lighting, or lack of it,
accordingly.)

"What's a funny thing?"

"Well . . . I always had this feeling that I . . . that my home,
my folks, were in the Middle West. But when I was working
there, I didn't feel anything. What I mean is, I kind of kept
looking for things I might recognize, but after a while . . ." He
shook his head. "There was nothing. It was just a place. But as
soon as I came here, to L.A., it was . . . Jesus, it must sound
hokey to you."

"Go on!" She ran her fingertips very lightly along the line of
the scar, and he turned his head into deeper shadow, since he
knew how closely she was studying him, and kissed it.

"You know that feeling you get? You're not sure if it's some
dream you had, or for real?"

"I have been here before," she said, naming the Priestley play
which she'd done in stock. "Perhaps you *were* here before."

"I don't know, but . . . something seemed to click. And then I
thought, Oh what the hell! What does it matter anyway?" He
smiled, putting a finger on her lips before she could speak. "I
was no Rockefeller, honey."

"You don't know *what* you were. And don't you ever
think . . . ? There might be people, nice good people, who
think they've lost their son, their only son. Grieving. Women
never get over that, you know. How can you bear to think that
there might be a sad, sad woman who still grieves for you—not a
mile away from here maybe?"

In the half-light, slanting across, the line of his jaw, the line of
the scar, was very hard, grim, hewn from cold stone. "Or," he
said, "I might have come from the most goddam terrible home
you ever knew. My mother might have been a tramp who
walked out on me when I was a little kid, before I ever knew her
maybe, and my father might have been some drunken bum who
never did a decent day's work in his life, and we might have

lived in some broken-down twenties duplex out on the east side—I bet you've never seen East Los Angeles, it's a ball-breaker—and I might have shared a room with a brother and sister, all of us lying awake every night listening to our old man screwing whatever drunken broad he'd found in one of the neighborhood bars . . ." He broke off, appalled at himself, appalled by his own imprudence, and even more appalled by the sense of release that this speaking of the truth had given him: a few seconds of naked truth embedded in the lie which he'd been living, even in his inmost thoughts, for so many years.

He thought, Jesus Christ, if this is the effect she's going to have on me I'd better call it a day right now!

Of course she had noticed it, the odd and unusual passion which had crept into his voice; she was a girl who noticed almost everything. She was still staring at him closely, but frowning now. He wasn't to know that having given herself to him, she was no longer the girl he had taken out to dinner. She had made her decision and now, for better or worse, he was the fifth living monument to Rose Maddox's lousy choice of men.

He said, "Oh hell, forget it! I told you, I don't care who I was."

She put her arms around him and held him close to her. "Don't worry," was all she said, "You were a P.O.W. for eight years, you were badly wounded and you lost your memory." She laughed wryly. "Every day I hear people saying, 'I went through hell.'" He felt her lips touch his cheek gently. "Well, you *did* go through hell, and it's all inside you, and it's all got to come out somehow. So let it all out on me, that's what I'm here for, that's why we met."

That did it! If he'd been horrified by his unguarded moment of truthful passion, it was nothing to the horror that grasped him as he felt tears, actual *tears* in the name of God!, rising up inside him.

He fought with them furiously, in a rage of fury, but it was useless. This no-good, lousy, two-bit Limey bitch had gotten to him, goddam her to hell and back!

She held him calmly while he wept; wept for so much more than she would ever know. Where was his mother, where was natural warmth, the only true reality . . . ? And his father, drunk, had hit him once, so that he went reeling back into the old-fashioned stove; his clothes had caught fire (he still bore the scars) and only his ten-year-old sister's presence of mind had saved him . . . And when his father was dying he'd taken money from his pocket, taken twenty-five dollars from the pocket of a dying man . . . What had it meant, that look on Jeff Kenny's face as the piece of sacking had covered it . . . ? "Will I remember, Dr. Kallman? Will I ever remember who I am?"

"Some of us would give a great deal to be able to start all over again."

He wept and she held him, and even in the midst of this storm of weeping his obsession, calm as an angel on a tombstone (whose?), said, "You see, we were right. This *is* the girl. Of course tears are embarrassing, but you couldn't have thought of a better way of testing her out. Look at her reaction! '. . . it's all got to come out somehow. So let it out on me, that's what I'm here for, that's why we met.' Jesus, man, it's *perfect!*"

Yes, even as he wept, cursing himself for weakness, and not yet knowing that for some women a man's weakness is his greatest strength, he knew that she was perfect. Luck, which had been his companion all through, was still at his side.

As the storm subsided (Thank God he hadn't been wearing the contact lenses, he'd probably have *swallowed* the darn things by now!) he began to realize that this outburst of unwanted emotion had served him better, as regards Rose, than many days of painstakingly planned manipulation. Already he felt as if they had known each other quite well for quite a long time.

Drying his eyes on the sheet, feeling the warmth of her encircling, protecting arms, he was well pleased with himself, with his old friend Luck, and even with the emotion which had stolen up behind him and stabbed him in the back when he was looking the other way.

If he could have known what was happening in the library of 234 Upper Canyon Circle at that moment, he would have been even more pleased. For it seemed that from every point of view his stars were in proper conjunction; the one, perfect, unalterable moment of time was almost upon him.

Six

Murray Forde, as solid as a rock and as immovable, faced Virginia in the kind of hoarse exasperation which, as far as she and she alone was concerned, served him for anger. He said, "Virginia, for Pete's sake! You say you'd like to pack up this . . . hotel and go to Europe again. You say the kid would like to go to Europe. I *live* in Europe. If that doesn't add up to one thing, you've gotta be Tarzan and me Jane."

Clearly, thought Virginia, eying him guardedly over an untouched glass of brandy, he wasn't Jane.

"Okay, so you don't want to marry me. Maybe you'll change your mind, I hope you do, and maybe you won't, but either way . . ." He spread huge hands at the obviousness of it all: they must both come to France and live with him.

Virginia wished that she'd warned Chris not to say anything to him about Europe; but there it was, she hadn't warned her, and at some time during their tour of Disneyland, it had all come out.

Chris herself, who had come downstairs in pajamas and robe, and had taken up position on the terrace outside so that she should not miss a word of this fascinating exchange, knew exactly when it had happened—as soon as she had clapped eyes on Disney's Matterhorn: "Maybe I'll get to see the *real* one when we go to Europe."

Virginia was not sure whether she had faced the truth of this situation all along but had refused to admit it to herself, or whether Murray had, this very minute, thrust the truth at her. Either way it was pretty absurd, but not half as absurd as it was going to sound if, as seemed likely, that intimidating ape-man forced her to put it into words.

She remembered now that a few weeks ago, the exact moment escaped her, she had been surprised to find that the death of her husband was more real to her, more immediate, than the death of her son; she had wondered at the time whether this made her an unnatural mother. She now knew the answer to that one: No, it didn't. But it made her something much more awkward, much more difficult to explain.

Being an honest woman, she searched her heart very thoroughly indeed before she even faced up to the situation in the comparative peace and quiet of her own mind. It all had to do with that letter, those two dirty pages which had appeared so many years, four to be exact, after the news of Jeff's death. They had seen a lot of wear and tear, those pages; they might easily have been found by somebody else and posted to her as an act of conscience or chance pity. It was far more likely that the official announcement of her son's death was the truth (the letter had been tauntingly unspecific about dates) and that the two crumpled pages in his handwriting were a cruel quirk of fate. And yet . . .

All right, so why had she never mentioned them to anyone else—never, to any living soul? Because the idea was ridiculous? No, not exactly. Facing an angry Murray across her elegant library, full of unread books, she had to admit that there was nothing in the least ridiculous about the two pages. What was perhaps ridiculous was that somewhere, buried very ·deep, hardly acknowledged even to herself, she believed . . .

She sighed deeply, facing the truth. A dogged, unreasonable doubt did still lurk deep inside her because of that letter. It was possible that Jeff was still alive.

Murray said, "For God's sake, Virginia, speak with me."

Out on the terrace, Joanne Christina sat down on the edge of a cold chair, carefully in case it should squeak, and hugged her robe more closely around her. There! They were at it again! It was beyond her why other kids didn't seem to realize what an unquenchable source of entertainment they had living in their homes with them: better than any old TV or movie, almost as good as Disneyland or the Ice Follies—to which Joanne Christina was addicted.

Personally, she didn't care whether they went to Europe with Murray or without him, that was her grandmother's business. And how! The idea of having to go to bed with any man struck her as pretty grim, to say the least, though sometimes at school she talked big about it just to shock the other girls, who, for all their tittle-tattle, were easily shocked. But the idea of having to go to bed with *Murray* . . . ! And how come small ladies didn't get squashed flat by big men like that? Those books of stupid pictures showing all the positions (a girl called Lorene had one, and in Chris's opinion a girl with a name like that would *need* one), those books were all very well, but no one was going to tell her that in all the preliminary rolling-about the small lady might not get under a big man by mistake, and slurp! that would be the end of her.

Not that Murray wasn't quite nice. He took her out and gave her hot-fudge sundaes, but then, all Grandmother's men took her out, it was one of the prices they had to pay.

Probably, if she knew how to avoid getting squashed, and if she could face it anyway, old Virginia would be better off married to Murray. She was fifty-six, though she pretended to be about ten years younger. (But come to think of it, she couldn't really believe anybody would fall for it, not with a granddaughter eleven years old; but this kind of lie didn't seem to count as a lie to adults. Just let her, Chris, go about pretending that she was *seventeen*! Oh yes, that would be a very different fish-fry!) Anyway, the fact was that Virginnypants was fifty-six, and it was really time she settled down; though if she could still manage to roll about with somebody like Leo, for whatever reason, then there wasn't much point in settling for someone like Murray until you had to. But as far as old Virginia was concerned, it didn't look as if she'd have to until she was on crutches, by which time Murray might have bitten the dust (men always seemed to die centuries before women) or he might not fancy her any more.

Chris would have been surprised to discover that her grandmother's thoughts, though differently phrased, were running almost parallel with her own. She knew that she was in many ways a fool not to marry again; she knew that this grainy, grizzled, gravel-voiced man loved her very much; would make no demands on her; would protect her and honor her in a way that Cass never had (Cass had depended on her). So why didn't she relax and let it all happen?

The answer to this one evaded her, as it always did. The reason lay very deep, and she was not a woman who believed in seeking out such things, digging for them and laying them bare; they lived deep because that was their natural habitat, and only fools dragged them protesting into the harsh light of day, or, worse, went and lay on couches so that so-called doctors could do the dragging. She had undergone a physical Caesarean, and that was bad enough, she had no intention of undergoing a mental one with or without a psychiatrist. She didn't want, at this moment, to marry Murray Forde, and that was that.

On the other hand, he was her friend, perhaps her only true friend, so why didn't she level with him about the letter and about the . . . What was it? The tiny seed of hope that somehow, somewhere, against all the forces of reason and likelihood, her son might be alive.

Well, the answer to that one also lay very deep, and she wasn't going to pursue it either.

Weary suddenly, and wanting to be alone, she put down her untouched glass of brandy and said, "You exhaust me, Murray. I feel as if I've been repeatedly hit over the head with a blunt instrument. I think I'll go to bed."

But as she passed him he did a thing he'd never done before: he laid hands on her; he laid one huge hand on her arm and stopped her dead in her tracks. "Is it that Leo?"

"Don't be silly!"

"Jesus Christ, I *love* you, Virginia—is that silly? Is love ever 'silly'?"

Now, of course, she felt ashamed of herself, but she had to escape from him. His maleness came out at her like painful shocks of electric force; she didn't like the pain, and she wasn't at all sure she liked maleness when it was that demanding. Not many women did.

Her voice calm, but only just, she said, "Please let go of me, Murray."

Outside on the terrace, Chris conquered an overwhelming desire to go nearer and try to see through the closed shutters. She knew that voice all too well; she bet that Murray had obeyed it.

After a while, during which they stared at each other angrily, Murray released her; his hand fell to his side like a dead weight. Of course, Virginia was by now even more ashamed of herself, and even more angry with herself for being more ashamed.

Shame made her overdo the proportions as she said, "Murray, with eighty, ninety percent of my being I . . . I'd like very much to marry you."

Still holding her eyes, and with that terrible perception of which he was at times capable, he said, "But with Cass it was one hundred percent, right?"

She hadn't even been thinking of her first husband, and in any case, only a very simple person (and Murray was also that) believed in hundred percents, but it seemed a possible way of escape, so she said, "Yes."

"But you'll think about it."

Anger vanished. She leaned forward and kissed him lightly. "You'd be surprised how much of the time I think about it. Goodnight, Murray."

At her bedroom door she paused, suddenly remembering her granddaughter; remembering her with a kind of pang which was rare in her relationship with that seemingly self-contained and unbiddable child.

She went along the hall to Joanne Christina's door and opened it quietly, then went into the room and looked down at the sleeping child. (The sleeping child had just, but only just, beaten her to it up the back stairs. The light had been on in Tony's room, he had probably heard her.)

Virginia realized now what it was that had caused the rare pang. The likeness of this small girl to her father gave all the explanation that was necessary.

But of course, she thought wearily, I'm a fool. It's ten years now since he was reported dead. And a letter is only a piece of paper. There are letters in existence that are hundreds of years old. Life can't be allowed to stop because of a letter. Not even another person's death stops life, however dearly you loved him, only your own. And at the thought of death, her own death, she wished she had not been so angry with Murray.

"Is love ever silly?"

No, Murray, it is not. Forgive me, but . . .

But!

The fear had come to him at nine minutes past ten A.M. exactly—at the exact moment of his waking up. It was violent, like a hand inside him, gripping a whole portion of his stomach.

He threw back the bedclothes and leapt out of bed, naked and trembling, and thanking God that Rose had not stayed all night, as most girls would have done, but had insisted on being taken home around two o'clock, tactfully leaving him to exhausted sleep. He had thought then that she was quite a girl. No, really—quite a girl!

But now all he thought of, in terror, was 234 Upper Canyon Circle and the certainty which had pierced him at the moment of waking: they had gone away, the house was closed, during the past forty-eight hours when he had been busy with the girl they had disappeared; everything was going to come crashing down around him in a terrible chaos of destruction and failure.

The pains were shooting up into the back of his head, threatening to split it in half; he gripped his head between both hands as he stumbled naked towards the phone, willing himself not to call the number which he knew so well but which he had never allowed himself to call, willing himself but knowing that in the face of this terror his will was helpless.

He dropped on his knees by the phone and stared at it witlessly. His hands moved out towards it; lifted the receiver; paused; dialed the number. It rang for an eternity, five times to be exact, before a man's voice answered, the Filipino, the manservant.

For a few seconds he was not sure that he'd be able to speak, but words managed to form themselves. He was thinking, Oh my God, why didn't she answer herself? They *are* away!

His voice said, "This is Adamson's Gourmet." He knew that she shopped there, had followed her often enough. "We have an order for two pounds of Scottish smoked salmon in the name Kenny. Now I wonder if you could help me, sir, because the boy put no address when he took the order, and we have three Kennys on our books. Was it Mrs. Virginia Kenny who placed the order?"

"I don't think so. One moment, I'll ask her."

The relief was so enormous that he fell across the bed still holding the phone. His heart was thumping like a pile driver, each beat shooting a needle of pain through his skull; sweat had broken out all over his back.

Footsteps approached the phone at 234 Upper Canyon Circle. The Filipino's voice said, "No, Mrs. Kenny didn't place the order, she isn't entertaining at home at all this week."

For a long time after he had tipped the receiver back onto its cradle he lay across the bed, as still as a dead man. Gradually the pain receded, assuming manageable proportions. He stood up, put on his robe, set a strong, a medicinally strong, pot of coffee to percolate, and began to pace about the apartment, deep in thought.

Every part of his being ached with a desire to act at once, tonight, but he knew that tonight was too soon. He had known Rose Maddox for only two days. No, less. Less than thirty-six hours. Now, that was extraordinary!

He came to a stop in his pacing, struck by the extraordinariness of it. Less than thirty-six hours, and yet he seemed to know her so well!

Obsession is relentless in its capacity for meticulous planning, for laborious hard work, attention to the smallest detail, but it doesn't know that it wears blinkers and can therefore only see ahead in an undeviating straight line. And so he was able to stand there, looking out of the window across Los Angeles under its metallic sheen of sunlight, and think, Extraordinary! Less than thirty-six hours, and I seem to know her so well! He was able to think it and suffer no qualms; because Rose was simply "the right girl," and whatever else she might be lay to one side or another of the undeviating sight-line, hidden from him as surely as the outsider coming up along the rails is hidden from the nervous favorite that leads the field, blinkered.

He poured himself a cup of coffee, sat down on the bed and dialed her number.

"Did I wake you?"

"Not exactly. I wish you were here."

"I wish I was, too."

"I have tremendously thick curtains; you don't have to know it's day if you don't want to."

"Sounds nice."

She laughed her soft laugh. "What are you doing?"

"Drinking a cup of coffee."

"Of course. Why did I ask?"

"Listen, honey?" Serious, businesslike now. "I'm getting nervous about this job, I'm going to go downtown and see what gives."

"I know the feeling."

"There was a guy down there seemed okay, I'll maybe ask him out for dinner."

"Meaning I don't get to see you tonight." She sounded disappointed but not all that disappointed; he was irritated to find that he would have liked her to miss him a little more than the voice implied; he really did like her a lot, she was a great girl. He said, "It may not work out. Shall I call you again later?"

"No, darling, don't bother. That girl, Lee—I told you about her, she's English too. I owe her a dinner, I may as well get it over." He wasn't sure about this; it wasn't an attitude he'd foreseen, and it worried him. Maybe there was some other guy; he couldn't afford her to have another guy just now. No, that didn't make sense; as long as she served her purpose, he didn't give a damn how many other guys she had.

Impatiently, because she was refusing to fit neatly into her part, he said, "I'll call you anyway. And tomorrow . . . Are you free tomorrow?"

She laughed again. "Dearheart, you are a nut! I'm free any time you want me. What does a girl have to do—cut off a leg to prove it?"

He replaced the receiver and sat staring at it, drinking his coffee and wondering what it was about the conversation that had been so unsatisfactory. The answer came to him under the shower. For a few unguarded seconds he had opened his heart to her, he had spoken the truth; after that, some tenderness in her had touched the trigger of all the emotion which fear and loneliness had rammed down inside of him like a charge of gunpowder; he had wept in her arms, wept for a thousand things, some of them barely remembered. Yes, and they had made love, twice, and it had been good; not just good as a release, it was always that, but good in some way which he didn't think he'd ever experienced before. All this made her something special, and something special was what his plan demanded that she should be; but more than that, she was real, she was the first real thing that he had allowed to happen to himself for many, many years, and he missed her, that was what it was all about: he missed her. It was as simple, as basic, as that.

Drying himself, he thought, Good! Now I know where I stand with her. The problem which she had seemed to represent had disappeared. As far as people, the human element, were concerned, only one thing was vital—to know exactly where you stood with them. That was how he had been able to kill Jeff Kenny, though in a funny way he had been quite fond of him. That was how he had managed to fool his fellow prisoners for so long. That was how he had been able to manipulate Drs. Kallman, Morton and McAlistair and their flock of assistants at the Institute.

Only by knowing where you stood, *exactly* where you stood in regard to all the pieces on the board, could you keep control of the situation.

Not many blocks away, Rose Maddox snuggled down into her comfortable bed for another hour's sleep, thinking that perhaps, after all, she *had* been a tiny bit naughty with him, a tiny bit too offhand. Poor love, she thought, now he's all mixed up, he doesn't know quite where he stands.

But then, in her experience, that never did any man any harm.

Murray Forde arrived at 234 Upper Canyon Circle equipped with a huge bunch of roses; he was not quite sure what he had to apologize for, but had a sneaking feeling that some kind of apology was necessary. He found that Virginia was not at home. Joanne Christina was splashing about in the pool.

Surfacing with a spout of water, she said, "It's beauty-salon day, Murray, you know that. And then there's lunch at the Bev Hills Hotel . . ." And she ended on a pretty good imitation of a party of agitated hens. Murray managed a hollow laugh. Chris, knowing so much more about the whole ridiculous situation than he thought she did, gave him her sunniest smile and added, "And then Leo called—you remember Leo, don't you? So I guess she might be seeing him after lunch. Or something." (She had to admit to herself that the "Or something" was masterly.)

She had said this in a spirit of experiment, and was sorry to see that she had produced an expression of anguished doubt on the man's ugly but pleasant face. She really quite liked him, she really quite liked them all, but honest to God they were too much!

The man whom the Aldington Institute had named James White drove out to Zuma Beach. As he had expected, the usual wind was blowing there, not strongly enough for discomfort if you chose the right place, but strongly enough to discourage other people, which was just what he'd hoped for.

He spread out his towel and lay down in the strong, clear sunlight. There was now nothing he could do until tomorrow evening.

It was odd, he had always thought that there would be an agony of indecision and soul-searching about these last few hours before the moment of truth, but he felt totally relaxed. He had expected his brain to be filled with last-minute panic fears and counterinstructions, but his brain was seemingly empty, even of the most ordinary thoughts. The planning was over. He had covered every contingency that his imagination could invent; every detail that could reasonably be checked had been checked. Of course, there were lacunae; it would be pleasant, for instance, to know whether Virginia Kenny had ever received that undated and unsigned wreck of a letter, to be sure that no one would ever check his (at present nonexistent) fingerprints, but he had long ago realized that in the interests of sanity, there were certain doubts which were best dismissed.

No, the fact was that he felt utterly at ease; everything now depended on one throw of the dice, and like all good gamblers, he knew that no amount of worry or incantation ever affected the behavior of those little cubes of chance.

He gave himself up to the sun, and the sun drew him into itself, enveloping his whole body and brain in a wonderful energyless mindless trance. And the last moments of that seemingly endless period of preparation spaced themselves out in the slow rhythm of waves, advancing to break in thunder and to draw back with a rushing sigh, advancing to break in thunder and to draw back . . .

Seven

Six P.M. He took a shower, making it last as long as possible. Six was a little early to start, but it was necessary for him to move now, to keep moving. He had delayed his return from the second day at the beach as long as Zuma had allowed him to do so, but this time the wind had not been on his side; around three o'clock it began to freshen and by four it was driving skeins of stinging sand southwards. Like the few other people who had braved it that long, he was sent running for his car.

Those two days in the sun had done him good. His tanned face now seemed to match up with the hair which, on his return from Denver, had seemed too dark. Yes, examining himself carefully in the mirror as he shaved, he decided that he looked naturally right.

He took the two photographs from their hiding place and propped them up facing him. "We Kennys," he said softly but aloud, "have to stick together."

His eyebrows were still a little too thick. Jeff Kenny's right eyebrow had seemed to lift higher than the other. He concentrated carefully as he plucked; he didn't want to give himself the slightest hint of artificiality, and he couldn't afford to draw the attention of Rose Maddox, that perspicacious girl, to any change in his appearance. That was enough.

Getting on for six-thirty. Time to call her.

"Rose?"

"If you're going to stand me up, I'm taking the next plane back to the U.K."

"Listen, honey, I think I may have landed that job . . ."

"If you're going to stand me up, I'm taking the . . ."

"Baby, be serious!"

"Believe me, I am."

"I have to meet that guy for about a half-hour, for a drink. I'll be free around . . . eight-thirty, quarter of nine, we can meet then."

"Fine. Where?"

"I haven't booked yet. Supposing I pick you up at your place."

"Perfect. I'd better get moving and put on a face, I look like the wicked witch of the west."

"Your place around eight-thirty. 'Bye, honey."

" 'Bye, darling."

He dressed carefully in a dark suit, cream shirt, dark tie. He went about the apartment silently, preoccupied; he was listening, within his memory, to the voice of Jeff Kenny. Because of the total concentration he had directed at it, the sound came to him quite clearly across the years, particularly a clipping of any word with a hard ending, like "back" or "could" or "mistake," words which most Americans usually extend; there was also a trick of using a longer "a" sound in place of the average American short "a." He had listened carefully to Rose and had realized that this was probably a habit picked up during his schooling in England.

Once or twice as he dressed he tried out some of the catch phrases he had long ago invented to acquaint himself with these tricks: "If you think I can dig a pit, man, you're making a big mistake," or, "Any man who can fuck a milk pan has no lack of advantages."

He had spent a lot of time worrying about the differences between his own voice and that of Jeff Kenny, but had come to the conclusion that these could be quite naturally explained. Certainly he'd never had a proper education, but then, in quite a different way, neither had Kenny. Any vocal superiority that rich young man might have acquired could well have been lost during the years when he was mixing with all kinds of men from all walks of life—first of all, in the Service, and then, more importantly, in whatever kind of existence he'd led during the nightmare period of lost memory and lost identity. And, contrariwise, as far as he himself was concerned, he had obviously made up for his early lack of education by the dedicated and peculiar self-education which he'd imposed on himself ever since he had snuffed out Jeff Kenny's life with a piece of gunnysack. And ten years was ten years.

He resisted a desire to hurry, even to run, as he left his apartment and took the elevator down to the garage. It was now three minutes past seven, and he knew from constant study of time factors that Virginia Kenny never left 234 Upper Canyon Circle before seven forty-five, not even when she was going to eat, for her, early. Usually it was around eight-fifteen; sometimes it could be as late as nine-thirty. He hoped, for the sake of Rose and the peace of their relationship, that it would not be nine-thirty tonight, but he knew that Rose would wait for him, and beyond that he didn't give a damn.

Of course, it was now out of the question to take up his old position on Mulholland Drive with a pair of binoculars; his friends the cops would certainly find that a little hard to take (he wondered if they would, in fact, recognize him), so he had to fall back on the only alternative, which was clumsy and uncomfortable. He drove up to Mulholland, and paused long enough at the crucial point to make sure that all was as it should be down at 234.

The terrace lights were on but nobody was out there. The cool north wind had reached this far inland. Through the binoculars he could see a woman sitting near the huge picture windows that edged the terrace; it was not Virginia Kenny; there were two or perhaps three men in the room. The Filipino manservant was dispensing the booze, so it had to be more than just a family evening, more than just a few remnants of Old Hollywood dropping in for a chat.

He realized that even though the north wind was quite strong on the bare exposed spine of Mulholland, he was sweating. Suppose that in spite of habit, in spite of the manservant's gratuitous information, "No, Mrs. Kenny didn't place the order, she isn't entertaining at home at all this week," plans had been changed. It had every look of a dinner party in its first stages. Or supposing she was going with these people to somebody else's house for the entire evening!

For God's sake, man, cool it! He could feel the pain beginning to uncoil in his skull, and the pain was something he could not cope with at all on this evening of all evenings. Cool it! So there's a change of plan, so maybe she *is* going out to a private dinner party, that's just too bad; you've waited ten years, you can wait one more night, Rose won't run away.

But all the same, he could not still the panic.

Ah, there was Virginia now! She passed across the window, laughing, wearing a long simple dress of what looked like very pale yellow.

He must not stay up here, gooping through binoculars. She was at home, she was dressed for dinner, that's all he needed to know. Get moving!

He drove to the junction and turned right down Coldwater Canyon. He kept telling himself that the statistics were all in his favor. In the first place, she ate out a lot more than most of the well-heeled people in Beverly Hills, who seemed to prefer the food at home. This possibly had something to do with loneliness. Whatever the reason, he had been checking on her for eighteen weeks, and Tuesday was her favorite night for dining out; eighteen Tuesdays proved it. On three of them she had stayed at home and entertained; on another three she had simply stayed at home; on two she had gone to dinner at other people's houses; on ten she had visited some restaurant or other, sometimes as a guest, more often as hostess; and that meant 55.5 percent against a next-best Tuesday likelihood of 16.6 percent. Compared with, say, Friday, this was high. The eighteen Fridays showed a dining-out potential of 22.2 percent.

By the time he had parked a hundred yards above the side road leading to Upper Canyon Circle, the headache was in full spate and sweat was drenching his back. He tried to cling to his statistics, but sense didn't really enter into it. The fact was that he was stark staring crazy, and the best thing that could happen to him would be if she never drove down that road at all; he was probably going to end the evening in a police cell anyway. Come to that, what *about* the police? Everybody knew how the Beverly

Hills cops just loved a guy who sat around watching other people's houses, waiting for them to go out to dinner yet! All he needed was a Beverly Hills Police prowl car—oh boy, that was *all* he needed!

Anyway, what was the good of a plan where he couldn't even see the place? They'd probably had seventeen martinis each by now and were busy pushing each other into the swimming pool! And how could he expect himself to think, let alone act, correctly when his head felt as if it were being fought over by a couple of teams of footballers. Maybe he should have brought some more of the pills with . . .

Headlights flashed over the trees at the bottom of the side road and Virginia Kenny's Lincoln came bouncing majestically down the steep slope into Coldwater Canyon.

By the time he had followed it to Sunset, every trace of the headache had disappeared, and he could hardly believe that he had ever suffered from that appalling attack of nerves; only the wetness of his undershirt bore witness to the silent agony. The time was fourteen minutes past eight, the statistics had not let him down, and with luck, he wouldn't be more than a few minutes late in picking up Rose.

Where were they going? They'd passed La Cappella, and it wouldn't be Riccardo's tonight; he *had* to dismiss that possibility, because it was the only place into which he couldn't follow them. Riccardo, it was said, had once torn up a fifty-dollar bribe in front of the very eyes of the poor schmuck who'd tried to wangle a table that way. In any case, to get to Riccardo's they'd have gone straight down to Wilshire and not along Sunset. Young's? No.

Were they heading for La Cienega Boulevard? It looked like it. So if Virginia Kenny was paying, and it seemed as though Virginia Kenny invariably paid, it was going to be Scotty's.

Less than a hundred yards ahead of him the Lincoln swung into Scotty's parking lot. He braked and followed as slowly as possible, curbing his passionate desire to find out how many cars were parked there. With a place like Scotty's, you could never tell, not even on a Tuesday. Was it full?

No—half empty, and a good few of the vehicles there would belong to staff. As he drove past the doorway towards a shadowy corner of the lot he saw that there were four of them; they were out of the big car and turning into the restaurant. A parking boy was getting into the Lincoln; they didn't like you to park your own, one of his colleagues was already coming forward to investigate the rogue customer who had just done so.

"You taking dinner, sir?"

"Later. I want to book a table. How's business?"

"Slow. You won't have no problem."

The bar at Scotty's faced the door, so that every time it opened, a number of heads turned to inspect the new arrival; this didn't worry him because he knew that Mrs. Virginia Kenny never sat at bars. Pre-dinner drinking went on at the table. What did worry him a little was that there were two rooms in this restaurant; the Kenny party was being ushered to a table in the larger of these, which was also the more popular. As he hung around waiting for Scotty's return (it was one of the few places where the owner was in constant command, which probably accounted for the highly quality of the food and service in comparison to most of the other hash houses on La Cienega) he saw that Leo was in attendance tonight; he didn't know who the other couple were, but had an idea that he had viewed the woman's face through his binoculars at some time during the past few weeks.

Scotty, returning, gave the young man who was waiting for him a quick and expert look, assessing the quality of the suit and tie, and pricing them both within a dollar or two.

"Sir?"

"I wanted to book a table for two in about . . . twenty minutes." (He hoped that Rose would be ready. Patient waiting while nails were painted or eyelashes refixed was not an ordeal he relished tonight.)

"Yes, of course."

"I like the big room, if that's possible. How about the booth in the corner?"

"I'm sorry, that's booked."

"The one next to it?" While the man consulted his list of bookings, he added, with what he hoped was a degree of shy and manly persuasion, "It's . . . ah . . . kind of a special date."

He didn't want to be too pushy about the placing of the table; men like this remembered every goddam detail.

"Yes, I can let you have that one. Shall we say nine?"

"Or a little before."

"Fine!"

He went quickly back to his car. It took him seven minutes to get to her place. He poop-pooped his horn, and she came out almost immediately, looking very good, very stylish in black; she certainly knew how to make the most of herself.

They kissed in the car. He could afford a minute or two for kissing if the drive back was going to take only seven minutes.

Rose said, "I missed you."

"Missed you too, honey." He was slightly shocked to realize that this was the exact truth, even though he had argued himself into what seemed to be a cool and detached attitude regarding her. She felt good and she smelled good and she looked wonderful; he sincerely wished that the evening was going to end up where she expected it to. In bed.

Scotty gave her a look of satisfied approval; at least he hadn't been wrong about the quality of that suit; she was English, too, which meant wine.

The booth was right, better than the one in the corner which he had at first wanted, less obvious. He let Rose sit facing the Kenny party, while he himself was angled slightly away from them, the left, the scarred, side of his face turned their way. This meant that Virginia Kenny would only look towards him when she spoke to Leo—fairly seldom, since, like any practiced hostess, she was spending most of her time talking to her male guest. Their hors d'oeuvres had just been brought to the table.

He asked Rose what she would like to drink. She settled for a Margarita, and he said he would join her. He felt icy-calm: not a trace of panic, and excitement only showing itself in the quick beat of his heart; he felt removed, like a scientist who has set some experiment in motion without knowing quite what the outcome will be, only that it will be extraordinary; it was almost as if he was watching all of them, himself included, on a slide under a powerful microscope.

Rose talked and he answered; they laughed; his hand found

hers under the table and held it; he remembered how she had been in bed and, in a way, wanted her in bed again; but all these were removed experiences, automatic, though he must have performed them quite well or she, with her sharp eyes and sharp emotions, would have seen through him right away. Later he was to find that he could not remember one word that either of them had said at this period of the meal.

The first time he was aware of Virginia Kenny looking his way was when he turned his head to order the wine; he felt rather than saw a sudden stillness from that direction; perhaps their conversation had languished for a moment too. At all events, he knew that something had happened. A second later he heard her laughing again. Perhaps he had been mistaken.

The second natural opportunity occurred when their first course was being taken away; he was able to turn as the waiter moved past him, turn and say, "Bring us some more bread, will you?" At this moment, if he had wished it, he could have met her eyes directly; she was looking straight at him, and even the glancing glimpse he had of her face as he turned back from the departing waiter told him that she had seen what he wanted her to see, what he had planned for all these years that she should see. Her reaction made his heart leap inside him.

It was odd that he had never thought about her reaction; he had just taken it for granted that there would be one. The reality of it, the starkness of it, was somehow shocking. For an instant he had glimpsed an old woman sitting where, a second before, there had been the beautiful and poised Mrs. Virginia Kenny in the full bloom of carefully preserved middle age. Yes, he was shocked—literally, as though some joker had attached a positive terminal to his nose and a negative one to his toe. Excitement quickened inside him. It was all happening with a kind of dreamlike exactitude.

Good God, no! His heart, from its wild beating, almost stopped. Terror struck him. *They were going!*

How he lived through the next minutes, or perhaps only seconds, he would never know. He could see from the very corner of his eye that they were all standing up, he could feel them standing up, he could tell from the people ahead of him that they were standing up, he could even see it in Rose's face, but he could not, he absolutely dared not, turn and look for himself.

He could, however, supposing he could find a voice, say to Rose, who was still staring past him, "What's the matter, honey?" He heard his own voice saying it.

Rose looked back at him. "Oh, nothing. Just a woman—rather attractive actually."

Somehow this gave him the right to turn. He saw, with a sick urge of relief, that the two men were sitting down again after standing politely as their hostess left the table. She was heading for the ladies' room in the corner behind the bar.

Of course! He had recognized the shock; what else would follow it but a retreat, she needed to pull herself together? And so did he, oh God, so did he!

She was gone a long time, perhaps five minutes. Watching Rose, he knew just when she returned; he could see the soft greenish eyes appraising the yellow dress, which was beautifully cut and worthy of any woman's appraisal. Now he knew that he must not on any account turn again. He leaned forward over his food, and kept his head averted, giving the girl all his attention; he knew, without knowing how he knew, that this was a very important moment.

More than once, Rose glanced past him at their table. What was happening there? A kind of hush had fallen over that part of the room, and whereas he had been able to catch stray ends of their conversation before, he could now hear nothing but the murmur of voices, muted against the talk of other diners.

Rose looked past him again, and he felt that soon she would speak of whatever it was that kept holding her attention. As a matter of fact, he knew what it was: they were talking about him, looking his way, perhaps repeatedly. The operation was leading into its crucial phase, and he must now be very careful how he acted.

At last she spoke. "It's funny . . ."

"What is?"

"That woman. Those people behind you . . ."

Should he look around? Would it be the natural thing to do? He wasn't sure; he didn't turn. "What's the matter with them?"

"I thought . . . I thought maybe I knew one of the men, he's rather like an actor I worked with. Years ago in England. But I think it's you."

"What do you mean, you think it's me?"

"I think they're talking about you."

It seemed to him that now he had to turn; he did so, brows raised as if in surprise.

He saw that they were all looking his way. Virginia Kenny had regained her composure but was still visibly shaken. This time their eyes did meet. As he turned back to his meal he was aware of Leo standing up. Things were beginning to move very quickly now. Panic stabbed him in the stomach, and a shrill voice in his head began to say, "This is it, this is it, this is it . . . !" very quickly, over and over again.

Looking down at his plate, he saw Leo's suit move into the line of vision. Leo's voice said, "Er, excuse me!"

He glanced up. After all those hours of watching through binoculars, he felt that he already knew Leo quite well. He seemed embarrassed, but why not?

"I . . . That's to say, we . . . Or rather a lady at my table seemed to think . . . Please don't consider this impertinent, but I wonder if you'd mind telling me your name?"

He turned from Leo's red face to Rose; her eyes met his, and he recognized with triumph that the look he had hoped to see was already in them. He turned back to Leo and said, "White. James White."

It seemed the correct moment to show them his face again, and he did so, smiling a little, shyly, as if to say, "Hi, folks, there seems to be some mistake."

Leo said, "I'm sorry, it's just that you're very like . . . like a friend of ours."

Shrugging, he said, "Sorry. James White. That's the best I can do."

Leo turned away. He could hear the other voices rising at the table behind him, but he was much too interested in Rose, in his choice of Rose as the correct person for this one moment in time, to pay any attention to them. She reacted exactly as he had planned: "But . . . but you're *not* James White."

"I told you, it's good enough for me."

"Don't be such a bloody fool, darling, they *recognized* you!"

"They thought they recognized me."

"Oh, for God's sake, it can only mean one thing, and you know it."

"I know nothing of the sort."

Her voice rose several notes: "James, they're going!"

"Let 'em go!"

She was half on her feet already, but he gripped her arm with a strong hand, holding her so hard that she winced. "I looked at them, Rose. They mean nothing to me."

"You don't *know* what means anything to you. Jesus, you *are* a nut-case!"

She shook off his hand angrily. A lot of people were looking their way now. More turned as she pushed her way past the table, upsetting her wineglass, which he caught in midair.

"Rose?"

But she was paying no attention; he turned again as she passed him. He saw that they were indeed leaving, Leo holding Mrs. Kenny's arm; all of them looked stricken. Rose, coming up behind them (My God, she couldn't have played it all better if he'd written and directed it for her!), said, "Please, I . . ."

They all turned, and the girl, not knowing which of them she was really addressing, spoke to Leo. "My friend . . ." She became aware, perhaps for the first time, of her audience; there was no one in the place who was not staring at the group now. "I believe one of you . . . thought you recognized my friend."

Virginia Kenny looked beyond the girl, and again their eyes met. He pushed the table away and got to his feet; moved up to them and took Rose's arm. "Honey, cool it, there's been some kind of a mistake."

Virginia said, "Oh, my God!" He knew, with another flash of triumph, that it had been his pronunciation of the word "mistake" that had wrung this from her. Not for nothing those hours of crazy practice: "Any man who can fuck a milk pan . . ."

Rose made an actress' gesture towards the gaping faces around them. "We can't talk here, it's ridiculous!" How divinely British she made that sound, and what presence she had! It was the first time he had seen her on the stage, and for the first time he realized that she was probably very good indeed.

Scotty came forward to take command. "Mrs. Kenny, I'm sure you'd prefer . . . The private room isn't in use tonight."

And so they faced each other among piled tables and chairs. A blackboard in one corner had been used for some business luncheon; on it (in illustration of what, for God's sake?) somebody had written Polonius' dictum: "Brevity is the soul of wit."

Rose was brief; he barely had time to try to interrupt her three times, and in any case, she ignored him utterly. Halfway through, Virginia Kenny stared about her wildly and Leo produced a chair; she sat down, looking away from them all, as he had seen her do so often on her terrace after she had spoken and while her guests were laughing; occasionally she would look full at him, and then away again, as if what she saw was too painful, too shocking.

". . . so you see," said Rose, "it's no good his saying that his name's James White. It isn't. That's just the name they gave him at this hospital place; and he's . . . he's got this thing about not caring any more *who* he was."

The other woman, who had a pleasant calming voice, said gently, "But *you* care."

"Yes, I care." She turned and gave him her full regard. "I'm sorry, darling, I had to do it; you must see I had to do it."

He spread his hands and said nothing. They were all staring at him now. It seemed that he had to speak, or they might all stand there in silence forever: "I don't know. I . . . I don't know."

The other man cleared his throat. He was the oldest person there, and obviously considered that it was time he behaved as such. "You don't . . . recognize this lady here?"

He gave Virginia Kenny a long look, which she was unable to return for more than a few seconds. He allowed it to be a very long look, because he knew that the longer it lasted the less they would believe him when he finally said, "No. I'm sorry, but . . . no."

The elderly man shook his grey head, tut-tutting. His wife said, "If only there was some . . . some proof, you know what I mean. A birthmark, or . . . I once knew a girl who was identified by her wedding band."

Rose turned her head sharply. He knew that she had already

thought of the medallion, about which she had naturally questioned him as they lay in bed together; so he was able to allow himself another awkward pause before saying, "It was all so long ago. I have nothing."

Rose went to him and stood confronting him, her honest eyes searching his. "You have. You know you have."

As if suddenly remembering it, as if instinctively, he let one hand go to his chest; he could feel the metal under his shirt. Holding her stare steadily, he said, "No."

The man also came closer. He was frowning, puzzled by the whole thing but doggedly determined to dig to the bottom of it. "What?" Getting no reply, he looked at Rose. "What does he have?"

Rose took his hand and removed it, gently but firmly; then she unbuttoned a single button of his shirt, felt for the chain and drew out the medallion.

For a few seconds of dead silence the golden eye gave them all its blank stare. Then, with a very quiet sound, no more than a sigh, Virginia Kenny slid off her chair in a dead faint.

Part II

The Waiting Snake

One

On the way back to Upper Canyon Circle, Virginia Kenny seemed disinclined to speak. Her friends naturally found this worrying and frustrating; all three of them were, for their different reasons, agog for reactions, suspicions, prognostications. She looked back, out of the rear window, and said, "Are they following okay? How stupid—one of us should have gone with them!"

Leo drove in silence, preoccupied with his own thoughts, which were entirely selfish. Virginia's other guests, Carl and Betty Lehman, were old friends who had retired to live in Palm Springs. He was a lawyer and had been Cass Kenny's business manager for many years; they occasionally stayed at Number 234 on their infrequent visits to Los Angeles to attend a play or a concert. Betty Lehman, who didn't like silences, this one in particular, said, "Are you feeling better, honey?"

"Yes. How ridiculous of me, I never faint."

"Heavens above, I don't call it ridiculous. A shock like that, after . . . How long? It must be all of ten years since he was reported . . . missing."

"I don't mean ridiculous in that way. I mean ridiculous because . . . because I knew . . . No, I didn't *know*, I had this idea that he wasn't dead."

Perhaps a trifle affronted (most of her men friends liked to think that she would always come to them with any troubles), Carl Lehman said, "You never told us that."

"I never told anybody. There . . . there was a letter."

"From Jeff?"

"Yes." She looked away, out of the window of the car.

The Lehmans exchanged a look; the very set of her head seemed to say that she was not answering any more questions. Leo, turning right into Beverly Drive, suddenly felt that he had ceased to exist, completely, just like that; it was a sensation that he had experienced often before, but this didn't make him like it any the better. He badly wanted to say something direct, sensible, comforting—and helpful to his own uncomfortable situation, but nothing occurred to him. Nothing, apparently, occurred to the Lehmans either, for they drove the rest of the way in silence, Virginia occasionally checking on the car behind, but otherwise gazing out of the window into her own thoughts.

Of course it was Jeff, she had no doubt of that, and of course he had changed enormously. Esther Woodhouse's husband had emerged from a prisoner-of-war camp in Vietnam, and Esther, who had naturally gone to meet him at the airport, had said that she wouldn't have recognized him *at all* if some helpful nurse hadn't pointed him out, knowing presumably that this might be the case; even then, Esther had said that her mind refused to accept him. He waved and they ran to each other and hugged and made all the correct outward movements, but it was days, Esther said, days before she fully comprehended that this man wandering about the house and sleeping in her bed was actually Vincent Woodhouse, the man she'd once married. And Vince hadn't even lost his memory.

She was shocked; the pounding of her heart told her that. She was possibly in a state of shock—why else had she fainted? But at the same time she felt quite calm; and this was not in her nature; she had never been one to keep calm in an emergency. Cass had been the calm one, and Cass had always been smitten later, sometimes a long time later, by delayed shock.

Jeff had come back. The doubt about his death, which had lurked deep inside her, refusing analysis, had proved to be right, and it was probably this doubt, kept to herself as a secret for so long, which now enabled her to behave in a rational manner. She wished that Cass could see her; he would be proud—and amazed!

But oh, how carefully she was going to have to feel her way into the situation that now confronted her! Even if he had turned out to be in full control of his faculties, she would have been forced to move carefully. Jeff was her son, and she loved him, and she would stand by him (*had* stood by him) in all kinds of trouble; but he wasn't an easy boy . . . man. He had as many imperfections as anyone else; perhaps rather more, if she cared to face the truth directly, and she'd *better* face it directly at this cataclysmic moment of time. The question was . . . My God, how cool, how almost clinical she was being when by rights she presumably ought to be overcome with a swooning joy. The joy was there; perhaps it would find its true expression later.

The question was, "Did a Jeff with no memory of the past pose more or less of a problem than a Jeff who could remember everything?"

She was glad to be able to shelve this complex and perhaps painful consideration in favor of many lesser ones, for they had now arrived at Upper Canyon Circle.

She preceded her guests into the house, switching on lights, summoning Tony to get drinks (he had never known Jeff anyway, thank God!) and generally steadying herself with the routine hostess performance. It gave her confidence; it gave her the ability to watch him evenly and without undue disturbance of the heart as he came in through the front door.

The first thing he saw, the first thing that anyone would see on entering Number 234, was the gilt Italian mirror on the staircase directly facing the door. She saw his eyes leap to it, and away to her face, and then back to it. He came to a dead stop, seemingly unaware of the people who stood around him in an expectant circle.

After a long moment he managed to stop staring at it, and again he looked at her; this time there was something so puzzled, so near (she could swear it) to tears in the brown eyes which she knew so well yet didn't know, that it wrung her heart. She said, "You mustn't . . . hold out against it, you know. That isn't fair . . . to anyone."

He nodded, his eyes still on her, studying her closely. Then once more he looked back at the mirror; he moved towards it slowly, mounting the short flight of stairs with what looked like enormous weariness until he stood right in front of it, as she herself would so often stand on her way to bed. He looked at himself in the mirror and then he looked at the mirror itself: the pattern of interlinking, formalized shells and seaweed that made it such an unusual and fascinating piece.

Rose, who had come in just behind him, the Lehmans, Leo and Virginia herself all watched him. Beyond them, Tony moved silently about the drawing room, only glancing once, politely, in their direction; then he went away.

Touching the mirror with a brown hand, he turned his head and looked at her again. "Rome," was all he said. (Information by courtesy of Mrs. Olga Rhinehart, real estate agent: "And of course she brought a lot of perfectly *beautiful* things back from Europe, they had two or three properties over there, you know . . . Like this but *gorgeous* mirror she bought in Rome, all done in seashells, I said to her as soon as I saw it, 'Well, if that golden beauty's ever missing, you'll know who to arrest,' that's what I said.")

Virginia Kenny said, "Yes, it was in the Rome apartment. Can you remember that?"

He shook his head, frowning, and came downstairs again. Rose went to him and took his arm; he gave her an uncertain smile. "See what you started?"

"I'm glad I started it."

He grimaced and glanced at the woman who was supposed to be his mother. "Please, you . . . you must forgive me. I guess I seem . . . rude. Worse. I wish I could *feel* something for sure."

"You will." She made it sound certain, but she was not certain, and there was a duplicity about her not being certain. It seemed terrible, but she must at all costs be honest with herself or there was no hope for either of them. She didn't know whether he wanted to feel something for sure; his own private world might be more pleasant than the encroaching reality; he might be resenting bitterly the demands of reality, and she of all people could hardly blame him.

However, the demands were obviously there; as they all moved towards the drawing room he saw her two Sheraton cabinets standing on either side of the library door. It was quite obvious that he recognized them. (Information by courtesy of

114

House and Garden, July 1958: "A House on Lake Geneva—the home of Mr. and Mrs. Cass Kenny." Thank God for all those pages of photographs! He had already noticed, out of the corner of his eye, the Buhl clock which, in Switzerland, had apparently stood in the center of the dining-room mantelpiece.)

He stood looking at the cabinets for a time; then again he turned and met Virginia Kenny's eyes. Frowning, he said, "The lake. There *was* a lake?"

She nodded. "What do you remember?"

"A big room, as big as this. Windows overlooking a lake. Oh yes, mountains. The room was . . . Were the walls a kind of . . . golden brown?"

She nodded again.

"And these"—indicating the cabinets—"stood on each side of a fireplace. And there were dark-brown chairs, and a picture of . . . No, two pictures of horses, and a portrait . . ." He broke off with a gesture almost of pain, looking about him wildly, like a man in a trap. "I just seem to . . . remember these things, but they don't *mean* anything."

Carl Lehman, who had himself stood many times in that golden room with the cabinets on each side of the fireplace and the windows overlooking Lake Geneva and the mountains on the French side, said, "Seems to me it means a hell of a lot."

But Virginia Kenny only echoed, "A portrait?"

He turned away from them as if these flashes of memory were too much for him.

"Who was the portrait of, do you know?"

He didn't answer for a long time; they saw only his hunched back. When he finally spoke, it was in a small faint voice, as if the words were staggering out of his mouth in the last stages of exhaustion: "I . . . I think it was . . . my father."

He heard the little flurry of exclamation, surprise, excitement behind him in the room. No thunder of applause from a packed house could ever have praised an actor more than this quiet sound praised his own amateur performance; he knew that he had played it well, but he was tired. Dear God, was he tired! The contact lenses were up to their tricks, and the tension of the whole evening was building inside his head to a really staggering attack of the old pain. It felt as if somebody were probing the back of his skull with a blunt needle; he knew with a terrible certainty that if he was called upon to continue the performance much longer, the pain from the wound and the irritation from the contact lenses might between them deflect his concentration, thus causing him to make some disastrous, perhaps irretrievable, mistake. He braced himself for a final effort, then wheeled around to confront them.

Presumably his face showed the pain, because the concern on all their faces (except friend Leo's—he'd have to watch friend Leo!) reflected it.

"I'm sorry," he said, "I must go. I can't . . . I mean, I know this has been a ghastly shock to you too, but I . . . My head!"

He looked in desperation at Rose, and she, wonderful girl that she was, leapt to his aid. "It's the wound. It gives him these terrible headaches."

He moved across the room to Virginia Kenny and for the first time confronted her directly, so that their eyes met and held. He said, "Why? Why should I suddenly remember that portrait, and not . . ."

"Not me." She spread her hands with a shrug.

He shook his head, then lifted a hand and ran it along the scar and round to the back of his neck. "If you only knew what this darn thing does to me. And don't you see, I . . . I can't tell now what I'm remembering and what I'm . . . I'm *seeing*. I'm seeing you and that makes me think I remember you. But do I? Do I?"

He had gone about as far as he could go; number seven in "Twenty-five Case Histories of Mental Disorder" on which he had based his performance was now exhausted, or, if it wasn't, he could remember no more details or symptoms. If Virginia Kenny had not at this moment suddenly reached out and put her arms around him he would probably have relapsed into silence like a tape recorder which has come to the end of its tape. It was an awkward embrace, but it saved the situation. She said, softly, "I think you remember me; I think maybe you remembered me as soon as you saw me, but . . . there's some block, some mental block. It *has* been a shock, for both of us. We need time, we *have* time, there's nothing to worry about."

Jesus, he thought, smelling her perfume, which was very pleasant, it's going to work, I'm going to win! The weakness which she could feel in his body as he leaned against her was not feigned; it had been a long, hard race, and he could forgive himself for feeling dead-beat now that he had staggered past the finishing post. For this *was* the finishing post, wasn't it? Wasn't it?

From a strategic position between a bougainvillaea and a banana palm, Joanne Christina watched the extraordinary scene through the big picture window with actual open-mouthed astonishment: old Virginnypants with her arms around some quite good-looking guy in front of an audience consisting of Leo, who looked as though he thought the arms would be much better employed around *him*, an unknown girl and those boring old Lehmans! What the hell was going on? Why hadn't she got out of bed at once, as soon as she heard them coming back (much too early), instead of leaving it, as was perfectly apparent, until the whole show was over: because the good-looking man was now moving away towards the front door, trailing the girl after him, while the Lehmans, who were seldom lost for a word, or ten million words, gaped at them like a couple of kids at a Christmas tree, silent.

Jiminy *Cricket*, she'd missed it! All because it was a cold night and she'd been chicken about getting out of bed! Virginia, the man and the girl were even out of sight now, far away in the entrance hall near the foot of the stairs. For a few seconds she played with the idea of trying to make the front porch before they arrived there; a handy clump of evergreens had given absolute protection on other occasions. Regretfully she abandoned the idea as impossible; the Lehmans might be as dumb as dingbats, but they weren't blind, and they'd be sure to see her as she sprinted around the far side of the pool. Furious with herself, she went back to her room.

He lay flat on his back in bed. He was exhausted, but it would be a long time before he slept; he hadn't even taken his pills, knowing that they'd be powerless in the face of his mind's tumult.

With her usual good sense, Rose had insisted that he drive her straight home; she could obviously tell at a glance that he was out for the count.

As they'd parted at the door of Number 234, Virginia Kenny had said, "You must come up tomorrow morning, and we'll have a long talk. Then, if you feel you want to stay . . . There are plenty of rooms here, it's up to you."

He would stay—it was the inevitable, and dangerous, next step. If he hesitated for too long now, it could lead to unthinkable difficulties: first, she might conclude that he was not her son at all, but a stranger who happened to bear a striking resemblance: second, she might call down upon his head a buzzing swarm of psychiatrists and specialists and you name it. He had to take the plunge, and he had to take it soon, even tomorrow.

So far everything had worked out as neatly as if it had been happening inside his own head; in comparison to the preparation, the actual event had seemed almost tame, even though it had put him under severe strain and held him there for about as long as he could bear. He knew that the tameness had existed *because* of the preparation; any non-actor given ten years' rehearsal could presumably turn in a pretty good performance; but now . . . Now, once he had taken the plunge, once he had stopped saying "Am I Jeff Kenny?" and had said "I am Jeff Kenny," he would find himself in a new and less well-rehearsed part. Every person he met, every word that they said and every word that he himself said in reply could be a trap. Of course, he need not (he dared not) give up his loss of memory altogether, but the gaps must not seem too convenient. Yes indeed, there was a lot of hard work still to be done, a lot of treacherous hazards to be faced.

He took three pills, realizing how badly he needed a good night's rest to sharpen his wits.

So far, so good. Very good! The contents of that house alone must be worth millions. Mrs. Olga Rhinehart had told him that the picture over the fireplace was a Velázquez, and he himself had recognized the one by the library door as a Degas. He would not yet allow himself any unduly comfortable thoughts, but he could already see light at the end of the tunnel. Sunlight. It promised, soon, to be a wonderful day.

But he dreamed of his youth. The cops had arrived in a prowl car and had taken him to the city morgue to identify the body of his father, who had been run down by a truck while blind-drunk. But when they lifted the sheet it was a young and beautiful woman who lay there covered in blood, and he knew, though he could not remember her, that this was his mother. Laughter made him wheel around, and there behind him stood his father with a whiskey bottle in his hand. And suddenly all the cops were laughing too.

He awoke more than once in a tangle of sweaty sheets, but the pills were strong, and at last he slept peacefully.

Virginia Kenny lay flat on her back in bed. She, too, was exhausted, but oddly enough, her thoughts, which had seemed to be running mad in her brain while she fended off the questions and advice of Leo and the Lehmans, had stopped rioting as soon as she had shut the door of her room. At this moment she had expected the *real* agonizing to begin, but it seemed that the agonizing had expended itself in the strain of keeping her composure in public, and that now, in blessed silence and solitude, she could clearly appreciate what had happened to her during the course of the evening. It was quite simple and quite astonishing; even in her exhaustion it made her feel ten years younger (just about as young as she looked, it struck her wryly). During the course of the evening, purpose had suddenly burst into the life of a woman who had been purposeless for longer than she cared to think; strength had entered into a woman who had for too long been vacillating in a comfortable but desolate little self-made vacuum.

She knew what she would do about Leo, she knew how she could handle Murray, she even knew how to leap the chasm that divided her from Chris. Jeff had come back, wounded in mind and body, and it was up to her to heal him. Perhaps she had known all along that this would happen; she believed in intuition. Perhaps her years of indecision, when she had seemed to float idly along on whatever current was the strongest, had simply been some inner sense warning her that she must wait, her time would come.

Well, it had come now. She would make a new life for Jeff, who had been lost, and a new life for Virginia, who had also been lost; and she knew, because her son was a changed man who had suffered, that the life she would make for him now would be better than the old one. Oh dear God, yes! Perhaps the things that had gone wrong had been her fault, perhaps his; none of that mattered now; what mattered was that the new life would be good. She intended to dedicate herself to that end, and nothing, but *nothing*, was going to stand in her way—not this time!

Two

There was no need for him to act the tense apprehension he felt when he was ushered out onto her terrace a little after eleven o'clock next morning. Anybody or anything might have been waiting there in the shadows: a consortium of beady-eyed lawyers, a gaggle of trick-cyclists, each with a portable couch under his arm, a "daughter," or even a "wife" in the form of that slut whom Jeff Kenny, for reasons as yet unknown, had seen fit to take unto himself. All he found was Virginia, his "mother" (no—time to do away with those inverted commas!), his mother, lying on a garden chaise, stitching away at a piece of needle-point.

Virginia saw no necessity to complicate issues by explaining that Joanne Christina had been taken out to the desert for the day by her old friend Murray Forde. (Since Chris adored the desert and Murray detested it, the departure had been a foreboding mixture of sun and thunder.) She merely said that she had seen to it that no one would disturb them unless they wanted to be disturbed.

This remark, more than the Rolls, the Lincoln and the Mini-Cooper in the carport, more even than the Velázquez and the Degas hung in the house, among others, brought home to him the luxury of being rich. People, faceless and obedient people, stood between you and the noisy, importunate world outside, and nobody would disturb you unless you wanted to be disturbed.

In his wariness it took him a little while to realize that her attitude to him had changed completely since the night before. Very slowly, his brain perhaps numbed by its own anxiety, the knowledge was borne upon him that she had accepted him; something, during the night, had resolved itself in her mind. She had turned towards him.

It took him a little longer to realize just what this meant in *practical* terms; she was no longer testing him, and so everything he said released from her a golden treasure of corroborative material. If he said, "It's funny, I can remember some of that house in Switzerland quite well, but some of it's . . . I don't know—kind of hidden around the corner," she would reply, "It was near Nyons, a rather nice white, almost Colonial house with a portico all along the front. Don't you remember the portico and the wisteria, you always loved the wisteria. Of course, it must be ruined now they've built that big freeway, practically across the back garden."

If he said, "I guess I didn't like that school in England, I can't remember it at all," she would say, "No, you hated it, but there was one boy you quite liked, he came to stay that last summer, South African; his father had something to do with copper."

Rome, of which he could create only the most sketchy of impressions, was brought to life by an immeasurable stroke of good luck when she handed him a large photograph album: this gave him the whole setup at a glance; more, it suddenly made the shadowy past quite real. He could even say, haltingly, "I'm . . . I'm pretty like my father, aren't I?" and win a tender smile for it.

Soon an opening appeared through which he could creep up on the subject of his wife and child. Awkwardly, for he *felt* extremely awkward about it, he said, "I guess you . . . don't know where Holly is now."

This produced a sharp look, even though the answer came softly: "Why? Do you want to see her?"

"Good God, no!" The horror had not been assumed, and it was approved of. "I just wondered what happened to her."

"She went east. Chicago first of all, then New York. She lived with some man in New York, a painter. They went to Europe together. That was the last I heard of her."

Looking away, he said, "I don't care about Holly, but I'd like to have seen the kid."

Virginia looked up at him sharply over her needlepoint. "Oh, really, what a fool I am!"

He found that he could turn and meet her eyes evenly now. "Chris is here, she lives with me."

He managed a startled look; then put a hand to his eyes and pressed the outside corners of them. "Jesus, yes. I can . . . What happened? You went to court, didn't you? You went to court on my behalf and they gave you custody."

It seemed to her that every moment he was remembering more and more; this was good, this had to be, but perhaps there were bounds—not to what he had to remember, it was obviously necessary for him to remember everything in the end, but bounds to how much he should be allowed or made to remember at one time. Quietly she said, "Holly got worse, you know; she was only on pot when you knew her, but later . . ."

He nodded, face averted. "Hash."

"Worse than that. This painter in New York was . . . was mainlining, I know that for sure."

He shook his head. "Poor Holly."

Turned away, he could not see the sharp look she then gave him, and so could not guess at its meaning, which was profound. Even then, though things were going very well for him, he had no idea of the thin ice, the delicate, tissue-paper-thin layer of ice upon which they were both so carefully tiptoeing.

Lunch was deftly and silently served to them by the Filipino under the shade of a vine-clad pergola. With every mouthful, he seemed to be devouring, gulping down, more and more facts; and the more he learned, the more the things he had only half learned, from Kenny as well as from his research, came to life and stood upright; were clothed in flesh and touched with the breath of life. Whole patches of the jigsaw puzzle were already blocked in, and he could see where other pieces, other groups of pieces, might be going to fit. Of course, it was a big puzzle, spanning as it did twenty-three years of a man's life. Long ago (it seemed long ago but was in fact only a few days) on the plane to Denver he had been uneasy about Jeff Kenny's years at the university in Los Angeles, and he realized now that except for the brief exchange concerning his "wife"—his wife and daughter, which had told him nothing he didn't already know—this period constituted a large part of the puzzle still lying scattered and unmatched all over the table. He realized something else, too. Whenever he tried to steer the conversation towards this area, Virginia Kenny gave the wheel a sharp twist and steered it away again.

After lunch, when she left him to sleep in the sun, he found himself disturbed by this fact; and yet . . . and yet, was it really so strange that she should want to avoid what was, in effect, a discussion not of his years at the university but of his disastrous and therefore painful marriage? Not really. It would be a callous woman who encouraged her son, her sick son, to recall what must have been the most unhappy years of his life. And Virginia Kenny was certainly not a callous woman.

On the whole, this explanation satisfied him; or at least it satisfied him up to a point—a point beyond which he must explore at a later date. In any case, what possible reason could he have for dissatisfaction? Things had gone a thousand times better than he had planned, even in his most optimistic moments. She had accepted him, she was on his side, of that there was no doubt. Equally, there was no doubt that this constituted eighty percent of the battle, perhaps more, because she was a stronger woman than he had suspected. Strong by nature and autocratic by reason of many years' wealth. Oh yes, Virginia Kenny would have been a formidable ally in any situation, let alone in this one, where she was virtually all that mattered.

At this moment an equally formidable female was approaching him at high speed across the Mojave Desert. Whether she would prove to be an ally or not, only time would tell; indeed, at this moment she was completely unaware of the fact that he constituted a part of her life. Joanne Christina had lost the day to Murray Forde. Oh God, why couldn't she grow up but *fast* so that she could have a car of her own and not have to rely on the caprices of fat ugly old men who moped about in the heat like stranded Eskimos, giving up the whole precious project before they'd even *heard* a rattler, let alone seen one, let alone tried to get it into her carefully prepared pickle jar!

124

Anyway, she could get her own back to some degree. Gazing out of the window at the hurtling desert (Murray was driving like a bat out of hell), she said, "Who's this new man that Grandma was kissing and cuddling and what-all with last night?"

The car swerved in a satisfactory manner, and Murray, who should of course have said, "How the hell do *you* know about a thing like that?" fell for it hook, line and sinker, and said, "What man? Where?"

"Oh, nothing. I thought you'd know, that's all."

Too late, by now revealed in all his nakedness, Murray said, "How do *you* know, anyway?"

"I saw them at it."

The car swerved again. At it! "How?"

Chris didn't answer, but began to sing with the radio which Murray had foolishly switched on: " 'I want to *be* happy, but I can't *be* happy . . .' " She had no sense of pitch and sounded like a corn crake.

Murray switched the radio off. "How did you see?"

Joanne Christina continued to sing, getting more and more out of tune as she went into the chorus for the second time; it seemed that she knew the whole lyric.

They were thus somewhat prepared, in their different ways, for the news which was to greet them when they finally got back to Number 234, just as they both, in their different ways, were aware of the change in Virginia, who came out onto the doorstep to greet them; there was a lightness about her; energy crackled in her wake. Chris, stumping off to her room in a temper, put this down to a probable super-session at the beauty salon. Murray, more jealous and therefore less charitable, put it down to a matinée in the sack. Both were soon to be disillusioned.

Murray, on the terrace, where he was preparing to take a desert-cleansing swim, stood stock-still, looking like a bullock that had just been pole-axed. "*Jeff!* Jesus Christ, Virginia, what's gotten into you? Jeff's *dead!*" while Chris, putting away her rattler-proof desert boots with care, looked up over her huge tinted glasses, her blue eyes round and glittering. Characteristically, she said nothing, but went and sat down on her bed, deep in thought. Such natural silences are not natural to adults, who like noise, exclamations, visible surprise. Virginia said, "It's a shock I know, honey, but isn't it wonderful news?"

Chris then did a very unusual thing; she took off the gigantic sunglasses without being asked to and laid them neatly on her pillow. Then she said, "I don't know. What I mean is, if I said to you, 'Alvin Acker's coming to dinner,' what would *you* say?"

"I don't know who Alvin Acker is."

"He's Number One for the second week and he's a total *smash,* but that's just what I mean. I don't know who Jeff Kenny is."

"Honey, he's your *father!*"

"I guess so, but I know Mr. Kiang better."

"You must feel . . . pleased that he's not dead, that he's come back."

"Uh-huh." It could have been the affirmative or the negative one, there was no way of telling. Then a gleam of light dawned, but not, as usual, the expected one. "Jiminy! Was that the man you were . . . ?" She broke off. What a crumb! That was the first time ever that she'd nearly admitted out loud that she peeked. There *had* to be something about regaining a father, to make her freak out like that!

"The man I was what?"

"Well, I'll tell you. I heard a lot of noise last night, so I went to the top of the stairs to see who was being mugged, and you were just saying goodbye to a man. Quite a wowee! Was that him?"

"Yes."

"Hm. He was pretty. Hey," she went on quickly, to forestall the inevitable correction about men being handsome etcetera but not pretty, "that Murray, he's worse than chicken, he's *hen!* Don't ask *him* to take me to the desert again!"

"Maybe your father will take you."

When her grandmother had gone she lay back on her bed and stared at the ceiling. In some ways it hardly seemed to matter whether she had a father or not, after all this time; she'd managed to get along quite well without one, and the lack had caused no undue inconvenience. Thanks to old Virginnypants! She made no pretense to herself about the thanks, however

126

casually ungrateful she might appear to be on the surface. She admired and loved her grandmother, and had lately come to realize just how much she owed to her. After all, you only had to look at other girls' parents to realize what a lousy unreliable group they often were. As for her own . . . Well, honestly, whatever old Virginia might feel, the less said about *them* the better!

On the other hand, he had certainly been a super-looking man, and there was always the remote chance that he might turn out to be human as well; he might even take her to the desert and help her to bag that rattler. The endeavor had gained in urgency because of Mrs. Ginsberg's nature class. Mrs. Ginsberg, long suspect in Chris's mind, had definitively proved last Monday that she knew absolutely nothing about nature and, what was worse, didn't even care about it. As judgment, it was only proper that Mrs. Ginsberg should be faced by nature herself—in the form of the rattlesnake.

Hi, Pa! Hi, Paw! There was also the question of Friday afternoon. How would the acquisition of a father affect that. Quite a bit, now she came to think of it.

She could hear old chickybid Murray grunting and groaning away down by the pool. Words rose to the surface of the general drone of disquiet: "Now see here, Virginia, are you *sure* about this?"

Pecking at her needlepoint, Virginia replied acidly, 'I think I'm old and intelligent enough to recognize my own son when I see him."

She had to say this with a little more force than she actually felt, because more than once during the course of the morning she had been gripped by a terrible sense of unreality. Of course that was natural; look at Esther Woodhouse! "*Days,* darling," she had said during their brief conversation at the beauty salon. "It was really traumatic; I mean, here was this man in my bed, and I kept thinking, 'Wait a minute, who the hell *is* he?' "

So the sense of unreality was natural. And it was also natural that he had changed. Oddly enough, she could accept the purely physical changes more easily than others, less easy to define. Twelve years was a long time; the boy of twenty-three, spoiled, a little selfish no doubt, had grown suddenly into a hard-bitten, hurt man of nearly thirty-five. There was something . . . yes, coarser about him, and yet he was more likable. His voice, his vocabulary even, had developed a rough edge. But why not? He had shared suffering, hardship, pain, with all kinds of men; they were more a part of him now than the easy, snobbish days of his youth. A good thing too, from every point of view!

In any case, now she came to think of it, why should he inwardly resemble the spoiled boy she had once known, loved and protected? He had lost his memory, lost all trace of his identity, so that although he was Jeff, he was really *another* Jeff. And so the doubts led her back to that one vital fact, the only fact that mattered: he had been born again, and this time it was up to her to see that he grew up properly, and not, poor boy, having to take second place to his father.

Well, there was no point in castigating herself for that. Any woman who had a child was forced to split herself; some gave the whole of themselves to the child, and the husband was left to suffer; she had tried to divide her love, but nature had made her the kind of woman who could not help giving more (perhaps too much) of herself to the man, the husband. No, it was not her fault, and yet only she could take the blame for it. And for anything that had happened later.

Murray returned from the cabana wrapped in white terry cloth. "I'll check the story. I'll check this . . . Institute and the place he worked in . . . Where was it?"

"Missouri. And . . . Murray?"

"What?"

"You'll check nothing. *I* will check."

Murray went to the bar which Tony had wheeled out of the house while he was drying himself. He mixed a bourbon and water, frowning. Virginia glanced at the frown; she knew him well. "Okay, let's have it."

"Virginia . . . Hell, I don't know how to put this. And if you say it's Jeff . . ."

"You'll be able to see for yourself in a few minutes."

"I don't mean *if* it's Jeff, of course it's Jeff, of course any mother would know her own son, but . . ."

"But?"

128

Murray scratched his wet head. "Jesus, I guess it's no goddam business of mine . . ."

Virginia smiled up at him, almost with tenderness. "Of course it's your business, you're my friend, my very dear friend. Do you want me to say what you're trying to say?"

The big ugly man took a great gulp of whiskey and stared at her. Long ago, when Cass had been alive, he could remember a Virginia like this. He ought to be glad that the boy's return had made such a change in her, but he resented it; he knew that she had moved further away from him—further than ever. "Okay. What was I trying to say?"

She stuck the needle into the tapestry and laid it aside. "You were trying to say that Jeff, the Jeff you used to know, and you only knew him a little, Murray . . ."

"Go on."

"You were trying to tell me that the Jeff you used to know wasn't . . . wasn't always a *good* boy. But I know that. You wouldn't put it past the Jeff you used to know to have *pretended* to lose his memory, all those things, just to . . . to escape, to play games, even to . . ." It cost her an effort to say it, but she managed: "Even to hurt me."

The man said nothing.

"You didn't know that *I* knew so much about him. Right?"

Murray made some kind of noise like "Hrrumph." It meant that he had certainly not known that she knew so much about her son's true character, and it also meant that he didn't know how much more she knew; come to that, he wasn't sure how much he knew himself, but he at least had been in Los Angeles for a great part of the time that her son had spent at the university, whereas she and Cass had been in Spain making some godawful movie about the Second World War.

There was the sound of a car coming up the steep incline towards the house. Glancing at her watch, Virginia said, "You'll see. He's changed, he's changed a lot."

His stomach contracted a little when he saw Murray Forde standing there, rocklike, bull-like, Caesar-like in yards of white. But there were going to be many tests like this, many unknowns into which he would have to feel his way like a man entering a strange room in the dark. As he moved forward he could feel a tension in the air, but she, thank God, came forward to greet him with real pleasure; at least this stolid adversary (some delicate sense told him that it was an adversary) had not turned her against him.

"Do you remember Murray? Murray Forde?"

Now, it so happened that this particular face, less jowls, had appeared in more than one of the Roman photographs, so he could say with confidence, but not too much confidence, "I think so. Didn't you . . . ? Didn't you have some kind of a striped shirt?" He glanced at Virginia, smiling sheepishly. "I hope you've told him I'm not a *complete* nut?"

Virginia explained to Caesar that he could sometimes only remember pieces of things and that the full picture only came later. To the younger man she said, smiling, "What shirt?"

He had to risk the fact that she might have looked at the photograph album before handing it to him, but even if she had, it could hardly have been more than a cursory glance, and the picture on which he was basing this particular fragment of returning "memory" had been of some woman; Murray had been one of several background figures; the shirt could hardly have caught her eye as it had (mercifully) caught his. So— "Stripes," he said. "White and yellow and pale-blue stripes. I think it was in Rome."

Murray recognized the shirt; he also recognized, with a sinking heart, the change in Jeff Kenny. As he turned to mix him a drink he saw the whole setup with absolute clarity: somewhere along the line Cass's son had lost his arrogance and whatever other undesirable traits had gone with it; and Virginia had seized on this, had found in it a cause, a crusade. Hence the change in *her.* He also had to admit that his immediate reaction against this young man had been unfair, simply yet another facet of the jealousy that Virginia could always inspire in him. The young man also said, "Thank you, sir" on receiving his Scotch and water; the young Jeff Kenny had not been accustomed to giving thanks, nor addressing his seniors as "sir."

He could feel Virginia's eyes on him as they chatted in the last warmth of the setting sun. The eyes were saying "See?"

Yes, he did see—more than she understood. He saw that if he was ever going to persuade her to marry him, and nothing but death would ever make him give up that intention, he would need this older, pleasanter, politer Jeff as an ally. No ally, no marriage, that was for sure!

The dark room, yet another dark room, had been entered safely; he had fallen over no furniture, smashed no precious vase and, unless he was much mistaken, he had found the light switch. Murray Forde had unfrozen; he had become almost affable—for reasons of his own, which would presumably become clear later. He was glad this metamorphosis had taken place before the child appeared, which she now had: a lumpy, perhaps undecided figure emerging slowly from the shadows of the house. He felt that he needed all the support he could get for *this* meeting.

Virginia noticed that the appalling masklike sunglasses were firmly in position; she also noticed, with tender amusement, that the hair had been combed, a rare compliment. Otherwise the entrance was as freakish and original as might be expected of this odd and original character, for Joanne Christina came to a stop a long way away: not for her the demure little-girl approach, so pleasing to adults, as she well knew. When the man she had been told was her father looked towards her and rose to his feet, she said in a small, perhaps nervous but certainly determined voice, "Would you mind if you came over here?"

He gave Virginia a quick look, and found her brows raised and a faint smile on her lips; then he turned and approached the stolid figure that stayed exactly where it was, back to the wall of the house as if expecting an attack from the rear. As he approached he said, "Hi!"

"Hi!" She lowered her voice. "I'm not being rude or cute or anything, but I don't see why I should . . . That Murray!"

"He seemed okay to me."

"He's a *hen!*" She regarded him carefully. He was certainly good-looking; he had a nice smile, but that didn't mean he was a human.

"Do you always wear those glasses?"

"Uh-huh."

"They make you look kind of interesting."

"I think they make me look a crumb. Come on, I'll show you something."

He gave a backward glance at the other two as she led him off the terrace. Bright as she obviously was, he hadn't for one moment supposed that she would recognize in him the bearded stranger whom she had obviously noticed watching and following her on the beach more than six weeks ago; but all the same, it was pleasant to have any doubt removed by her casual and not unfriendly attitude.

As he followed her up the wide staircase he noticed that she was not a fat or lumpy child at all; the little figure under the extraordinary clothes was lithe and shapely; he guessed that the face, under the preposterous glasses, was probably as revolutionary.

She took him to her room, which was like that of any other well-to-do pre-teenage youngster, except that it boasted rather more books than was usual in the electronic age, and was a good deal tidier than average. From a closet in the corner she took a large glass jar which had probably once contained pickles or preserved fruit; the metal top had been pierced with holes.

"Now," she said, "do you think I could get a rattler in here?"

He thought it unwise to show any surprise, but considered the jar seriously. "Not a big one."

"A small one?"

"Sure."

"Will you take me to the desert and help me get one?"

"Why not?" She studied his face for a long time in silence. He added, "But I tell you what—there's a kind of cage thing that hunters and snake-people use, it would be a whole lot easier and a whole lot more comfortable for the snake, why don't I get one for you?"

"Would you do that?"

"Sure."

"And would you take me? Help me?"

"I just said I would."

So he didn't just *look* like a real person, he actually was one. Come to think of it, why not? He was her father, for Pete's sake! She smiled; her smiles were rare, and very revealing—perhaps rare because she knew they were revealing. She said, "What will I call you?"

"I don't know." They both considered the subject for a time. He was thinking, Boy, was I right not to underestimate this one. He said, "How about 'Jeff' until we get used to each other?"

"Grandmother won't like that."

"Yes, she will." He was almost as surprised as she was to find that he had enough confidence to say this; but it was a true confidence, he was sure that he could get his own way about a lot of things. Already!

Chris was thinking that this was interesting, the idea of having a counter-authority around the place. "Okay then. Jeff. I'm Chris."

"Hi, Chris!"

They shook hands; it was really an absurd gesture, but somehow it seemed the most natural thing in the world.

"Now," he said, "you do something for me."

"Like what?"

"Like you take off those glasses and let me see what kind of a face you have."

She thought about this for a moment. In view of the promised trip to the desert, and the offer to get her a snake-box, not to mention the possibility of possessing a parent who might turn out to be entirely human, she could hardly refuse. She took them off.

Even though he had seen a colored photograph of her mother, he was surprised at the clear strong blue of the eyes. What shocked him, however, was their likeness, color apart, to his own, the same cool, if not cold, and appraising regard. It was interesting that the comparison extended itself from there into different realms: she hid her eyes behind the huge tinted glasses, he hid his behind contact lenses; for their own very different reasons they both went about the world masked.

He was suddenly sure that he and this child would always understand each other very well. He was not mistaken.

Three

Rose had fallen asleep. He reached across her and twitched open her curtains, which, as she had once told him, kept out the day so efficiently. A shaft of late low sunlight struck across the room. It was six o'clock; time for him to be going.

He looked down at her sleeping face, frowning. He had been surprised at the strength of his desire to be with her again, surprised and forewarned. At first he had thought that the desire was purely for escape; there was a constant built-in tension up at Number 234. Well, of course there was; he couldn't afford to be off his guard for a single instant: every move he made, every word he spoke, had to be scrutinized first, readjusted, censored, rehearsed, all in a fraction of a second. Luckily he had his mental disturbance to fall back on; they expected him to be confused, and confused was what he very often was. But all in all, it had worked out perfectly; every minute of that long period of preparation had been well spent.

There was something about Rose asleep, her head pillowed on his arm, which was oddly reassuring; the sleep itself was a sign of trust: she trusted him—better than he trusted himself! With her he could (almost) relax.

The relationship with Virginia had developed, not quite along the lines he had envisaged (and, had he known it, not along the lines that she had envisaged either), but it *had* developed, that was what mattered. There was affection, a kind of reserved affection which had initially worried him a good deal. Was she unsure? Had he made some small but disastrous mistake? No, it seemed that this was an attitude which she had decided to adopt; he wasn't sure why, but there were indications that it had something to do with their previous relationship; even he himself had suspected that Jeff Kenny had been a spoiled young man who had only to click his fingers in order to be given whatever he wanted by his adoring parents; perhaps the coolness, the loving coolness, had something to do with that. And then Murray Forde had said something at dinner last night which led him to believe that Jeff Kenny's manners had improved during the lost twelve years—that Jeff Kenny had improved in more ways than one.

This had given him food for thought. It struck him, not for the first time, that though he had observed Kenny very closely during their brief time together, he had not really researched him in depth, as he had researched, for instance, his mother. The reason for this was simple: Kenny was dead, there was no chance of having to meet him face to face. On the other hand, the reason was not so simple when he began to consider it more deeply: there had been hardly any research material at his disposal. This was perhaps natural; he had been little more than a boy when the Air Force had snapped him up. Film stars and their wives live in a world of publicity; their children do not; in fact, they make sure, if they are wise, that their children do not

The explanation didn't altogether satisfy him. He had made a mental note to search the house, casually, at his leisure; if there was anything to know about young Jeff, it would most likely be found lying on a bookshelf or tucked away at the back of a drawer, or in one of the pigeonholes of his mother's Chippendale bureau.

In other respects he had no cause whatever for complaint. He had been given one of the two elaborate guest wings of the house as his living quarters, self-contained, private to the extent of having its own patio and small swimming pool. Here there was absolute peace. Here, if he was undergoing one of his agonizing headaches, Tony the Filipino manservant would bring him exquisite meals on a trolley-table glowing with the finest linen and sparkling with crystal and silver. Here, flowers were always fresh and cool, the morning came glimmering with the sound of birdsong, his clothes were always clean or pressed or polished, and the sounds of the house came to him muted, if at all. Even the telephone was his own, no mere extension but a private line. He was living, as he had for so long dreamed that he would, in absolute luxury. All this in three days! What could he not accomplish in three months, three years.

But it *was* a strain. Virginia was one hundred percent on his side, with whatever slight reservations he had noticed in her attitude to him; it was essential to keep her there. Murray treated him with guarded good will, but could be caught out every now and again giving him an inquiring, perhaps even puzzled, look; he was not sure what this meant, and naturally, it made him uneasy. It could mean no more than the fact that the big, unprepossessing man was in love with Virginia, which was certainly the case, and was wondering how the reappearance of her son would affect this state of affairs. Or it could mean other things.

This might not have been so unsettling if the child, Chris, had not behaved in her own peculiar variation of the same manner; he would become aware of somebody watching him as he lay by his own private pool, and eventually, after a good deal of searching, he would find the small face, shrouded in its tinted glasses of course, gazing at him from the shadow of some bush.

Yet why should they not watch him, examine him, all of them? He was an extraordinary phenomenon: a son, a possible stepson, a father, who had appeared miraculously out of a cloud of smoke in a roll of drums. Hey, presto!

There was no reason at all why he should be disturbed by any of the reactions; and of course, there was every reason why he should be disturbed. At least friend Leo of the steely eye had been conspicuous by his absence; he didn't see why Virginia should deprive herself of that pleasure, if it was a pleasure, on his account, but that was up to her. He had caught the tail end of one heated telephone call, which could only have been with him, but Virginia had ended it abruptly and replaced the receiver with vigor when he hove into sight.

As for the outside world, he had so far seen nothing of it; he didn't know whether this was a matter of chance, or of Virginia's

136

powers of organization, keeping the outside world at bay until she considered that he was ready to meet it; either way, it suited him just fine: the less publicity the better. And he needed those long periods of rest and relaxation in the sun; he needed them to recharge himself for the next meeting, the next dinner, the next encounter with Chris, who occasionally inched out of her hiding places like a friendly animal and settled down by his recumbent figure with some private occupation or other. Thank God she was not a prattling, prissy, sassy child! Thank God for her long preoccupied silences, even if the questions or statements when they came were usually startling: "The tortoises are doing it. You know, having sex—do you want to see?" Or, "Look, I've made a forked stick! You bang it down, crunch, just behind the rattler's head, so then he can't move, and you can slip your hand under his neck and Zonk! Into the box!" (The rattler hunt was planned for next week. He had been surprised to discover that he meant to see it through.) Or, "Have you ever been in a place where there was a poltergeist?" (His answer had been "No, honey," and a quick withdrawal to consult the dictionary.)

Oh yes, life at 234 Upper Canyon Circle was all he had expected it to be from the point of view of creature comforts, but it was a strain. And there had still been no discussion of his financial situation.

Rose said, "A penny for them." He hadn't even known that she was awake.

"I was remembering how I laughed at you for deciding I was a Rockefeller. You weren't far wrong, were you?"

"Well, that little yellow dress didn't come from Sears and that rock on her finger didn't come from Woolworth's. Anyway . . ." She reached up and gave him a kiss. "You have style."

"Style my ass!"

"You have a nice ass too."

He laughed and kissed her back. "And I'd better get it out of here quick, it's after six."

He got out of bed and began to dress. "By the way, you're summoned to brunch on Sunday—do you want to come?"

"Of course. Actually, your mother asked me the other day."

He looked at her sharply. So there'd been talk behind his

back; there *were* things going on of which he had no knowledge. "When?" He tried to make the voice less sharp than the look which she had noticed.

Rose regarded him in silence for a moment. "She . . . They've been checking on you, darling."

His stomach plummeted. A cold and deadly fear filled the cavity where it had once been. "Checking?"

"Well, of course."

"They? You mean she and Murray?"

"Dearest *heart,* don't look so stricken. You've just said yourself she's a very rich woman. I think it was his idea, she didn't seem too enthusiastic. He's very fond of her, he obviously doesn't want her to make a fool of herself."

"When was this?"

"Day before yesterday."

He was furious with himself for revealing even a corner of his fear to her—particularly now that it was gradually seeping away. The day before yesterday was, in the present nature of their various relationships, a long time ago. And whatever they had discovered could only have been reasonable, even encouraging, since Murray had been more friendly towards him yesterday, following the check, than he had been the day before. This must mean that he at least was satisfied. Did it also mean that they had stopped short of checking the fingerprints? It seemed possible, particularly as Virginia Kenny had not been "too enthusiastic."

His stomach was slowly clambering back to its ordinary physical position. He could appreciate that Murray would certainly have bullied Virginia into making the proper inquiries; he himself had expected it. Heavens above, hadn't he long ago laid a trail for such inquiries to follow? Hadn't he in fact been doing just that for the past ten years or more, ever since he had snuffed out whatever feeble glimmer of life had still burned on inside Jeff Kenny?

He felt all right again now, but as he kissed her goodbye he made a mental note to do a little checking himself; he needed to know what they had found out and from whom. Virginia herself would tell him that; she'd tell him anything he wanted to know, as long as he went about it the right way. "See you on Sunday, honey. I'll pick you up around eleven-thirty."

"Fine. I can't wait to see the palace."

"And maybe if I drive you home, you'll ask me in for a cup of tea?"

"Maybe I will."

He felt good as he went out to his car. That desperate moment of fear had been salutary; the return from it had forced him to appreciate all over again the beautiful position in which, by the sweat of his brow and the intense application of his intellect, he now stood. They could check until they were blue in the face—everything was covered, everything was going to be all right.

His confidence might have been less pronounced had he known how Joanne Christina had been spending this, Friday, afternoon.

Pete, who cleaned the pool, arrived about one-thirty, as he usually did. The job had taken him an hour, so that his departure coincided happily with the after-lunch siesta. Her grandmother was lying down prior to a visit to the beauty salon, long postponed; Jeff had driven away on private business. Chris took the usual precaution of dropping some vague and un-heeded remarks about wanting to see her friend Jane. Unheeded or not, they would be remembered later if her absence was called to question. Then she met Pete at the usual corner of the drive, climbed into his pickup and ducked low onto the seat beside him to evade any hostile watching eye that might be around. (This was how, by chance, her Friday departures had also evaded the watching eye of the bearded man who had once, some weeks ago, taken such an interest in all her movements.)

Pete drove her to the usual bus stop on Pico before going on to minister to various pools in Cheviot Hills. Chris left the bus at the corner of Oceanview and walked down it, parallel with the ocean, of which it had no view whatever, until she came to a small side road leading directly towards the beach. It was called Majolica Drive, perhaps because of its proximity to Venice (California) that grand, impractical and now ruined American dream.

The houses were tiny, built of wood, with a wealth of twenties detail which would have delighted the heart of any aficionado of that period. Number 7, outside which Chris came to a stop, boasted an Art Deco stained-glass window at the top of the door, representing a swordfish leaping spectacularly against a setting, or rising, sun. It was a neat house, neater than many of its neighbors, but the din of construction from the vast marina complex not far away, and the rapidly approaching chunks of modern apartment buildings, seemed already to pronounce its doom.

She knocked on the door. After a moment it was opened by a woman; she was in her early thirties, but could have been much older. With one exception it was a face of almost superhuman blankness; it looked as though it had been practicing lack of expression all its life; the lines below the eyes and from the sides of the nose to the corners of the mouth were deeply scored, and the skin was parchment-colored, only faintly touched by a trace of sun; it was free of make-up, from which it might indeed have benefited not at all, and the hair was featurelessly neat. The exception was the eyes. If Jeff Kenny had been alive, he would probably have recognized his wife, Holly, by the faded yet still extraordinary blue of the eyes. There wasn't anything else about her that he would have recognized.

Virginia Kenny left the beauty salon without a trace of the uplifted spirits which it usually induced in her. She wasn't in the least looking forward to the meeting with Leo which was about to take place. The fact was that she didn't like any of the purely official duties engendered by Jeff's return, even though the actual pleasure of having him back was growing day by day. It seemed that his loss, following so quickly upon the loss of her husband, had activated some defense mechanism deep inside her, with the odd result that only now, now that he was with her again, did she fully realize how much she had missed him. It was exciting, the most exciting thing that had happened to her for many, many years; every day they grew closer to each other; every day she could see him venturing a little further out of his protective shell, just as she herself ventured a little further out of hers.

She hated this ride to downtown L.A. only slightly less than she hated downtown L.A. itself; but the least she could do was to let Leo choose the ground for their last meeting. She wished now that she had driven herself in the Mini; this grandiose performance in the Rolls, with Tony driving, didn't suit her mood at all. The fact was that nothing suited her mood very much these days except the hours she spent with Jeff.

She was annoyed with Murray because he had made such an undercover (*underhand,* in her opinion) cloak-and-dagger performance about "checking," as he called it, on her son. It would have been so much more civilized to conduct the whole performance out in the open, with Jeff in attendance. Anyway, she had had the satisfaction of seeing everything proved conclusively aboveboard and correct. Well, naturally! What on earth did he expect?

Dr. Kallman had left the Aldington Institute, but his assistant had verified all the details and expressed delight that a line could be ruled under the case of poor "James White." If Jeff needed a checkup at any time, he had only to take a plane to San Francisco and the Institute would be at his disposal.

Susan Sackville Inc., of Greenstown, Missouri, had said that he'd always been a conscientious worker and that they'd been sorry to lose him, while their doctor, traced after a good half-dozen calls, had proved to be more than pleased that the young man's vacation had ended up so happily for all concerned.

Rose Maddox—a charming girl, pity she was an actress!—had corroborated all these details, drawing them, as it were, into a neat bunch. How fortunate that Jeff had happened on such a nice, natural, outgoing person! And how nice to know that his taste in ladies had improved that much: out of all recognition!

Really, the whole thing had been perfectly ridiculous, and when Murray had started rumbling about fingerprints, she had put her foot down sharply and heavily. Wasn't it enough that he was a sick man—did he have to be treated like a *criminal* as well? Alex Feldman, her lawyer, had agreed with her (naturally; he knew that she could change lawyers with a stroke of the pen, even if Murrays were more difficult to dispose of), so that at last the field had been cleared of the clutter of practicalities which men found so reassuring.

She could see that Tony, who loved driving her about in the Rolls, was most disappointed that she wasn't entertaining him with the more absurd pieces of gossip which the beauty salon invariably imparted; usually they laughed about these all the way home, but today . . .

Leo was waiting for her in a corner of the deserted businessmen's bar (phony oak paneling and a phony log fire in the baronial grate), where they had met before. His long face told her that he already knew what she was going to say, and she wondered why she had found it necessary to come all this way to say it in person. Well, you had to be an utter louse to put paid to an affair on the phone, though she knew a lot of women who had done so.

Of course there would be no actual scene. Leo had known how much he meant to her right from the start, and she didn't flatter herself that she meant any more, qualitatively, to him. It had been a mutual convenience.

However, he did seem to find her *reasons* a little difficult to grasp. "Okay, honey, if that's how you want it, but I think it's crazy. Jesus, he's a big boy now, he knows what it's all about."

"He's not well, Leo. It's a very difficult situation for him anyway, and I . . . I can't confuse it any further."

Of course what he ought to be saying was, "Then don't! Come to my place, and he'll never know." But this was the one thing he could never say. His place! That crummy hole! Ah yes, where was the Château Lafite now? And where the expensive perfume he had loved to sniff, the delicate hand-washed sheets he had loved to stroke, the exquisite Fabergé clock by the bed, with its tiny, glittering, diamond-studded pendulum that had twinkled away the hours of dalliance with such an excess of luxury?

"I owe it to him, Leo. I . . . It's very difficult to explain without going back—far back into the past, and there's no point in doing that. I made . . . mistakes then, and I'm not going to make them again . . ."

He hadn't been listening to her, not really. He was thinking, Oh well, at least I have the Mercedes.

And finally she was gone, leaving a last whiff of that perfume.

It was five-thirty; by rights he should go back to the office for half an hour to check on a few things, but fuck the office! What he needed was another Scotch. And then another. And by this time other men were coming into the bar, a sprinkling of women—not the kind that held any interest whatever for him. Another Scotch, and he began to feel better. The Mercedes would be a great help, a very classy sprat to catch—who could tell?—an even classier mackerel. The idea pleased him and he smiled.

"Hi, Leo, what's the joke?" "Hi Leo! Bartender, give this gentleman here a Scotch, he looks thirsty."

He liked this time of the evening; they were all regular guys, and they were all glad to have finished work. Also, it was Friday; the weekend stretched lazily ahead, and if you got stinking, so what? It was your own time, your own hangover.

On the other hand, there was this seesaw sensation, hardly new to him but unsettling. Up—and to hell with Virginia, to hell with her beautiful house; come to that, it wasn't a house at all, it was a goddam museum, full of antiques; and guess which was the biggest antique of all? Ha ha! Down—and Jesus, he was going to miss all those great restaurants, and that expensive perfume, and the beautiful little clock twinkling away in the corner of his eye while he made love to luxury in a melée of sumptuous sheets . . .

Hi, Leo! Hi, Burt! Hi, Leo! Hi, Dan!

Dan Harrap. Was that Dan Harrap? Sure it was—as fat and as bland and as avid for tidbits as ever. Dan Harrap, ex-Harvard, social snooper for the Los Angeles Sunday *Times.*

"You look great, Leo, how's your glamorous girl friend?"

Well now, how exactly was she, as far as fat Dan Harrap was concerned? She was probably very interesting as far as fat Dan Harrap was concerned, even though she'd said, "Now please, my dears, I know I can trust you. Thank God," she had said, "that I was with three friends I can trust," lumping him in with those godawful old pachyderms called Lehman. The trouble with rich people was that they thought you'd always do as they wanted, and the trouble with poor old Leo was that he generally did.

"So please, my dears, not a word about any of this, not to a living soul. You all saw the kind of state he's in; he's not a well man, he's sick. So please, not a word. Promise me."

So they'd all promised, like the load of punk pricks they all were!

"You look great, Leo, how's your glamorous girl friend?"

He was going to be bitchy, he could feel it coming on; but why the hell *shouldn't* he be bitchy once in a while, huh? Everybody pushed him around, yes they did. Whoosh, *down* went the seesaw! Poor old Leo, good for a quick lay, and then out into the cold again. On the beach, washed up, getting too old!

"Now please, my dears, I know I can trust you . . ."

Oh yes! So *how* do you know, Madame?

"You look great, Leo, how's your glamorous girl friend?"

"Well now, Dan, I'll tell you a little something . . ." Why the hell should *he* care because a spoiled brat called Jeff comes lumbering back from the dead in an expensive suit with an adoring British broad on his arm? ". . . a little something interesting for your column. Remember her son, Jeff, the one who was killed in Vietnam? Well, he wasn't killed at all, he . . ."

Quite obviously Dan Harrap was not particularly impressed. In the first place, he knew more about Leo than Leo thought he did; in the second place, he found the whole thing rather distasteful (ex-Harvard); he even toyed with the idea of ignoring it altogether, but knew that he wouldn't do this because he was also a good newspaperman. Of course, it would have to be checked out; no one but a fool would believe everything Leo Faber said, even if he was sober, and the Widow Kenny was not a member of the community about whom you printed inaccurate pieces of news. By the time he had checked, it would be too late to make this Sunday's paper. He might, therefore, give it an inch or two the Sunday after, if it hadn't by then been splurged all over some weekday edition.

In any case, he repaid Leo's little confidence with one of his best Harvard looks, which implied more clearly than any words that he thought Leo a son-of-a-bitch and a shit to boot.

Down went the seesaw! Leo the rat! Okay, so why should he care what they thought of him? The seesaw rose again, slowly.

So what the hell, they could all go screw each other; and screw Dan Harrap too, if that's how he felt! Who does he think he is, anyway, the ghost of Hedda Hopper? Hey, that's funny! Listen, you guys, do you know who Dan Harrap thinks he is? He thinks he's the ghost of Hedda Hopper. Hedda Harrap. Hey, that's funny, isn't it? Well, isn't it?

Four

Joanne Christina Kenny sat under a banana palm at the edge of the rock garden watching the tortoises. She wasn't sure whether they had yet achieved perfect union; she wasn't even sure that they ever would, what with all that dead weight of shell and the fact that the gentleman tortoise was nearly half the size of the lady. Presumably they did in the end, or there wouldn't be any tortoises at all, would there?

If only Pamela would stay *still* for a moment or two! It was really very contrary of her to keep clambering about the rock garden just at this time, when normally, for weeks on end, she would remain stationary, doing absolutely nothing. Percy, of course, was frantic. Poor thing, he'd been trying for *days* now! Chris had brought him some nice cool milk—he looked as though he could do with it!—but he had ignored it absolutely. And he liked milk. Truly, sex was a terrible and cruel business.

She stood up, while she was on the subject, and bounced up and down on her toes a couple of times to see how the boobs were coming along. Evidently they weren't.

From the house behind her came an urble-burble argle-gargle of adult voices. Skinny, hideous, *sinister* Alex Feldman, her grandmother's lawyer, had arrived just as they were finishing lunch, accompanied by a beautiful young Jewish assistant of some sort, with eyes like melting balls of treacle toffee. When she saw young men who looked like that she understood for a brief second that boobs and so on might at some moment become necessary extras.

She knew what they were discussing because she had listened for a few minutes outside the window; it was all to do with Jeff's money: apparently Grandfather Cass had started various investments and stuff for him long, long ago when he'd been a kid. She hoped that everybody was starting investments and stuff for *her*, so that as soon as she was of age she could take off on her own and do a few of the things she really *wanted* to do.

Meanwhile, there was this problem with her mother. Honestly, adults could make problems out of but nothing; they could sit down on the beach on a nice sunny day when God was in his heaven and all was right with the world, and Wham! within about two minutes they'd managed to create a problem.

Come to think of it, the whole business with her mother was a problem; had been ever since the day it first started. That must be . . . nearly a year now. What happened was this: Miss Mannering's, where she went to school, was way out the other side of Santa Monica Boulevard, so that Tony or her grandmother or some male attachment, if available, had to collect her and bring her home; they weren't always on time. Well, Tony was on time, always, but nobody else ever was for about a thousand different reasons. She objected to sitting around in empty classrooms or, worse, making polite conversation with some distracted teacher or other who really wanted to be at home in the sack, or on the beach, or whatever teachers do when they're not teaching; so she'd walk up the street to Santa Monica Boulevard and go to a place called the Ice House and eat something cold and delectable until whoever-it-was arrived. She did this practically every day.

The second time she saw this woman in the Ice House she got this well-known feeling that somebody was about to kidnap her. (Come to think of it, she probably *wanted* to get kidnapped, subconsciously, the way she was always thinking about it—but by a man, not by a woman.)

Anyway, here was this straggly, scrawny kind of woman who always wore very dark shades and was always staring at her; or rather, was never staring at her when Chris looked her way, but was always staring at her when Chris was looking at something else. She was often in there. In fact, it seemed she was in there every single day, but actually, she averaged three out of five schooldays, which was enough.

Sometimes she would leave before whoever-it-was arrived to collect Chris, and sometimes whoever-it-was would arrive first; this was all according to the buses. There was a bus stop outside the Ice House, and this weird female would catch the bus going to Santa Monica; it was supposed to be there at three fifty-five, but owing to the vagaries of the Los Angeles public transport system, it never was. Anyway, this was her bus; she always caught it, always sat up front.

Joanne Christina, tired of the frantic tortoises, went to the edge of the pool and dabbled her feet in it. She couldn't remember whether she had ever been scared of the woman or not; she rather thought not; there had been something odd about her, but more sad than scary. But anyway, after nearly three weeks of this silent, distant scrutiny, this is what Chris did.

She made an excuse at school, saying that she was being collected twenty minutes earlier than usual; then she walked quickly up to Santa Monica Boulevard, but not by the direct route straight up the street; she went around the other two sides of the block and hit Santa Monica further east, about three hundred yards away from the Ice House. Then she ran up to the next bus stop, which was fortunately by a gas station where she could use the phone. She called Number 234 and got Tony a few minutes before he set off to pick her up; she told him that she was going to visit with one of the other girls (omitting to say which) and that this girl's father would drive her home in time for supper.

Then she waited for the Santa Monica bus, getting on it and finding a seat right at the back, where she hid herself behind an old copy of something called *The Gay Lib Express*, which she'd found in the trash bin fixed to a lamppost near the telephone booth. As they approached the Ice House she took a quick peep and was just in time to see the weird woman coming out of it to catch the bus as usual, she sat as far forward as possible. She never looked around once.

The bus went right down Santa Monica Boulevard to the

ocean and then turned left; about a mile further on, the woman got out at the corner of Oceanview and walked quickly away down it, staring at the ground, as if she was late for a very important meeting and was thinking out what to say when she got there.

Chris allowed the bus to start again before jumping to her feet and crying, "Oh, stop! Please stop. I'm terribly sorry!"

The driver jammed on the brake and cursed her, but quite good-naturedly, as she tumbled out—well past the end of Oceanview, so that even if the weird woman *had* looked back, she would have seen nothing.

After that it was easy to tail her the half-mile to the corner of Majolica Drive and to watch as she let herself into Number Seven.

Once the door had closed, Chris made a circuitous advance upon the house, ending up with her face pressed to the worn wooden fence which enclosed the shabby yard. The yard was full of junk: there was an old refrigerator and several wooden packing cases, a mattress with a hole in it, an ancient TV set with no tube, part of a canoe, and many other things equally fascinating, which were hidden by long grass and weeds; there was also a line for hanging out the wash.

Chris had to wait for what seemed like hours, but was in fact about twenty-five minutes; she was quite secure, being hidden from prying eyes by the blank wall of the house next door, inside which somebody was beating the hell out of a piece of iron. (This was a sculptor, at least he called himself a sculptor, whom she met later.)

At the end of this time she was rewarded by the sudden appearance of the weird woman carrying a basket. From the basket she took various damp and sad-looking pieces of underwear, male as well as female, which she pegged to the line. It was only when she turned, having completed this job, that Chris caught a glimpse of her eyes (she was no longer wearing the dark sunglasses) and was struck instantly and violently by their brilliance.

Well, really, it could hardly be coincidence, could it? Joanne Christina had once possessed a mother who had gone away, never to be heard of again; this woman, of about the right age to be mother to an eleven-year-old (though it was impossible to tell what age she actually was), came day after day to the Ice Box and sat gazing at her; and she had, set into her ravaged face like a couple of sapphires, these eyes which Chris had never seen anywhere else but in her own reflection.

Argle-gargle, urble-burble. Would they never stop yakking away there inside the house? So Jeff had a lot of bread piled up in some bank or other! So hand over the key and let him get on with it!

Anyway, after that, Friday had become Majolica Drive day because of Pete the pool man who could lift her half the way there. She came back by bus, to the Beverly Hills Hotel, and thence by taxi to the bottom of Upper Canyon Circle; if anybody asked questions, there was always Jane, who could be relied upon to lie effectively in case of emergency.

There was no way of telling just when the weird woman became aware of these Friday surveillances or, having become aware of them, decided to make herself known. There was an adult problem to do with Court Orders and, of all things, Conscience involved in this. But eventually, on the sixth Friday, she suddenly came out into the yard and stood staring with those eyes right at the patch of fence behind which Joanne Christina crouched peeping like a cross between Mata Hari and a scared rabbit. "Why don't you come on in and have a Coke?" was what she said.

The inside of the funny little house was much tidier than the yard, and it was very clean. But it had a desperate air about it, as if nobody had ever cared for the things it contained. Everything, however clean, was slightly worn or slightly chipped or on the point of peeling. It was the first time that Chris had ever been inside a house that was let furnished at a really cheap rent. It seemed that nothing in it *belonged.* It made her feel desolate, and perhaps it even scared her a little, but then, the woman who had been (was still?) her mother made her feel desolate too, and now that they'd actually met, scared her a little sometimes.

They never spoke of money or of Number 234; they never spoke very much of anything. Holly Mitchell, as she now called herself, though she had never married Mitchell, was appalled by what she had done; she didn't even try to hide this. It seemed that she worked, as a typist, almost next door to the Ice Box, and had one day looked up from her work to see this (to her) instantly unmistakable small girl walking past her window. A little later, Virginia Kenny, equally unmistakable, had stopped in a white Lincoln to collect her. She told the child of all this with no visible emotion. "Of course I shouldn't have done it. I promised, I promised in a court of law, so you mustn't say a word to anybody, you do see that, don't you? It was actually *illegal* for me to follow you into that ice cream place. Do you understand?"

"Yes." It was stupid, like so many adult situations, but perfectly understandable. "There was a girl at Miss Mannering's, and her father was told by the court that he couldn't see her ever again, and he came and took her away, and they flew to France, and there was a terrible row, it was super!"

"Well, it wasn't super for the girl's father, so please . . ."

"I won't say a word to anybody. I promise. I have dozens of secrets, you'll see, I spend practically my whole life keeping secrets."

Since then they had met perhaps twenty times. Chris didn't know what the weird woman got out of it and she didn't even know what she got out of it herself, but somehow it was important for them to see each other on Fridays; for fifteen minutes, for an hour, two hours, even though they hardly ever spoke, and when they did, it was always about generalities.

Chris liked it best when they sat on the beach; this was not only because the house depressed her, it was also because of the man in the house; he was never mentioned either, but she knew he was there. Once or twice she had heard him moving about, *shuffling* about, he sounded like a very old man; and once she had heard him coughing; and once there had been a kind of groaning noise which had made Holly leave the room for almost ten minutes. She came back looking even more pale, more tense, than usual and said, "Why don't we go on the beach for a while?" So they had walked down to the marina in silence.

It was funny, really; she didn't know why she kept going. Just that it was important.

Perhaps they had both been waiting, waiting without knowing why or what for. And the moment they'd been waiting for was the moment, yesterday, when the weird woman had closed the door and Chris had said, "My father, Jeff, he's come back."

The face which looked as though it had been practicing lack of expression all its life continued to remain blank. Almost. There was a quick intake of breath, an infinitesimal widening of the faded but extraordinary eyes, a long moment of utter stillness, as though life had finally departed from that already seemingly lifeless body.

"He was a prisoner-of-war for years and years; he was ill; he lost his memory."

The weird woman expelled her breath very quietly, with enormous control, and said in a controlled and very quiet voice, "What . . . do you think of him?"

"He's nice. He's going to take me to the desert and we're going to catch a rattler."

They walked along the beach and then out to the end of the Venice fishing pier. There was a pleasant breeze and the sky was bright blue. The Pacific was in a teasing, sparkling mood, showing all the charm and none of the steel. Standing at the end of the pier, watching the patient old men and the less patient kids, neither of whom ever seemed to catch anything, Holly eventually said, "I have to speak to him. Once. Just for a few minutes. But if you tell him who I am, he won't come."

Chris was visualizing a far more awful eventuality than his failure to appear. "No, you mustn't! Don't you see? When he gets back, back to Number 234, he'll *tell*." Her blood, usually an even-temperatured liquid under the iciest conditions, ran cold at the thought of that revelation and of the scene with her grandmother which would follow it. The recital of those Friday absences! Holy *mackerel!*

"No. He won't say a word." There was hard certainty in this. The small girl understood at once that her own situation in the face of Virginia's incredulous wrath would be nothing compared to the situation which this blank, bony woman would have to face—a courtroom situation.

"I promise you he won't say a word. Not to her, not to anyone. But I must see him. You must bring him to me."

Five

This was the life! Good God in heaven, this was the life!

It was a soft, clear day with a gentle breeze, just enough to ripple the pool and to stir the leafy shadows that lay across the terrace, just enough to make the palms rustle and sigh. A perfect Southern California day, and a perfect Southern California setting, and beautiful people in beautiful, light, crisp clothes, lolling in the pleasant heat of midmorning with glasses of champagne in their hands.

Virginia, judging her time, and thinking of her son's age group, had let the dinosaurs rest by their own pools and had asked the new young sensation to join them with his pretty wife; she had done this for Rose too, knowing that the meeting could do her no harm professionally and might do her a lot of good.

Even Murray was happy, because he was yet another of those Americans who (inexplicably to many others) loved England and London in particular, and Rose therefore delighted him. Yes, quite a day! Even good old Murray was happy!

Rose looked great; it was obvious that she could rise to any social occasion with ease, and he was looking forward (but lazily, without tension) to the afternoon, when he could drive her home and make love to her. For the first time he was filled with actual confidence; for the first time he felt that he was indeed Jeff Kenny. The details of his financial situation, into which the lawyer, Feldman, had conducted him, as into an Aladdin's cave, had exceeded his expectations to such a degree that for quite a while he had been literally speechless. Luckily, when Mr. Feldman was around nobody else was required to speak very much, so that he had been given the opportunity to get used to the idea, in silence, that he was a very rich young man indeed; among other things, he owned two apartment buildings and a sizable chunk of land at the northeastern edge of the San Fernando Valley, where building was already in top gear.

It seemed (and here a note of despondency had entered Mr. Feldman's voice) that he had managed to make a severe but not disastrous hole in this money structure during the two years following his twenty-first birthday and preceding his absorption by the Air Force; but (more brightly) Mr. Feldman had by his own brilliance patched the hole and practically doubled the sum that remained. Good solid investment.

The champagne sang in his blood, the sunlight danced on the terrace, the light breeze stroked the pool into a million glittering points of light. Good God in heaven, this was the life! This was what he had striven to achieve.

Chris was absent, but Virginia had assured him that of all social occasions, Sunday brunch was the one that most immediately drove her into hiding; she might or might not appear with the actual food; her usual habit, apparently, was to eat her share in the kitchen with Tony. (Chris, had they known it, was at that moment sequestered in the second, unused, guest wing, talking to Holly Loring-Kenny-Mitchell on the telephone.)

Rose, bless her, was now in seventh heaven, because it appeared that the sensational new male star had seen her play when it was on Broadway and had thought her performance superb—and Jesus Christ, she didn't really have that old bastard Matt for an agent, did she? He'd talk to his own agent first thing Monday morning, fix up a meeting.

He stretched in the sunlight, smiling to himself. Virginia caught his eye, and thought to herself, "That's better. Every day he gets better." He transferred the smile to her.

A wonderful day. A wonderful life.

At about this time, Dan Harrap of the Los Angeles *Times* was eating *his* brunch with his wife at Scotty's restaurant on La

Cienega, Scotty (who liked to see a Harvard tie every now and again) in attendance.

"Seems like you had quite a drama in here the other night, Scotty. Virginia Kenny."

"Well, I'll be darned, Mr. Harrap, you certainly get to hear of things, you really do."

"My job. What happened?"

Scotty hesitated. It was one of his rules never to discuss one customer with another, but on the other hand . . .

As if picking up his thought by psychic means, Dan Harrap said, "Good publicity, Scotty . . ."

And at about the same time, on the telephone in the second, unused, guest wing of Number 234 Upper Canyon Circle, Joanne Christina said, "Okay, I'll try. If it doesn't work, you'll know they all got too stoned."

She replaced the receiver and went out onto the guest patio, where all was quiet and calm compared with that argle-gargle going on beside the main pool. She stood there looking across to Jeff's suite, frowning.

Something wasn't quite right about this whole maneuver in which she had now got herself involved; she didn't know why she was doing it, any more than she knew why she had felt that need to make the Friday visit. It seemed that as you got older, there were these things you felt compelled to do or not do; she hoped that eventually you learned what was wise and what was unwise, what was kind and what was cruel, because at this moment she was all at sea, filled with a sense of uneasiness and doubt. She would have liked to talk to somebody about it, but that was impossible. Her grandmother must never know that she had met Holly once, let alone time after time; and Jeff . . . "If you tell him who I am, he won't come."

She went to look for Pamela and Percy. The search was complicated by the necessity of keeping out of view of all that socializing on the terrace, and anyway, she couldn't find them. So what? She wasn't very interested in tortoises today.

Returning to her room, she examined the rattlesnake cage listlessly; in her present mood she somehow doubted whether the promised hunt would ever take place. Like a lot of other

155

things, it was probably just a kid's dream. In fact, she was filled with childish wishes for escape, but an unchildish awareness kept telling her that the thing she wanted to escape was in her own head, and therefore inescapable.

Gazing down at the adults by the pool, listening to their laughter, she thought that if this was what they had to put up with, the way she felt right now, it was a wonder they ever managed to laugh at all. For almost the first time in her life she felt a twinge of sympathy for the adult condition.

There was thus a very real pathos about her when she finally intercepted the man who called himself her father as he returned, after the meal, from a visit to his own private bathroom. "Hey," he said, "where have you *been*, I've missed you."

"I hate"—a gesture towards the terrace—"all that."

He had recognized her aloneness; before he could raise his guard against it, it had flung him reeling back into his own childhood. Sunday afternoon. His father drunk, the shabby house untenable because of that big menacing uncertainty; if you went in, he might embrace you in a whiskey-sobbing embarrassment of self-pity or he might give you a straight left which would knock you down the steps into the yard. No telling which. An appalling uncertainty.

Recognizing his recognition, Chris said quickly, "Will they all go soon, will you take me down to the beach?"

He looked out of the shadowed hall in which they stood, across the glare of the sunlit terrace, at Rose sitting in the shade; that was what he wanted, that was what he'd been promising himself all day. And yet . . . He looked down at the small girl and saw, or thought he saw, it made no difference, something of the uncertainty and the desolation of his own youthful loneliness.

Rose was secure; she was his any time he wanted her. The champagne, and the excellent wine which had followed it, said, "Now!"—but they also said, "Remember?"

"Okay, chipmunk, I'll take you to the beach."

Chris had seen the look towards Rose and had interpreted it more or less correctly. "Alone," she said. "Just you and me?"

156

"Sure." He knew that Rose could not be lured within a mile of the beach on a Sunday; she loathed crowds, above all.

But her understanding, when he explained the situation to her, was so quick and so complete that he found himself being annoyed by it; he wanted to be wanted more. Of course this was ridiculous; he had chosen her in the first place *because* of her understanding, and could hardly start resenting it now. All the same he did resent it: "What are you doing this evening?"

Even as he said it he realized that this was the first time he had felt secure enough in his new position to dare leave the house in the evening—in the quiet hours when people chatted idly of this and that, in the quiet hours when thoughts arose, when a thought might so easily flower into a suspicion. Behind his back!

"I'm washing my hair."

"Couldn't that wait?"

"Of course."

Virginia smiled a mother's approval upon his evening arrangements. Murray smiled too; he planned to leave for Europe again soon, and was happy at the thought of having Virginia to himself for a few hours.

So he drove Rose home, a silent Chris in the back seat; and then he drove Chris down to the beach, Venice Beach, which seemed to him an odd choice, but it was her outing and she could go where she pleased.

Her silence, however, continued. Glancing at her, he found the small face unusually preoccupied behind the gigantic glasses. "What's the matter?"

She looked up at him, a long look full of concentrated thought. "Nothing."

But when he had parked the car and they were moving towards the crowded stretch of sand, teenagers squirting Coke at each other, anxious fathers shepherding unruly broods, earnest fishermen of all ages from nine to ninety heading for the pier, she suddenly came to a halt, leaning against a wall on which somebody had scrawled in red paint "Krishna Loves *You.*" He glanced back at her and was struck by what seemed to be an expression of physical pain; for a second he thought that one of the passing kids must indeed have given her a slap. He went back. "Chris, what *is* the matter?"

Again she gave him that look of extreme concentration. "I promised I wouldn't tell, but—" she heaved up a deep, an enormous sigh—"I guess I have to. If I don't, it's . . . it's not fair to you."

The sidewalk was narrow and people were bumping into him. He was keenly aware of their awkward position, pressed against "Krishna Loves *You*" in order to avoid the sweating Sunday crowd. "Let's go sit on the beach and talk, huh?"

"*No!*" He could have sworn that she wasn't far from tears.

"Honey, what gives?"

"I . . . I promised somebody I'd . . . bring you here, but . . . It's not too late, you can still go back."

He gazed at her in amazement, touched with perhaps a little fear (fear was never very far away from him), as her childhood struggled with whatever was going to follow it, all beneath the benefice of Krishna amid a surge of hot, sandy, shouting people. Venice Beach on Sunday! What a place to choose.

"You promised who? Why? What do you mean?"

Chris told him.

It was like a series of well-aimed punches: to the stomach, doubling him up, to the chin, lifting him again, and smash . . . full in the face, sending him reeling back against the ropes.

Holly! Jesus Christ, the one thing, the *one thing,* he had been sure he'd never have to face. Holly, the pretty bitch who had trapped Jeff Kenny into marriage for the sake of his money. Oh yes, he knew who'd made that hole in the bank account that had so worried lawyer Feldman. Holly, with her pretty little face and her insatiable appetite . . .

He grabbed his panic-stricken reactions and pulled them back into some kind of order. Of course the kid was right; they could get into the car and drive away, and there was nothing that the woman could do. She had been defeated in a court of law; she raised her head now at her own peril. This was obviously the sensible action to take; but on the other hand, it would only be sensible in the most limited way. Holly herself would remain, a mystery and a possible threat; running away was hardly the action to be taken by a man who could prepare and carry out that ten-year-long vigil.

Confidence, a little of the confidence which had seemed so

158

absolute a few hours before, came creeping shamefacedly back; he had locked away the panic and could now think reasonably again. His *mother* had accepted him, for God's sake, so why not his ex-wife? It was an eventuality he could have done without, but since it had arisen, there was nothing to be gained by avoiding it and everything to be gained by meeting it face to face. Never in ten thousand years could this woman force a rift between himself and Virginia Kenny, and that was the only thing that mattered. As for the rest, obviously he must find out what she was up to, and if it was blackmail, God help her! He'd put Feldman onto her so quickly, she would never know what hit her!

He looked back at Chris, who had been watching this storm of feeling sweep across the man's face. He smiled. "Thanks for warning me, honey, you're a great girl." ("And," he might have added, "you bring my own youth so darn close that I can smell it." That was odd. What the hell did the youth of a poverty-stricken kid in East L.A. have in common with the luxurious youth of a small girl in Beverly Hills? Answer: youth.)

"Shall . . . shall we go home?"

"Hell no, let's go meet her."

As Chris led him through a side alley, into Oceanview, and along it towards Majolica Drive, he prepared himself for the encounter. What did he expect? Something loose-mouthed, wide-hipped, flopsy big-breasted, the prettiness evaporated, but still potent in a dim light, still provocative enough to enable her to get a man and haul him back to this shack which they were now approaching. The plush apartment blocks of the marina would soon advance and crush it underfoot like a cockroach. And a good thing too; the kid wasn't the only thing around here that reminded him of his youth.

He stared in disbelief at the taut, blank-faced woman of no age who opened the absurd door, stained-glass swordfish leaping against the sun. The sea breeze molded her cheap cotton dress to a seemingly fleshless, breastless body, and the very dark sunglasses on the parchment face reminded him of a skull's eye-sockets.

This was true shock. Something in this boded ill, he could feel it in his bones. His heart pounding suddenly, he looked at Chris. "Got any bread, honey?"

"Yes."

"Go get an ice cream, huh? See you back at the car."

To an already-retreating child, the woman said in a flat and featureless voice, "Ten minutes. Ten minutes is all."

He followed her into the pathetic house. He knew the smell of it, the feel of it; he knew the battered furniture that had never been any good in the first place, the television set that was ten years out of date, the rattle of an ancient refrigerator from out back in the kitchen, the flimsy curtains that were four inches too short owing to repeated washing between rentals.

They faced each other in the desolate living room. The woman, as if wishing to give him proof for an unspoken disbelief she could see in his expression, took off the sunglasses, revealing her extraordinary eyes; he accepted the proof, and he accepted the deeply scored lines beneath the lower lids.

"Jesus," she said, "you didn't even have the decency to get yourself killed properly, did you?"

The wariness which had gripped him at the sight of her ran tingling through his whole body; it was possible that his initial panic had been more reasonable than the confidence which had superseded it.

She moved, nearer to him and nearer to the light from the single dirty window; she turned her face so that this light, brilliant and unflattering from the cold blue Pacific sky, fell directly onto it, showing him the flaccid unhealthy skin, the deep lines, the yellowish smudges like healing bruises under the eyes, the ruin in all its cruelty. He calculated that she was thirty-one, but it was hard to believe. She knew that no words were necessary; the face, the emaciated body, the bleak blue eyes holding his with a sideways glare, told all there was to say.

"Satisfied?" she said.

He still remained silent. There had been many other situations into which he had been forced to feel his way with extreme care, but none like this. In this situation he sensed violent, almost physical danger; he wondered how Jeff Kenny would have reacted.

"You knew me, you cold fucking bastard, you knew me,

pretty stupid little Holly; you knew I might get stuck with it, but did you care, did you shit?"

He would like to have backed away from this unanswerable cold venom, but in the tiny room there was no space for backing, and in any case, some intuition made him stand his ground.

"Oh yes, it was all kicks for you, wasn't it? Anything was kicks for you, you perverted fucking bastard! A little hash, a little speed, a touch of acid here and there. All kicks for gorgeous Jeff Kenny, and if anybody happens to get stuck with it, what does gorgeous Jeff Kenny care? Why don't you say something, cat got your tongue?"

It was almost as if Jeff Kenny himself reached out across eternity with the right words, even the words he would have used himself. He heard his own voice, tight and angry: "I've nothing to say to you. What do you want, money?"

"Oh my God, money! That's the key to it all, isn't it? Money buys the kicks and money hushes up the mess, and money keeps the cops quiet, and money socks it to stupid little Holly so she can get stoned again and shut her mouth. No, keep your fucking money. And don't look so scared, darling, Holly won't tell Mummy." She came very close to him; he could smell alcohol on her breath, and a strange odor, not unclean but . . . he couldn't place it. "I've one thing to say to you, Jeff, just one thing. You leave that kid alone. You start playing games with that kid, *any* kind of funny game, and I'll raise the roof. I'll start hollering and I'll holler so loud and so long, you'll hit every goddam headline in the whole of God's beautiful country."

The anguish on her face was terrible to behold at that moment, but again he knew what Jeff Kenny, this new and unexpected and altogether shattering facet of Jeff Kenny, expected him to say: "You poor bitch, you couldn't do a darn thing, not one darn thing. You're full of shit, you always were."

The look on her face gave him the uncanny feeling that he was indeed being controlled by the man he'd killed all those years ago. The look on her face brought confidence surging back. "You listen to me," he said. "Okay, so I was a crazy kid, we did a lot of stupid things—you weren't so hot on the accusations then, were you?"

161

She opened her mouth but no sound came out; he knew he'd hit the right track. "Whatever you did to yourself after I'd gone, *you* did, Holly. Not me, you! So you suffered—well, *I* suffered too. You've changed, and so have I."

She gave a gasp and turned away; it took him a moment or two to realize that she had done so to hide tears. He flung his advantage at her trembling back: "I love that child, I wouldn't harm her for the world. And you . . . A fine mother you turned out to be, anyway!" It was his turn to go closer, even though he couldn't bear the smell of her. "Don't blame that on drugs, don't blame me because you took to the mainline, *I* never did that." (He didn't know whether he could trust what Virginia Kenny had said about this, but it was all he had to go on. It seemed she had been right, there was no denial.) As she turned, falling over a chair, she fumbled for the dark glasses, found them, rammed them back onto her face, but not before he had seen how ravaged, almost deathly, it had become.

He should have felt sympathy for her, poor ruined creature; he should even have felt grateful, because she had presumably revealed Jeff Kenny as no amount of research, no amount of talking to Jeff Kenny himself, had ever revealed him. But he was scared; she'd knocked the props out from under him, and he was reeling about, blind, on a battlefield where a thousand misconceptions had been slaughtered by a handful of bold realities—for he had no doubt that this wreck of a woman was speaking the truth. Any sympathy he might have felt was trampled underfoot by fear and anger and disgust; the abject house, the smell of alcohol, the utter desolation of it all, brought back his youth, not mildly, almost nostalgically, as Chris had done, but with a savage, kicking fury. This wretched sniffling creature that had once been pretty Holly Loring could never know what she had unwittingly released in the man who had never been her husband; he could, at that moment, have seized her miserable skinny body and shaken the life out of it, kicked it to a pulp, and known, while he was doing so, that it was his own childhood that he was erasing forever.

He took a grip on himself with difficulty; his head was aching as if it would split, and as usual, the contact lenses were playing up in sympathy. He wanted to get out of this house, away from this woman, at once, without delay; but he knew that he had to see the whole horrible scene through to some kind of uneasy conclusion. He said, "Chris is safe with me, you know that as well as I do; her grandmother's done a fantastic job, the job I couldn't do, the job you wouldn't do . . ."

"That . . . bitch!"

"There's only one bitch around here, and it isn't Virginia Kenny. And you mark this, Holly: if you raise your voice or your head, I'm going to put a hundred lawyers on to you and they're going to pick your bones clean. Do you understand me?"

She was snuffling and moaning to herself. ". . . the clinic, and I beat it. I beat it, but look at me! God helped, you won't believe that, or maybe belief helped, I guess it doesn't matter *what* you believe. I need to see her, I really do, Jeff, honest to God, I need to see her. Nobody need know, nobody need ever know."

"That's up to the kid, isn't it?"

"I'll keep my mouth shut in front of her. I always have. You can ask her, I've never said a thing to her." She stumbled back to him and grabbed his arm with fingers like a bird's claw. "Don't stop her coming! Just a Friday every now and again. There's no harm in me, I'm . . . I'm burned out, Jeff."

He shook his arm free in disgust and said again, "It's up to her." He needed to get away now; he needed to think; he needed to search the battlefield, finding out which of the misconceptions were dead, which needed surgery, which could be dispatched with a merciful bullet. He needed to be alone for a while, before that ride back to Beverly Hills with Chris. The child was too bright, she saw everything; he had to regain some kind of composure before being subjected to her clear eye. "Okay, here's what I'll do. I'll tell her to come and see you right away, and whatever she decides . . . that'll be that. Okay?"

She peered at him for a moment with genuine surprise. Then nodded to herself. "Yes. Maybe you *have* changed."

He didn't want her to find the change too surprising, so he added, as he might have added to his father, "And for Christ's sake, don't have another drink before she comes. And rinse your mouth out, you stink."

He moved past her very quickly, unable to stand her for

another instant; he pulled open the door . . . and a figure shot past him in the bending position, ending up with a crash against the TV set, but mercifully, not putting its head through the tube. A man. A youngish man who could not, it seemed, recover his balance, but fell forward onto the floor and rolled over, upsetting a cheap and flimsy chair. A youngish man with long hair and a ravaged face who was, at a guess, and he could make a pretty informed guess after those years in Vietnam, suffering from hash—or even heroin—withdrawal.

A trump card. His, not hers.

She bent swiftly, putting an arm around part of the sprawling figure; her sunglasses had fallen off, and the blue eyes raised from the floor were anguished. "I'm helping him, he's cutting it now." And to the lolling head: "Why didn't you stay upstairs like I said, what were you doing out there?"

"He was listening, I'd have thought that was obvious."

"Chris has never seen him, she doesn't know that he exists, we usually go on the beach. Oh God, you can't think I'd ever let her know, and he . . ." She looked down at the helpless man, who had now begun to shudder uncontrollably—a look, not of affection, certainly not of love (she was beyond all that), but of enormous understanding and compassion.

He recognized without self-criticism that she was a good person, better than Jeff Kenny had ever been, far better than he himself had ever been or ever would be. He said, and it was all he had to say now, "Take care. The last thing *you* need is a visit from the police, right?" And, as he turned out of the door, "Get him out of the way, clean yourself up, she'll be here in five minutes."

At a little after four on a Sunday afternoon the Sandpiper was almost empty. He didn't need the alcohol, he needed to get away from sun-glare and noise and the agitated movement of hundreds of overheated people. Here, in the beer-smelling darkness of this typical Los Angeles bar, you couldn't tell whether it was midday or midnight; time ceased to exist, and by some freak of luck, even the jukebox was silent.

He thought back to Jeff Kenny, lying in his corner of that hut. Had there been indications . . . ? Yes, perhaps. A certain attitude, a certain scorn for other people which had occasionally peeped through his utter dependence on other people, one in particular. It had been so easy then to misread signs. Certainly his attitude to his ex-wife had been abrasive, but then, most men had abrasive attitudes to their wives, ex or not, it was all part of the men-together syndrome. And sometimes there had seemed to be a faintly contemptuous glint in the brown eyes, a glint of "What would you know about such things anyway, you dumb ignorant bastard?" Or was this hindsight? Was he simply being wise after the event?

Probably, now he came to think of it, he had known very little of the true Jeff Kenny. How could a sick man, a man too weak to leave his mattress in the corner, reveal anything of his true self? Perhaps as he slid into semiconsciousness . . . But that rambling, often obscene monologue, to which he had once listened so intently, had been long ago; and in any case, it was almost impossible to remember disconnected scraps which had no rational meaning. If he could play them back on a tape recorder, he might discover many fragments which would be revealing in view of what that wretched woman had said. His memory was not a tape recorder; it failed him.

However, he could understand one thing very clearly now: his inability to come to grips with the life which Kenny had led during his time at the university, here in California. The lacunae had struck him as odd; they were more than odd, they were downright sinister. He could find out very little because Kenny had made sure that there would be very little to find, that was obvious.

So what did he now know that had laid waste so many misconceptions? He knew that Kenny, like many another rich young man, had set about wasting his time at the University of Southern California; the evidence seemed to indicate that he had wasted it on the usual things, drink, girls and drugs; he had become a well-heeled decoration of the so-called subculture, and at some time during the trip he had met and married Holly Loring; but whereas he had been a young man of some character, and one who had eventually had to submit to the discipline of the Air Force, she had been a weak-willed girl; what had been a kick for him had become for her a way of life.

A tragedy certainly, but not a very unusual one. Children who played with fire got burned; it had been that way, with variations, all through history.

He began to realize that his stroll across the battlefield had not been quite the terrifying experience he had expected; the misconceptions which had fallen in the face of reality were better dead, and though many of his conceptions about Jeff Kenny had suffered wounds, they seemed to have profited from the experience. If he cared to look at it one way, there was nothing, however terrible, he could learn about this young man that didn't actually help him in the final reckoning. After all, he *was* Jeff Kenny, so he might as well know whatever there was to know about himself.

As he left the bar, his drink untouched, and went out into the glaring, blaring day to meet Chris, it occurred to him that on the whole he was quite pleased to discover that Master Kenny had been a good deal less than perfect. They were more alike than either he or anyone else had guessed: brothers under the skin as well as upon it. No wonder Mother Virginia had treated him with that odd kind of reserved affection—how much did she really know? And Murray's attitude of suspicious hostility settling into more friendly but still guarded watchfulness now made a lot of sense. (How much did *he* know?) Oh yes, a number of things were going to clarify themselves greatly in the light of wretched Holly's disclosures.

Chris was already sitting in the car, sucking gloomily at an ice cream. As he got in beside her he said, "Well, how did *that* go?"

She considered the ice cream in silence, then threw it away. "I hate pistachio, don't you? I think she's batty—was she batty when you were married to her?"

"No. She's been . . . ill."

"Freaked-out, I wouldn't wonder."

He said nothing.

Chris sighed. "She was pretty, I've seen pictures."

"Yes."

"She's got some man or other in there, you know. I've only heard him, he was having a fit or something upstairs. I'm not going any more, she doesn't want me to."

"Is that what she said?"

"Yes. There's an ice-cream parlor near school—I guess we'll meet there sometimes, I don't know."

"Don't you care?"

"Nope. Can we have the radio on?"

After a while she began to sing along, tunelessly. Then: "I don't care what you say, I think she's bats. You sing too."

They drove slowly back from the squalid clutter of the beach to the cool, green orderliness of Beverly Hills, singing all the way.

Six

The rattlesnake had warned them of its presence, of its awareness of their presence, by a faint ominous whir. The man and the small girl, tiny figures in the vast shimmering landscape which was the rattlesnake's world, not theirs, came to a halt, listening. He made a gesture to Joanne Christina, motioning her to move behind him; she did so with alacrity. They both took a few paces forward. The snake whirred again, but this time the sound seemed to come from another place.

The desert heat fell on them like a positive weight, and rebounded from the floor of the ravine with almost equal power. A hawk hung motionless above them in a burnished sky from which the sun seemed to have bleached every trace of blue. The rattlesnake again announced its awareness of their presence, its resentment.

He had done this kind of thing before, in his youth, part of the savage dare and counter-dare of those idiotic days. After he'd left home . . . Home? After he'd left that shambles he called home in East L.A., he'd taken a job at a desert gas station, outside Barstow; he and a guy called Ramon, half-Mexican, had gone rattlesnake hunting. Hunting each other in fact, since the basic idea had been to see who turned chicken first. He had forgotten the outcome, but it had happened only a few weeks after leaving home. His father had taken one quart too many and lay on his bed, dying, unable to move.

He remembered how he had gone into that room and picked

up his father's pants; he had taken twenty-five dollars from the pocket while the man on the bed had watched him in silence. That was how it had ended: he had stolen twenty-five bucks while the dying man had watched him; then he had gone to Barstow and taken this job.

Now he had two hundred and fifty thousand dollars in his bank account, and a lot more where that came from; now he had everything he had ever wanted, including a Ferrari, and yet he kept remembering the past. Why was the past more immediate, more real for him now than it had been at any time during the last ten years? He could even recall the expression on his father's face when he had looked back at him from the door. Why now?

The rattlesnake was silent, biding its slow, cold-blooded time under the bludgeoning sun.

In a whisper, Chris said, "It's gone." As he shook his head he thought that he had detected a very slight note of relief in her voice; it made him smile. The rattlesnake gave them another, sharper warning.

He looked back at the child—her small figure was tensed in expectancy; excitement and fear battled together on the smooth face. He didn't know what it was about her that moved him so much, struck at his heart.

The wrecked woman who had given birth to her had probably said it all that hideous afternoon: money was everything and money was nothing. Except for creature comforts, and this kid didn't know what they were because she had never had to go without them, there was little difference between his childhood and hers; neither of them had possessed parents. The fact that Virginia Kenny had done a wonderful job was neither here nor there; a father was a father and a mother was a mother, and no child could go without either, not when it came to the crunch; and the crunch was life when childhood was over. Oh yes, that was the crunch.

What did this crazy snake mean to her, anyway? Come to that, what did it mean to him?

Standing there under the violent sun, with the snake, the sun's creature, dangerously at hand, he felt a tremendous surge of fellow-feeling for this child, so tense, eager and afraid behind the

169

huge tinted glasses which she used as a barricade against life. Something had pierced his heart. He had never known love, so it was hardly surprising that he didn't understand that what he was feeling for the small girl was an aspect of love.

She looked up at him, biting her lower lip, the precious snake-box clutched against her stomach. He whispered, "Now you stay here, understand? Don't you move from here until I shout for you."

"But . . ."

"No buts, honey. Right here!"

"Okay."

As he moved slowly forward to a shelf of shaly rock where he was pretty sure the snake was hiding, he wondered what kind of an expression would sweep over Virginia Kenny's face if she could see them now. Absolute, uncomprehending horror. Of course she'd be right, it was a crazy idea in the first place, and only a couple of crazy people would think for one moment of implementing it.

He remembered suddenly the first time he had hit his father back. How old had he been? Fourteen, just fifteen. Had to be; he hadn't turned sixteen by the time he walked out. Nothing so utterly fantastic about it really—socking a drunken man not a great deal bigger than you were, the only wonder was that he'd never done it before; the best target had seemed to be the belly; his father had collapsed like an ill-set jello, slumping back onto his bed and sitting there with an indignant expression on his face.

He remembered that he had tensed himself for retaliation, watched by the other two kids, his sister Fran and his brother Joseph; but no retaliation had been forthcoming. Their father had stumbled towards the bathroom, but had started vomiting long before he got there. They were all quite used to this; Fran cleaned it up almost automatically, while their father, locked in the bathroom, had wept.

(Where were they now? Fran had written to him once while he was in boot camp; she was working in a bar in San Diego, and a sailor had asked her to marry him; she didn't know what had become of young Joseph, the County had sent him to one of their schools. Christ, what a family!)

170

The rattlesnake sounded its full warning. He came to a dead stop, searching the ground below the cleft of rock, but with rattlers, how could you tell?—they were great ventriloquists. He glanced towards Chris, who was leaning forward in absolute concentration, mouth slightly open, a tiny and absurd figure in her huge boots, with an enormous panorama of desert behind her.

There!

The camouflage was so perfect that it was as though a section of rock itself was moving, or as though water moved across the face of the rock. A big one.

He raised the forked stick. Not the one Chris had made, something a good deal stronger. The rattler had come to a stop in shadow; it had paused in the action of moving away from him so that its head wasn't facing him; then it slithered two yards forward into sunlight and was still again.

He couldn't afford to take his eyes off it now—only twelve or fifteen feet separated them, and it didn't take a rattler very long to move that far. Without looking at her, he signaled Chris to stay still. Now they must all wait. If the snake didn't move again, it would mean that it had forgotten the danger which had once seemed to threaten it. Movement was danger. Lack of movement was rock and the drowsy sun, the empty desert.

They waited. The snake made no move. He stood with his forked stick raised, like some crazy Statue of Liberty, and Chris remained hunched forward over her box.

Sweat trickled down the small of his back; sweat trickled down his forehead and into his eyes. The glare was getting to him; at times he was willing to swear that there was no snake there, but then he blinked and saw it clear again.

Time stopped. There was no sound, not even the whine of a high jet. The pounding of his heart was so loud that it sounded in his ears like the pounding heart of the desert itself. What the hell was he *doing*, anyway?

He knew what he was doing: he was tempting Providence in the shape of a dangerous snake; he was balancing Jeff Kenny, and his killing of Jeff Kenny; he was balancing all that was left of Kenny's wife, all that misery, and the Ferrari, and the two hundred and fifty thousand dollars in his bank account, and the investments which wily Feldman had made, and the constriction of the heart which that odd little girl had just aroused in him, and Rose, and the luxury of Number 234 . . . he was balancing all these against the possibility of this snake twisting on him like a whiplash and reaching, perhaps, above his boots.

That was screwy, that was *really* nutso! But—and he certainly hadn't known it until this very moment—it was the truth. He was asking the snake a question.

He took two paces forward, one on sandy soil, one on a flat stone. No sound. The snake hadn't moved; its tail had not even sighed in warning.

He took another pace on to firm rock. Nine feet now; he was well within the danger line. Through trickling sweat he saw that the snake had not stirred; it was dozing. Now he would take three more steps and he would strike; the neck was lying on gravel, which meant that the fork would hold it. The first step would be to that patch of soft sand, the second had to be as far as that slanting outcrop of solid rock, the third . . . was in the lap of Providence.

Three steps. He tensed himself, and he sprang forward. The soil was fine, but there were loose pebbles on the rock and his foot scattered them. The snake began to move as he began to take the third step; its head lifted and swung around; the powerful body coiled. The man slammed down his forked stick, and realized a fraction of a second later that he had missed the neck. He heard Chris cry out as the snake let loose its powerful coil and shot at him. Providence lifted his leg for him in the nick of time and he felt the solid blow, the uncoiled force of the snake's body as it hit him, burying its fangs in the tough leather only a couple of inches from the top of the raised boot.

It seemed that the fangs had not expected to contact anything half as solid; the snake was convulsed in the effort to extract them, and in that paralyzed moment of convulsion, the man seized its writhing tail with both hands and jerked the body upwards with all his strength, tearing the fangs loose and whirling the wriggling body, slamming it down onto the rocky outcrop.

This might have killed it or it might not have killed it; he took no chances, but reeled forward and brought his boot crashing down on its head.

During this, Chris had reached him, gasping but still clutching her box. "It got you, it got you, are you okay?"

"Yes, I'm okay." But he sat down at once by the smashed head of his adversary and took off the boot quickly, then the sock. People had died before because the poison had reached some tiny scratch; people, sucking the poison from another's wound, had not known that there was a little sore place inside their mouths; they had died too.

The man and the small girl examined his leg carefully. The venom oozed on the inside of his boot where one of the fangs had just penetrated. At the sight of this, Chris looked up with a sharp intake of breath; their eyes met.

"Wow!"

"Wow's right." He noticed for the first time that she was no longer wearing the glasses; her eyes, in this utterly clear desert light, were truly astonishing. He also noticed how the color suddenly ebbed from her cheeks; she glanced away.

"It's okay, honey, it's over."

"Yes, but . . . One inch, one *half* inch!"

"No. There was the sock, it's a thick sock." But all the same it had been a close thing; and where had that sly bitch, Providence, placed her bet? She'd known all along that the snake would give no answer.

Dan Harrap of the Los Angeles Sunday *Times* was irritated, but he knew that in journalism what had happened was an occupational hazard. He'd spent the entire morning polishing a romantical piece on Jeff Kenny's return from the dead. It hadn't been an easy job: in the first place, Cass Kenny had been gone a long time, and his name wouldn't even be a memory to many readers unless they'd happened to catch him recently on the Late Late Show; in the second place, the Widow Kenny kept herself to herself, neither making nitwitted marriages with younger men, leading to newsworthy disaster, nor behaving in any of the other ridiculous ways by which a number of her peers kept their aging faces on view; in the third place, though there

173

was no doubt that young Kenny had got up to some pretty disgraceful tricks before going out to Vietnam, it was all old stuff now, and you didn't drop snide hints about veterans who had suffered for their country; also, it was worth remembering that Alex Feldman was the family lawyer, everybody had a healthy respect for Mr. Feldman.

So, what with one thing and another, it hadn't been an easy story to write, and Dan Harrap had finally settled for a lump-in-the-throat angle which had worked out pretty well. And then, just as he was about to send the opus along to his editor, came the news that this silly bitch had committed suicide out at Malibu; and here were *all* the newsworthy angles—sex, drugs, drink, promising young star (she had no more chance of being a star than of turning into Batman, but that was the word you always used)—and the net result was that his Jeff Kenny story would have to be cut from four hundred lines to about fourteen, which would kill it stone-dead. Hardly worth printing, really, but there'd probably be a corner for it somewhere.

After a scrutiny of the map and a little searching, they'd found a straight stretch of secondary road with a decent surface; it undulated across the desert like a grubby piece of grey ribbon for six miles without a bend. So he'd let the Ferrari go, and boy, *did* she go!

The sudden lunge of speed had left both their stomachs behind. Only now, as they sat in the declining sun outside a battered old hamburger joint, situated in the middle of nowhere, did their stomachs come toddling along the road to join them. They were silent, each occupied with his own thoughts. The dead rattler, in its box, had been deposited in the shade; Chris wanted it to be in exhibitable condition when they got home, and was even now wondering whether she could keep it for a few days in the refrigerator of the unoccupied guest suite without Tony's discovering it there.

She glanced, apprehensively for her, shyly for her, at the man who sat silently drinking his beer beside her. He was about the only adult she'd ever known who didn't yak-yak-yak all the time anyway.

"Want another Coke?"

She shook her head, staring. The large sunglasses had eventually been retrieved, but one of the lenses was smashed, she must have put a foot right on it as she ran forward to see if he was all right. *Was* he all right? She had heard such terrible stories about rattler poison . . .

"You okay?"

"Fine." He turned his head and looked at her, startled all over again by the blue of those eyes. "Quite a day, huh?"

She regarded him for a moment or two before saying, "It was the best day I ever had in my whole life."

"Good."

"But . . ."

"But what?"

She looked away from him; looked up at the two tall rustling eucalyptus trees that stood guardian over the shack. "I guess I . . . I was pretty darn stupid, wasn't I? The whole rattler thing, I mean. I was stupid to . . . to ask you to do it."

"So? I did it."

Again the beautiful blue stare that would, that must, quite soon begin to take its toll in the world of men. He grinned. "That makes me pretty stupid too."

"Why did you?"

If ever there was a kid for searching questions . . . ! And they couldn't be evaded, they couldn't be answered with easy clichés, he'd discovered that already. Why?

"I guess," he said at last, "I guess a lot of people set themselves . . . risks—just to make sure they're still there."

"Who's still there, the people or the risks?"

"Both. But I meant the people. Sometimes, when you get older, you . . . you get this feeling that you don't really exist, so you do things to prove to yourself that you do. Crazy, really."

"*I* don't think so."

In the silence that followed, it struck him that perhaps, without her knowing it and certainly without his knowing it, she had just made him give the reason for everything he had done since the idea of taking her father's place had first popped, alive and whole, into his head. In a sense he had never existed in his own right. The poverty, fear and uncertainty of his youth had pushed him out into the world with no equipment of any kind; he hadn't even known that he possessed a brain, an intelligence,

175

until the determination to become someone else had revealed them to him. He had stumbled from lowly job to lowly job without any sense of his own existence; he had worked and eaten and slept and, occasionally, had sex without the faintest idea of himself in relation to these humble functions; he had been absorbed by the Army; he had marched here and there, he had fired guns, he had worked and eaten and slept and occasionally had sex as before, but he had never existed. Only at the moment of becoming someone else, Jeff Kenny, the father of this child who sat by his side—only at that moment had he begun to achieve identity.

The irony of it made him smile. He was a gigantic, living, ironical joke. And the few moments, the half-hour, the time out of time that he had spent alone with the rattlesnake (the child and Providence being mere onlookers) proved it.

Dan Harrap's Jeff Kenny story (courtesy of drunken Leo, who, when he came to read it, didn't even remember that he'd spoken to Harrap that evening) had come down in the world since its inception. Tacked on to the end of a column of newsy tidbits it now read:

IDENTITY REGAINED!

Nice to hear some really good news amongst the bad. It was certainly Surprise Night at Scotty's on La Cienega when Virginia Kenny thought she'd recognized another diner as her handsome son, Jeff, whom many will remember. Jeff was reported missing believed killed in Southeast Asia.

The young man proved to *be* young Kenny, wounded when his plane was shot down, and a prisoner up to the end of the war. He had been suffering from complete loss of memory, and had given up all hope of discovering his lost identity.

So Lady Luck smiled on the Kenny family, and we know our readers will join us in wishing them much future happiness.

Come to think of it, this happy ending could have come right out of one of Cass's old movies. Too bad he couldn't have been there to join in.

It wasn't very much, but it was enough. The Los Angeles Sunday *Times* was probably incorrect in assuming that there were many who would remember Jeff Kenny, but there were a few. Oh yes indeed, there were certainly a few.

One of these was a thin sandy-looking man in his middle thirties; his hair, neatly cut and unremarkable, was the exact color of dry sand, high above the tide line; it even had something of the dry texture of sand; his face was lightly touched by the Californian sun to match the hair, and nature had seen to it that nothing should mar this one-colored effect, giving him sandy eyebrows, dry lips only a shade darker than his skin, and eyes of a light hazel fringed with pale lashes. He was a man that most people never looked at twice, unless he gave them reason to do so; those that did were inclined to be struck, eventually, by the eyes which they had previously ignored, for on closer inspection they proved to be very keen, very level in their regard, on final analysis, somewhat alarming. In the bars, clubs and discos (yes, discos) which he occasionally attended, this one-colored man was known as Clifford. It said something about his character that nobody ever called him Cliff.

The somewhat overcute four paragraphs in the Los Angeles Sunday *Times* affected this person in an odd way. He stood up abruptly from his breakfast, which on Sundays he always ate in his living room, usually by the open window giving onto a small balcony. He stood up and then remained exactly where he was, staring at the column with his keen eyes, his face screwed up into an extraordinary expression, which, if he had just stepped on a thumbtack wearing only his socks, would have been one of pain

Then he turned away from his half-eaten meal and moved across the immaculately tidy, characterless room, dropping page after page as he went, until, by the time he slumped down onto a sofa without even seeing it, he held only the one page which had so afflicted him. Eventually, having read the four paragraphs over again, he dropped that too; then, abruptly, he raised his two hands and pressed them over his face, bending almost double, so that hands and face all but rested on his bony knees. It was a position which might have been mistaken for one of extreme grief, but in fact it was no such thing; it was, as nearly as possible, the exact opposite.

Seven

At 234 Upper Canyon Circle the telephone calls had started on Saturday evening. By eleven o'clock on Sunday morning they had become a bore, and Virginia had instituted Tony as an oriental answering service; she had not realized just how many friends and acquaintances she possessed, dotted about the Los Angeles basin. (Interestingly enough, only five or six of the calls were for her son.)

Occasionally, if the caller had first of all managed to pass through Tony's sieve, and if they had at some time known Jeff, she would pass the receiver to him with a grimace, and he would say a few polite words; in this way it never really mattered to the person on the other end whether he knew who they were or not (and of course he never did); a formality had been observed, a gesture made and accepted.

As for his own friends, Tony inscrutably judged four of them to be unsuitable, and the other two, both girls, soon found it embarrassing not to be remembered by a man whom they had both, by the sound of it, known rather intimately many years before.

He wondered wryly whether Holly had seen the column. He could visualize exactly the expression which it would produce on that wreck of a once-pretty face. He thought about her quite a lot off and on; he could understand her better than any of the more glossy characters of the Kenny world; in many ways she and he were alike: both had known despair, poverty, abuse. He had already made arrangements for money to be sent to her regularly, though he had a feeling that she would probably refuse to accept it.

He could not pretend that the four paragraphs in the newspaper hadn't caused his heart to give an uneasy lurch. They were a complication he could have done without, even though he had long ago prepared himself to deal with something a good deal worse; after all, there'd been no guarantee that he wouldn't hit the headlines, it could so easily have happened. In that case, he had even foreseen the worst contingency of all: the remote possibility that (a) somebody had survived the savage bombing of that first camp, that (b) this same somebody had known Jeff Kenny, that (c) this same somebody had known about Jeff Kenny's death (unlikely, since deaths were purposely kept quiet in the interests of morale), that (d) this somebody had managed to live through the remaining years as a prisoner, (e) chanced to live in Los Angeles, (f) chanced to discover the unimportant paragraphs hidden away on an inside page, (g) chanced to be the kind of person to do something about them if he did discover them.

As far as he'd been able to tell at the time, or find out later, none of the fifty or so men in that first camp had ever reappeared at the bigger one outside Hanoi. It was quite possible that none of them had survived the attentions of their compatriots in the B-52's, and he would have taken any bet that the nine men in his own, and Kenny's, hut hadn't done so, because it had received a direct hit—the one which had saved his own life by depositing him in the shit-pit. Yes, on the whole it would be surprising if there was anyone around who could successfully piece together that particular Chinese (or Vietnamese) puzzle. By Sunday midday he found that he could read the four paragraphs in the *Times* without undue concern.

Here were the Lehmans, calling from Palm Springs and insisting that they must have a word with the dear boy. The dear boy was relieved to be able to speak to somebody whom he didn't have to pretend to remember dimly. And here was Scotty calling from his restaurant, where, judging from the background noises, Sunday brunch was being celebrated in a haze of Bloody Marys—Scotty diplomatically ensuring that Mrs. Kenny was not irritated by the publicity, and that he stood in no danger of losing such a good customer. Of course, Virginia was completely unfazed by the whole thing; it was a mere zephyr compared to the gales which had occasionally swept over her household during Cass's lifetime.

Watching and listening, he felt confidence strong inside him. It seemed possible that this woman really was his mother, that this house really was his home. As for Chris, they had obviously sealed some pact during that crazy day in the desert, the day of the rattlesnake: she was his friend and he was hers; she liked to stand close to him, even to lean against him; he liked to put an arm around her, feeling the fine delicate child's bones. Neither of them, in their different innocences, knew that they loved each other, but then, love is a bond that sometimes requires a test to make itself known.

Virginia had taken him shopping in Beverly Hills; it seemed that she wanted him to have a wardrobe as extensive as her own. At a certain moment their eyes met, over a bolt of lightweight Scottish wool, and he had known, as he now seemed to know most things, that this was the right time to speak, while the tailor was elsewhere, searching for an even finer cloth. He said, "I remembered . . . last night . . . I remembered some of the things, pretty stupid things, I did when I was here before, at U.S.C."

There was no way of judging how much she'd discovered about his relationship with Holly, about the life they had once led together; it was evident from her expression that she wasn't about to tell him. All she said was, "I'm sorry, in a way. They're best . . . forgotten."

"I guess I was . . . different in those days."

"Yes, you were." He was glad she sounded so positive. On the other hand, he thought he caught a glimpse of something else in her eyes as she turned away to finger a length of tweed, something more profound, unsettled as well as unsettling.

Virginia was thinking of that first night when she had lain on her bed, thanking God that Jeff had come back, that she was to be granted another chance; all the errors, of omission, which she had made in his youth would now be erased; she would give him all the love and attention which she had then failed to give because, in those days, Cass had claimed everything.

Yet how much *could* you go back? Sometimes she wondered. Sometimes she wondered whether it was possible to go back at all. The past was past; the things that were done in the past were done. Irrevocably? She tried not to think so, but a doubt haunted her.

If he had returned as the Jeff she had known long ago, nothing would have been possible; for better or worse, mostly worse, that Jeff was formed. It was only the change in him that gave her hope; war and wounds, both of body and mind, had changed him utterly; he had lost his memory, and this surely meant that he had lost *himself.* A person was simply the sum of the thousand things they had thought and done; remove what they had thought and done, and it followed—didn't it?—that you were left with an innocent nothing. And it was this nothing, this clean slate, which had initially made her so happy—in which she had seen a possibility of salvation for him and for her. But if he was going to remember all the past . . .

Oh yes, that was the kernel of it. She was afraid—yes, afraid, better to admit that honestly—afraid that if he remembered, he would automatically return to being the man who owned those memories. In that case, she had certainly been kidding herself; in that case, there was no going back, no hope for him and no erasure of guilt for her. Merely a return to square one. And at this thought panic filled her. The profound and unsettling something which he had glimpsed in her eyes had been panic.

Then it would all disappear, draining out of her mind like an evil mental pus; he was back, and he had changed; no matter what he remembered now, no matter what specters arose gibbering from the past, this new, changed and strengthened Jeff would rise above them. Watching him, standing alone in thought on her terrace, or laughing with Chris, or being courteously polite to some of her old friends, who probably bored him to death, she was filled with contentment and hope again. It was more than a son whom Providence had returned to her, it was a son metamorphosed into the kind of man she had always wanted her son to be.

Nowhere was this more evident than in his relationship with Chris. Nowhere was the proof of his being Jeff Kenny—the kind of proof which dear old Murray had so unnecessarily demanded—more obvious. He had done wonders for the child;

even in that horrifying business of the rattlesnake he had achieved a wonder; the dreadful sunglasses, smashed during the fracas, had not been replaced. There was a new and perhaps beautiful little girl about the house, with astounding eyes. Virginia was constantly being astounded by them.

Murray was preparing to go back to Europe. He had naturally not said anything about her going with him (another Jeff-given bonus), but she knew he thought about it all the time. Released from the pressure of his overpowering will, Virginia could now peacefully consider the idea of crossing the Atlantic herself. Jeff would probably enjoy it; places that he had known and loved when he was a boy might even complete the healing of his mind, and the trip would remove him from Los Angeles with its store of memories which were better not remembered. Yes, it seemed to be a good idea from every point of view. Chris was at an age to change schools anyway. Perhaps a quick decision . . .

Of course, there was always Rose. Virginia had no idea where Rose stood in her son's heart; he kept her to himself. Knowing what she did of men and women and their always delicately balanced relationship, she suspected that the girl's feeling for him was deeper than his for her. It seemed unlikely that they would ever marry, she had her career and he his memories of Holly, but it was always a possibility.

Last Sunday, in the course of that successful brunch, the fear of him (of that other Jeff in him) had suddenly raised its head, as it often did when he was being particularly charming. It apparently liked to spoil simple moments of pleasure. In panic she had turned to the girl for reassurance, leading her away from the others, trying to discern in that young mind some echo of her own disquiet. "Does he . . . does he ever seem to get . . . depressed when you're together? Depressed for no reason?"

Rose had been surprised, not by the question but by the panic which she had recognized. "No. Why should he?"

Yes indeed, why should he? Clear young question confounding the stupidity of an old woman's confusion. "He . . . In the old days, he . . . had troubles, you know. His wife . . ."

"I don't think he worries about her. Considering what he's been through, he seems marvelously . . . in control of himself. Altogether."

The fear withdrew a little, biding its time. She hated it; she must fight with it and destroy it once and for all—before it destroyed their relationship.

Rose said, "He's giving me a wonderful present, did you know?"

He was giving her a car; Los Angeles without a car was a total impossibility. For a week, ever since that afternoon, he had tried to argue her into buying something that suited her personality, but Rose would have nothing but a Volkswagen Beetle. She was adamant. In the end he had contented himself by making out a check for considerably more than the Beetle would cost, but Rose would only discover this, in delighted confusion, when the time came to pay. She planned to pick the car up first thing on Monday morning.

Meantime, as Sunday afternoon continued in a jangle of congratulatory telephone calls, a few of Virginia's closer friends decided to drop in, many of them wishing to take a look at the returned prodigal. It was for him a sure proof of his confidence that not even this worried him unduly. He was confident and he was charming, and if he occasionally caught them exchanging looks of surprise, even of shock, this only made him turn up the charm a little higher, made him more studiously polite. They had come expecting to meet the man whom Holly had revealed to him (though almost all of them had never actually seen that man, only heard about his antics), and they found this handsome, grave, polite, shy (yet confident) charmer. Their exchange of glances gave him a good deal of amusement.

Before very long the friends had persuaded Virginia to call other friends; by six o'clock there were some seventy people on the terrace or in the big room giving onto it, and Tony, having summoned help from a number of the guests' houses, was performing the kitchen miracles for which he was justly famous.

Rose, looking cool and beautiful in a new white dress, arrived at six-thirty. High on his wave-crest of success, he greeted her with unconcealed affection and delight, so that, since she was the only person there who was *his* friend and not his mother's, her entrance was any actress' dream. Watching him as he steered her through this smart rich crowd, she was suddenly overcome by the realization that this was really all her doing. If he had had his way, they would have sat quietly at their table in Scotty's while Virginia Kenny and her party had trailed away; the opportunity would have been lost, perhaps forever. This was her doing, and she was proud of it: proud of him, proud of herself. In addition, her last visit to this house, and the change of agent which had ensued, was now paying dividends: she had been given the plum part in a prestigious television play, which could only lead to greater things, since everybody in town was talking about the better-known actresses who had been turned down in her favor.

The party, like most unplanned parties, was high-spirited and amusing. For him it was a mountain peak on a clear day; all around, in every direction, the fine prospects stretched away to promising horizons. Yet when he led Rose from the noisy terrace, down the wide shallow steps to the water garden, she noticed that a shadow had fallen over him.

"What's the matter?"

He looked at her in the growing darkness. He very much wanted to tell her what troubled him, but of course that was impossible. All the same, how odd and disturbing it was to find that every moment of success in this new life which he had stolen was counterbalanced by a memory of the old life which he had worked so hard to lose; so that up there on that terrace, glittering with light and laughter, he had suddenly remembered with shocking and painful clarity his sister, Fran, and his small brother, Joseph. They were all three of them holding solemn council in the dusty, abandoned yard at the back of the dump they had called home. He himself must have been sixteen by then, Fran a year younger, a pale ungainly girl with big eyes, and Joseph twelve; the subject had been whether or not he should leave home. Up there on that terrace the two pinched young faces had suddenly been as clear to him as the face of Rose herself, perhaps more clear. The memory, almost forgotten, had pierced him to his gut. Joseph had been wearing one of his old sweaters, still too big for the bony little frame. Joseph had never possessed anything new, anything he could call his very own, in all those years; always hand-me-downs.

"What's the matter?"

"I . . . was wishing Chris would come out and join us."

"Won't she?"

He shook his head.

"Maybe if I find her, talk to her . . . ?"

"No. She hates parties." The look he gave her now was a strange one, almost distraught. In spite of his success, he still seemed to her to carry this air of being a man lost, a little boy lost, and it touched her very deeply. So far she had managed to keep her feeling for him on a fairly even keel; they had come together out of a mutual need, and that need was still there; the meeting of their bodies was beautiful and gentle and satisfying; but now, for the first time, she felt a fear of actually falling in love with him, even of actually *being* in love with him, and a deep instinct told her that this was not wise—not now, not yet.

Almost as if he sensed this thought in her, as if he wanted to pour a little cold water on it, he said, "And I was wishing . . . You'll think I'm crazy. I was wishing that Holly could be here, but of course she'd never come, and she'd hate it if she did."

He had been quite honest with her about Holly, and partially honest with her about the Jeff Kenny whom Holly had presented to him; he had wanted to test her reaction, wanted her to tell him how much, in that case, Jeff Kenny had changed. This, bless her, was exactly what she had done.

"You, and the kid, and Holly. It's funny, you're the only three who seem . . . real to me. Really real." This honesty (as near as he could get to honesty) seemed to make the dismal past recede a pace or two into the elegantly designed shadows of Virginia Kenny's water garden. Rose's face at least became more substantial than the wan faces of his sister and his young brother. He made an extreme effort to banish them altogether. "When do you pick up your Rolls-Royce?"

"I wouldn't have a Rolls if you paid me. Everybody in them, even young people, look as if they're on their way to their own funerals."

"You never know. You're going to be a famous actress." He leaned over in the darkness and kissed her lightly. He knew nothing about love, it had never entered his life; he was the kind of man who, after sleeping for a long time with one woman, might suddenly find that he couldn't do without her; and that, for such a man, is love.

185

She said, "We'd better go back. It's your party."

He gestured towards the parakeet chatter above them on the terrace. "They're doing just fine without me." But they went back, slowly, hand in hand up the wide steps. On the way she said, "It's going to be pale yellow, my Beetle. Pale kind of creamy yellow with brown seats."

He laughed. Her choice of car still struck him as funny. Neither of them could know that this Volkswagen, already waiting for her at the dealer's among a hundred others, was Nemesis. He had thought to find Providence in a snake, not understanding that Providence is never where you look for it. Providence and Nemesis, fatal sisters, were already sitting side by side in the back seat of a small German car, waiting for someone to take the wheel and drive them to a certain destination they already had in mind.

Perhaps five minutes after they had rejoined the party something quite incredible happened; it started with a sudden silence from the direction of the house, followed by a sudden burst of chatter. He turned to see what was going on. Rose turned. Virginia, just beyond them, turned in a turning of heads. At first they saw nothing unusual, but then people moved at the edge of the pool, and there was Murray walking forward with an outstretched hand and a wide smile on his ugly face—walking forward to welcome the new guest. It was Joanne Christina, and the good Lord alone knew what soul-searching and doubts, hesitations and final decisions, had gone into this materialization. She had tied back her straggly hair with a brown ribbon, and she was wearing . . . He heard Virginia let out a slow, soft gasp. She was wearing the coffee-colored caftan embroidered with gold thread which Murray had brought her from Morocco. She took Murray's hand and came forward, shy but determined, awkward but beautiful.

The sand-colored man known as Clifford worked for a real estate agency in the San Fernando Valley. The attitude towards him of the other people in the office was also monochromatic: nobody liked him very much and nobody disliked him very much. As far as his employers were concerned, he was trustworthy and reliable: others came and went; Clifford stayed. If it ever struck them, or anyone else, that nobody could be quite as blank, reliable and trustworthy as that without having something to hide, they disregarded the thought, which thereupon faded and expired.

On this Monday morning when Clifford slid quietly into his boss's office and announced that he had four properties to show, and some private business which needed attention, his boss did not question the fact that he wouldn't be seeing Clifford for the rest of the day; neither did he notice that though Clifford had four properties to show, he nevertheless took five keys from their hooks.

He drove a small and unremarkable Toyota, dim grey in color. His first action after leaving the office was to go to his bank in midtown Los Angeles, where he collected, after due ceremonial, a small black strongbox which had been reposing there for some years; this he locked into the trunk of his car. Next he went to a somewhat seedy, but in reality prosperous, camera store on Seventh Street, where he rented various paraphernalia which he also locked into the trunk of his car.

He ate a light lunch with minimum calories and whiled away the time in thought until a few minutes to two; then he drove unhurriedly to the corner of Highland and Melrose, where a most unlikely character was waiting to be picked up: a very large and battered-looking young man in his late twenties who answered to the name of Bart, but only answered to it if the name was shouted very loud, because he was hard of hearing.

There is nowhere quite so suitable for shouting instructions to a slightly deaf person as a car caught in the midst of the Los Angeles lunchtime rush hour, so the man known as Clifford turned on the radio and shouted loud and long, only pausing at traffic lights when other cars drew up alongside the Toyota. By the time he had finished they were driving up Laurel Canyon—into Lookout Mountain—up to the top of it—then left, then right, then left and left again until they were well and truly entangled in the warren of hilltop roads which wend their way in and out of the heights above Sunset Boulevard.

Eventually they executed an abrupt left turn into a perilously steep driveway and came to a halt. The two men took everything from the trunk and carried it up a steep flight of steps and onto a wide patio, ducking under clumps of leaning bamboo. With the real-estate part of his mind, perhaps an eighth of the whole, Clifford made a mental note to get the place tidied up a little before he had to show it to the next possible buyer. Not that there was much chance of selling it the way things were at present; it was too large and too remote—the one-time escape fantasy of a one-time successful film producer, who had just been able to live in it for a week or two before Twentieth Century-Fox, his employers, had foundered for the umpteenth time, leaving him on the breadline. The patio commanded a tremendous view south and west, but at the moment, since the basin was full of yellow layers of smog, it was not very impressive.

Inside, the empty house was desolate and forlorn. The floor of the hall had developed a slight tilt, result of an earth tremor possibly, or of the humbler but unceasing work of gophers.

The man called Clifford tried an electric-light switch and was pleased to see that the company had acted with its usual speed and efficiency following the call he had made to them, in the agency's name, the night before: power had been reconnected. He put the strongbox down on the floor and unlocked it; the sight of its contents affected him with such violence that he curtly ordered Bart out of the room and onto the patio; it was not his habit to show strong emotion in front of other people.

When the big man had gone, he rested a hand on each side of the open box and leaned there for quite a long time, his eyes closed; this kneeling attitude gave the impression of earnest prayer, but he did not believe in prayer, he believed in hard work, self-discipline and meticulous attention to detail. When he felt sure that he was in complete control of himself again, he began to sort out the contents of the box. It did not strike him as odd that after all this time he could remember the details of every single article it contained. He had cultivated his memory; it was one of the things which accounted for his success, even in that dull eighth of his being which was concerned with real estate. As for the other seven-eighths . . . He permitted himself a small smile as he began to arrange the contents of the box in neat stacks on the bare floor.

Rose was absolutely delighted with her Volkswagen. The pale cowslip-yellow was almost her favorite color, and she had by now recovered from the delightful shock of finding that the check he had given her to pay for it was much too large. Her first and immediate reaction on taking the wheel was to drive the adorable object up to Number 234 and show him its perfection. The sisters Providence and Nemesis sat quietly in the back seat, invisibly biding their time, which was to come as the traffic lights on Sunset, just before the Beverly Hills Hotel, turned red at her approach. Rose brought her darling to a gentle stop; at the same moment, among the cross-traffic released by the lights, she saw him drive by, not twenty feet away, heading south towards Santa Monica Boulevard. He was not lording it in his magnificent Ferrari, but sat hunched up inside the Mini-Cooper which Virginia and her manservant used for shopping.

Rose had no intention of allowing her thanks and her proud demonstration of the gift to be deflected by mere chance. When the lights changed, she broke several absolute rules of the road by veering over to the left lane amid a fanfare of horns; she was thus able to make a left turn and give chase. But despite the movies, it is not easy to catch up with another car in a busy city, particularly if the other car is a specially designed and surprisingly fast little object like a Mini-Cooper, and it soon became obvious to Rose that if she wanted to speak to him, she'd have to wait until he came to a final standstill. But he showed no sign of coming to a standstill, and after a few miles the excitement of the chase began to pall on Rose—or rather, to be more exact, it subtly changed its form; she realized that the sensible thing to do would be to turn around and go home, visit the market, iron the dress which she planned to wear this evening when he was taking her out to dinner.

Why didn't she take the sensible course? Could it be because curiosity had crept in somewhere? Following a man out of curiosity was not at all the same thing as following a man out of desire to give him a kiss and say thank you.

Come to think of it, why was he driving that funny little car anyway? Why not the Ferrari, of which he was so proud? And why was the set of his head and shoulders, when she managed to catch an infrequent glimpse of him, so tense and intent? And where in God's name was he going, leading her past the downtown conglomerate, which she knew only slightly, into a ramshackle and desolate area which she didn't know at all, and which, from the look of it, she never wanted to know.

It seemed that a lot of Mexicans lived here, as well as a number of black people. The white members of the community had about them a look which she was at first unable to place, until, brought to a stop by traffic lights, she was given the opportunity of studying it more closely. A youngish man was standing on the sidewalk with a paper sack of groceries under his arm; she recognized on his face an expression which she had seen often enough in her days as a penniless actress when she had stood in line with the rest of the unemployed to collect whatever aid the state was willing to give them—it was a look of despair, and even in her confident youth she had been able to recognize it as a particular kind of despair which saw no hope at the end of the line.

Uneasiness stirred at the back of her mind but curiosity still dominated the foreground and was more compelling. What was he doing here? It was obvious that he had chosen the Mini because his Ferrari would have attracted too much attention in these parts, would indeed have been thoughtlessly ostentatious.

They drove on, turning off the main street into a decayed and sagging residential area where the tottering houses had about them the particular dead, dusty air which unloved and unre-paired dwellings so quickly acquire in hot climates. These looked as though they had never been loved, never repaired, since that sad day in the late twenties or early thirties when building had been completed. They sat amid littered dust in a wasteland. Had there ever been grass, a tree? If the man at the traffic lights had been carrying his groceries back to one of these, no wonder his face had expressed quiet despair without hope.

The Mini-Cooper was slowing down. Was this . . . could this conceivably be his destination? Out of the uneasiness at the back of her mind crept the thought that perhaps this joyless street had meant something to him during the time when he had wandered aimlessly, with no memory, following his release from the Aldington Institute. Yes, perhaps that was it.

In the full and ashamed knowledge that she was now spying on him (there was no other word for it), she drew her car up against the curb some three hundred yards behind him in the lee of a big broken-down old Chevrolet. What was he doing now?

He was sitting in the tiny car, one arm resting on the open window, the hand pressed to his mouth. He was staring across the dusty, potholed street at the miserable dwelling where he had spent his youth. He didn't know what had driven him to come back here; perhaps it had been inevitable from that very first moment, so many months ago, when he had once again clapped eyes on Los Angeles from the driving seat of the battered pickup. No, he had barely thought of this wretched place in those days; his eyes had been fixed in obsession on one single point far away on a distant horizon. Only since he had reached that point, only since he had become Jeff Kenny with all that becoming Jeff Kenny implied, had he begun to feel this urge. Only last night, in the middle of the party which had marked his hour of triumph, had he known that his plain sister, Fran, in her torn dress, and his small brother, Joseph, in his hand-me-down sweater, had been calling him back here. But for what?

The miserable house taunted him, with its peeling paint, patched stucco, staggering fence, its patch of dust scattered with old beer cans, scraps of waste plastic, pieces of cheap broken toys. What ghost did he think he was going to lay to eternal rest by coming back here? His own?

He shook his head, gazing with a leaden heart at the door out of which he had emerged daily on his lagging way to school, out of which his father had thrown him bodily more than once, out of which his mother had tiptoed that early morning when she had abandoned them all for good, out of which he himself had set forth into an uncaring world with twenty-five dollars stolen from the pocket of a dying man.

Staring at it, he felt the upward thrust of tears, but no tears came to his eyes; he had wept once for all this, lying in the soft arms of a girl, and once was enough, too much. But then, before he could stop it, before he could even recognize what it was, he was seized by an emotion more terrible than any tears, an emotion so appalling and so unexpected that his head jerked upwards as though he had been hit. *Regret?*

Jesus Christ, no—that was impossible! There was nothing to regret here in this scabrous disgusting dump, not one single solitary thing!

But the quiet yet wounding pang persisted and would not be banished by mere anger. If his mother had been a different woman, if his father had never hit the bottle . . .

If, if! The word only made him angrier. But where was young Joseph now? And why had he never answered Fran's letter from San Diego?

All right. *If* things had been different, he would never have hit his father back, never have taken those twenty-five bucks (following that council with his brother and sister in the dusty yard), never have walked out into a bum's life where, six years later, he would kill a man by putting a dirty piece of sacking over his face, where, ten years after that, he would have twenty-five thousand dollars in his checking account and all the rest of the crap that went with it. He would never have killed the rattlesnake.

In anger he would have liked to get out of the little car, cross the street, walk in through the front gate of that obscene house with all its obscene memories, grab the corner beam between his two hands and shake it so that the stucco would crack and fall away, and the roof would sag in a clatter of breaking tiles, and the whole decayed structure would come thumping down in clouds of rotten dust and a splintering of worm-eaten wood.

Okay, so no ghosts had been laid to rest, but he wasn't sorry he'd come back. Coming back had dealt him the absolute ultimate surprise: he had experienced a pang of regret, a pang of loss, for his own youth. After that, what the hell could surprise him ever again?

Three hundred yards behind him, in the new yellow car which had been his gift, hidden from view behind a bulky old Chevy, realization had suddenly come to Rose; uneasiness had crept out from the back of her mind, conquering curiosity. She had remembered.

192

They were lying side by side in his bed on that first night, at the Sunset Plaza Apartment Hotel, and she was scolding him for his lack of interest in his identity. Didn't he realize, she had said, that his parents might be living within a mile of where they lay, good people grieving for the loss of him. And what had he said in reply? "Or I might have come from the most goddam terrible home you ever knew . . ." Something to the effect that his father might have been a drunk and his mother a tramp, and he might have had to lie awake at night with his brother and sister, listening to his father screwing whatever drunken broad he had managed to pick up in one of the local bars; and . . . yes, she could hear the bitter edge to his voice as he said it: 'We might have lived in some broken-down twenties duplex out on the east side . . . I bet you've never seen East Los Angeles," he had said, "it's a ball-breaker."

A tiny voice of self-interest tried to intervene, telling her that she had no proof, that all this was a ridiculous illogical leap into the dark, that she was out of her mind, that she didn't even know if this godforsaken area *was* East Los Angeles; but the tiny voice held no confidence and was quite unable to stand up to the huge wave of anguish and, yes, horror that towered over her. For after he had spoken, what had he done? He had wept. Nobody, and certainly not that man, wept in the wake of an idle comment. No, he had wept for the truth, and it was the truth that hung above her, falling slowly upon her, threatening to engulf her entire world.

Before she knew quite what she was doing, she was out of the car; she was moving quickly down the sun-scorched uneven sidewalk towards him.

She would have liked to stop. She would have liked to go back to her car, get into it and drive away from this dreadful place and from the even more dreadful thoughts which were already crowding into her mind; but she could not do so—for if he had indeed been born here . . . if he had lied to her . . . if he had used her to . . . The thoughts were unbearable; as yet she couldn't even begin to consider them; she merely knew that she must look into his face and demand an answer—and in the moment of knowing this, she also knew that she had been completely dishonest in her assessment of her feelings for him: she loved him. Love and the demand for his immediate answer were indivisible; one could not live without the other.

When she was perhaps a hundred yards from his car, hidden from him by other shabby vehicles parked along the curb, a woman came out of one of the houses carrying a rug which she began to beat against her fence, dust flying. This sudden activity made him turn, lost in the past and its meaning; he gave the woman a glance, then turned back.

He turned back just as Rose passed the woman and came within his range of vision, but by that time his regard was again fixed on the house across the street. He didn't see her, but she, bending to look into the car, saw him; and what she saw froze her to stone and stilled the hand which had only just begun to move forward to tap on the window. What she saw was his eyes, reflected in the car's rear mirror; they were turned to one side, it was true, for if they had not been turned, they would have been looking directly into her own. They were turned but they were fully visible, and (since he had taken out the tiresome contact lenses, as he usually did when there was no chance of being observed) they were their true cold grey.

For an insane moment she thought that it was all a huge mistake, that she had simply been following the wrong man. Then she backed slowly away, watched the faint interest by the woman, who had finished beating her rag of a carpet; then she turned and ran, stumbling a little, back to her own car. Her invisible passengers had vacated the back seat during her brief absence. Their work was done.

Eight

The telephone call came just after six o'clock that evening. He was already dressed for his date with Rose, wearing one of his magnificent new suits; he was chatting idly with Virginia while Murray fixed them both a drink. From force of habit Virginia lifted the receiver. A quiet well educated man's voice said, "Mrs. Kenny?"

"Yes."

"This is Johnny Adams. I only just heard the news about Jeff, I was . . . Jesus, I was bowled over. Is he there? Any chance of a word with him?"

It was a nice voice, it inspired confidence; also, the deluge of calls had long since dried up; there had only been three others all day. She held out the phone to him, saying quietly, "Adams, Johnny Adams."

He shrugged and took it from her, preparing himself for the usual polite routine. "Hello."

"Jeff? How are you, how's tricks?" There was something about the use of the word "tricks," as well as the intonation placed upon it, that struck a little warning bell somewhere inside him. "Johnny who?"

"Hey, that's a great name, why didn't I think of using it. Johnny Who." Virginia Kenny would not have thought the voice so nice had she been able to hear it now.

He said, "Listen, I'm sorry, but . . . I have this memory problem, you know. I don't seem to be able to place you."

195

"Well, Jeff, I must in all honesty tell you that if I had memories like yours, I'd probably develop a problem myself."

This was danger. His stomach dropped away, but he braced himself and parried the quick thrust of fear. He had prepared himself for this, trained himself over a period of many years; he knew what to do. Aware of Virginia's eyes on him, of Murray coming across the room with a couple of drinks in his hand, he even managed a passable laugh. "No, seriously, I didn't catch your name. Was it Adams?"

"Adams, Ackenbacker, Asshole, call me what you like. We need to meet, we have a couple of things to talk about."

He took the drink which Murray was offering him and forced a good gulp of it into himself. "We do? Like what?"

"Like old times, Jeff. But of course you can't remember old times, can you?"

He was trapped between two possibilities: the first was that the owner of this voice knew nothing worth knowing, was playing a hunch; if so, and if he refused a meeting, the whole problem might melt into thin air; the second was that the owner of this voice knew everything, had been in that first camp, had even been in the same hut, and by some miracle (like the one which had saved his own life) had survived the bombing, and in this case it was vital for them to meet right away. Playing for time, he said, "Look, I have a date this evening, and I . . ."

"Sure you do. With me. So where do we meet and when?"

Virginia and Murray were talking quietly together; he was amazed that his tense anxiety—it was not fear, not yet—hadn't communicated itself to them. He said, "I guess I could fit it in. How about . . . the Beverly Hills Hotel, the Polo Room?"

"Very suitable. To your new image. What time?"

"Say . . . six-thirty."

"Great. And come alone, won't you? No stupid little tricks, you'd be the loser." The line went dead.

As he replaced the receiver, Virginia said, "Who is he, he had such a nice voice?"

"Guy I knew in the Air Force." The answer struck him with its black irony even as it comforted Virginia. For her the Air Force constituted a period of safety and innocence, for him it could only mean disaster.

He finished his drink and went back to his own wing of the house. Needless to say, that damned headache had gripped him with its iron claw; he took a couple of pills before dialing Rose's number. Usually she answered her phone at once, like all actresses for whom the telephone is a lifeline, but on this occasion it continued to ring. He thought that she was possibly in her bath; he couldn't know that she was sitting on the bed, hunched over her drawn-up knees, staring at the shrill instrument with thoughtful eyes. Eventually she lifted the receiver.

"Look, honey, something awkward's happened, I'm afraid I have to call it off tonight. There are these people I have to meet . . ."

Rose wondered whether, within that complicated angling of mirrors and eyes, he could possibly have seen her, bending forward witlessly beside the Mini-Cooper. No, for if he had, he would have reacted straight away; the situation would have been as full of danger for him as it was full of shock for her.

". . . to do with family business, you know how it is."

She didn't know how it was; she didn't know how anything was, not any more, but she said, "Yes, sure."

"I'm terribly sorry, Rose, I'll make it all up to you later."

"It's okay, I . . . have things to do." That was true enough; she wasn't quite sure as yet what those things were, but certainly she had to do them.

He stopped the Ferrari halfway down Coldwater Canyon and lay back in the seat; somehow he must organize his reeling thoughts, consider possible courses of action. In the first place, he was rich enough to be able to pay out large sums in blackmail without being hurt very much; but even as he reasoned in this way, another part of his being rose up in fury for God's sake, he hadn't planned and worked so deviously and cleverly for ten years in order to give away great chunks of the reward to the first rat that came crawling out of the sewer of the past! He thought wistfully of his Luger, locked in a suitcase and hidden away at the back of the closet in his bedroom. Would he use it? No! Why not, he'd already killed once? It was odd how that gentle killing still didn't seem like killing to him. An act of deliverance, a friendly gesture.

Would he kill? Perhaps, if there was no other way out.

He closed his eyes, willing the headache to succumb to the pills he'd taken before leaving the house. The main thing was to relax, to see what it was that faced him, jumping no fences until he reached them. He had fashioned this whole glittering edifice with his own cunning and intelligence; he was a man to be reckoned with, and his adversary, whoever he might be, would do well to consider that.

He felt better. He drove on down the canyon to the hotel, went into the bar and settled at a reasonably private table.

Which of them would it be? Ray, the college boy who had sat daylong in his corner, silent and alone and, some said, half around the bend already? Or tall, rangy Mike, with his Chicago slum background and his quick vicious readiness to pick a fight? Or Sam, with a Texas drawl and a Texas superiority which had so maddened all the other men in . . .

The shock was absolute when the sand-colored individual who called himself Clifford materialized out of the semidarkness of the bar, pulled out a chair and sat down opposite him. His floundering brain told him at once that he didn't know this man at all!

The first reaction was an enormous surge of pure relief. So luck was still on his side, after all, that same luck which had initially demonstrated its friendship by dumping him in the shit-pit. He could have laughed out loud.

Overwhelmed by relief, it was not perhaps surprising that he didn't immediately perceive the meaning or the danger of this non-recognition.

Rose still sat on her bed in the same position, knees drawn up, arms resting on them, chin resting on arms; she had been sitting like that for more than two hours now. Intense thought, intense agitation always affected her in this way; she could not understand people who paced.

It was the eyes which kept coming back to her; somehow the whole problem was contained within those steely grey eyes. (Why had she never noticed the contact lenses? They weren't all that difficult to detect. Why had no one else noticed them? Of course, the Californian addiction to sunglasses must have helped him enormously.) With the eyes, and the shock of seeing them for the first time, had come that agonizing moment of insight—she loved him. Love had been recognized, accepted and extinguished, all within a single minute. Yes, extinguished, for how could she love him now? How could anyone love a man who didn't exist? Or a man who did exist, but who existed elsewhere?

Oh dear God, how right she had been about him on that second evening together! She remembered how she had sensed in him something actorish as well as wily; she remembered how she had rationalized those faint suspicions. (Of course he would appear to be other than he pretended; of course there would seem to be an actorish quality about him, and of course he might even seem to be a liar . . . He *was* other than he pretended, he *was* acting and he *was* lying. Since he had lost his true identity, what else could he possibly do, poor man? Actors had to create parts, and sometimes that seemed a big enough ordeal, but this man was having to create an entire life.)

Oh, Rose, Rose! And you had thought yourself a dumb cow *then!* No wonder the tiny gnome of reason who dwelt inside her had stumped into his little house, slamming the door and locking it behind him!

The wound made his eyes water, did it? Poor darling! It was the bloody contact lenses that made his eyes water, you stupid bitch!

No wonder he had looked at her so sharply, no wonder he had reacted in something like fear, on that occasion when she'd told him that Murray Forde and Virginia Kenny had been checking up on him. ("Dearest *heart*, don't look so stricken. You've just said yourself she's a very rich woman. I think it was his idea, she didn't seem too enthusiastic. He's very fond of her, obviously doesn't want her to make a fool of herself.") Oh yes indeed, no wonder he had looked stricken!

But what an actor! Grudgingly she had to admit it. What about that first scene up at Virginia Kenny's house? What about that bemused half-recognition of the Italian mirror on the staircase, of that pair of Sheraton cabinets? What about the stumbling memories that these had seemed to release? ("A big room, as big as this. Windows overlooking a lake. Oh yes, mountains. The room was . . . Were the walls a kind of . . .

199

golden brown?") Jesus, what a performance—she was forced to admire it in spite of herself.

But what about the knowledge, the rehearsal behind the performance?

Ah yes, this was where the chill thoughts began, the cold questions. If, with his steely and calculating eyes hidden behind contact lenses, he was not Jeff Kenny, who was he? She had seen East Los Angeles now and she knew that he was right. A ball-breaker. Admiration slipped under her guard again; she shook her head in admiration, but turned away from it towards darker things. In order to assume the identity of Jeff Kenny he must have known that Jeff Kenny was dead; and . . . It always came back to the implacable grey eyes. Seeing them, she had known a moment of shock and fear; she could perfectly well believe that this man was capable of killing. If so, who else might be in danger? Who else besides herself?

This thought made her angry, for some reason she couldn't understand. Anger lifted her off the bed and onto her feet.

He had used her as mercilessly and as implacably as he had used the Italian mirror and the twin cabinets. He had angled for her, and hooked her, and set up that situation at the restaurant so that she would act in exactly the way he wanted her to act. Devised, Written and Directed by . . . By whom? X.

Anger pushed her towards the mirror so that she must look at her face. What was it, what the hell *was* it, about this woman confronting her that caused every man she cared for to take a long sharp knife and plunge it, sooner or later, into her back. But none of them had done it quite like this, so coldly, so calculatingly, at the same time using her body as a convenience when it suited him to do so.

It was anger, and perhaps a little self-pity (and who would blame her for that?), which made her throw on a sweater and a pair of jeans, run a comb through her hair, and slam out of the apartment. Only when she saw her Volkswagen sitting out in the street, so innocently yellow, so guiltily given, did she come to a dead stop. Anger suddenly gave way to grief. Yes, she *had* loved him, but what the hell was the good of love now?

The man who called himself Clifford (or Johnny Adams, Ackenbacker or Asshole) said, "Okay, where do we start?"

The man who called himself Jeff Kenny said, "I guess that's up to you." The relief had drained away and the new danger had introduced itself into his brain: if this man had never known him in Vietnam, and that was a fact, he had known him before Vietnam, which meant that it really *was* Jeff Kenny whom this man had known.

With the sense of danger came a quick mental glimpse of the ruined woman who had once been Jeff Kenny's pretty young wife. "Oh yes, it was all kicks for you, wasn't it? Anything was kicks for you, you perverted fucking bastard." It was the echo of that voice which took the sense of danger and turned it into fear; he was beginning to realize that he had been warned, more than once perhaps, and he had ignored the warnings.

In his quiet monotonous voice, with its odd mixture of cruel sarcasm and dreary dispassion, the monochromatic man opposite him said, "I hold all the evidence about you and Marianna. All we have to decide is just how much you're going to pay to stop me sending it to the police."

What was it about this character, his voice, his whole attitude? Who did it all remind him of, and why? Cautiously he said, "I . . . This loss of memory, it's . . . it's no act, you know. There are whole areas I really can't remember."

The pale uninvolved eyes rested on his face and studied it carefully; there was no way of telling whether he believed the lie or not. "You've managed to remember a couple of things since your mother recognized you in that restaurant."

"Not at first. Only when she . . . she and other people reminded me." He knew the reply he was asking for, knew that however appalling it might be, he had to ask for it. It came: "Then *I'm* going to have to remind you too, aren't I, Jeffty?"

Anything might be going to happen now. He tried hard to prevent his imagination from making wild guesses; he tried to let his brain rest, because he knew that before very long he was going to need all the energy and cunning that it could produce. Guessing—that this man had known him in Vietnam—had already exhausted him once; he must learn from that mistake. Wait and see, that was the watchword now. Wait and see, and then think and wait again, and *then* act after due consideration.

They had taken his car ("It's not every day that people like me get a ride in a Ferrari, Jeff") and they had driven up Laurel Canyon, up Lookout Mountain, into the hills, which he didn't know. "Make a left. Make a right. Make another right. Left at the next stop sign, then fork right."

He took it easy, slow, giving himself time for rest, composure. But who *was* it this dusty individual reminded him of so strongly?

"Okay. Another two hundred yards, where that tree hangs out over the road. Right here."

He cut the motor. Silence. Somewhere a mockingbird was imitating a nightingale, raucously. He followed the other man up steep steps and onto the big patio. Visibility had cleared since the morning; a jet could be clearly seen as it came down, winking, towards International Airport some ten miles away. The western part of the city was laid out at their feet in a quivering, flashing pattern of multicolored lights, a fantastic sight.

Clifford knocked on the door, which was opened at once by Bart. He looked slyly at his guest. "Big, isn't he?"

"Yes."

"Professional wrestler. If you see what I mean."

The echoing emptiness of the sprawling house took him by surprise. Clifford gestured him towards the living room, flicking on lights. Bart withdrew. He saw that one corner of the floor was covered with papers and folders. A 16-mm movie projector was perched on an upended black strongbox. He was pleased to discover that he had regained his composure; the conscious effort he had been making ever since they'd left the hotel had not been wasted. But the sense of danger was still there, stronger now, and so was the fear. Wait and see, and then think and wait again, and then act.

The other man had picked up one of the folders; from it he took a photograph, held it out. "Marianna."

Okay, so it was Marianna, a pretty if somewhat zany-looking girl leaning against a wall and smiling. Nothing exceptional; he had rather expected Jeff Kenny to have better taste.

Clifford held out another picture. "Marianna."

His heart contracted and missed a beat. It was undoubtedly the same girl, but she was lying naked on a bed, and it didn't take an expert to see that she was not asleep, she was dead.

"Copy," said Clifford flatly, "of one of the official police photographs."

Something in his eyes as he glanced up must have revealed pure surprise, for the other man looked at him more closely, a long, searching, contemplative look, before saying, "Well, I'll be darned, you *don't* remember her, do you?"

"I told you I don't."

"Mm."

He had just noticed, as people usually did after a while, that the eyes, though so pale a fawnish green, were ringed with an extraordinary dark line; you only noticed this when you were quite close to him, so that only when you were quite close to him did you realize how piercing, all-seeing and totally without feeling the eyes were. This seemed to say something profound about his whole character; he seemed to be saying, "What does it matter how you think of me when I'm far away from you? When I want your attention I shall come nearer, and you will give me your attention."

In silence he held out a sheet of paper.

A cutting from the Los Angeles *Times*; the headline yelled, "Girl Dies at Drug Party." His eyes skipped over the report: ". . . in the Hollywood Hills . . . so far unidentified, the girl was found to be dead by her hostess, Frances (Frankie) Reissler, when she tried to wake her the following morning . . ."

"A nice cover-up," said Clifford calmly. "Don't tell me you can't even remember what it cost you?"

He stared blankly over the press clipping. He was remembering Holly's voice in that cheap rented house a block away from Venice beach: "Oh God, money! That's the key to it all, isn't it? Money buys the kicks and money hushes up the mess, and money keeps the cops quiet, and money socks it to stupid little Holly so she can get stoned again and shut her mouth." Oh yes, he'd been warned all right.

"How . . . How much did Holly know?"

Clifford tut-tutted old-maidishly, shaking his head. "Oh, come on, stop kidding."

"Honest to God, I'm not kidding."

Again the close, piercing stare—followed this time by a sigh, of acceptance perhaps. In a more patient, explanatory voice he said, "Holly didn't know a thing, how could she? You weren't on speaking terms, I don't think you'd even been home in two, three weeks."

He moved away, kneeling to find another press clipping among the neatly arranged piles on the floor. The act of turning his back evidently reminded him of something, for he paused, looking up at the other man. "By the way, in case you should be getting any corny old ideas, there are copies of all this"—indicating the folders and the film already threaded into the projector—"in another strongbox in my bank. Usual thing—they go direct to the police if anything happens to me."

He straightened up with what he'd been looking for. "Frankie Reissler was a good girl; she never split, not even when the pigs grilled her. She covered for you, and I covered for you, and the money did the rest. You were never even mentioned. Look! Look there!"

He looked, and read something about intercourse: "There had been intercourse with a man or men unknown."

"Frankie went back to Germany. I hear she's doing pretty well. Bright girl!" His flat emotionless voice made this sound as if he were discussing the progress of his daughter in high school, prior to the showing of some cozy home movies, for he flicked off the main light and was moving towards the little projector.

The short clip of film was disgusting, but it was roughly what he had by now been led to expect. He'd read that they often took film at those parties in order to get a kick or a laugh out of them later. He wondered what kind of a person would get a kick or a laugh out of this particular film.

Amongst other figures and other rococo details, there was Jeff Kenny staggering about nude with the girl, Marianna, in his arms, also naked of course, both of them obviously stoned out of their minds and Master Kenny with an erection. Then there was a cut to some mercifully muddled shots of legs and buttocks writhing around on a bed, recognizable by the bedspread as the one on which the police later photographed Marianna dead.

The projectionist's voice, unemotional, said, "They didn't find a single fingerprint they could use. Frankie and I did a pretty good job on that. The girls thought your name was Perry, I said you were just a guy I'd met in a bar. Oh yes indeedy, we covered

204

up for you but *good,* mister. Now watch this, I stop-framed it!"

It was a single brief shot, but the stopped frames made it seem endless; they also made everything hideously clear. Jeff Kenny was standing up from the bed, minus erection; as he turned out of frame, grinning with loose-lipped drugged idiocy, the camera held the bed and the girl lying there. Her position was exactly the same as in the police photograph taken the following morning: she was already dead.

Clifford said, "Wouldn't look too good in a court of law, would it?"

The film flickered to an end; he flipped on the lights, and they stood looking at each other in the bare room.

It was not the man himself, not the nauseating revelations, not even the blackmail, that made him feel so weak, drained, unutterably weary; it was that during the course of the film he had suddenly recognized the thing which had been taunting and evading him ever since the man had pulled out a chair and sat down facing him in the hotel bar: he had suddenly realized who it was that the man reminded him of so strongly.

Himself.

All this, the neatly stacked folders, the press clippings, the copies of police photographs, the film, the stop-framing, the empty house, the big man waiting outside the door in case there was trouble, the duplicates in another stronghox, the flat passionless voice, the direct regard of those uncanny eyes—all this indicated painstaking, sometimes dangerous and always methodical hard work, hard planning, hours of careful thought over a long, long period of time.

They differed only in one important respect. This sandy individual had faced a moment of terrifying disaster which had brought all the plans, all the work crashing around him in ruins. Jeff Kenny had been reported killed in Vietnam. My God, what he must have suffered then! And what dizzy ecstasy must have seized him when he had turned a page of yesterday's Sunday *Times* and read those four paragraphs!

"Wouldn't look too good in a court of law, would it?" The voice was not cruel, it held only a trace of ironical pleasure. Like the pale eyes, it was uninvolved, just as he himself had been uninvolved, even in the actual killing of Jeff Kenny. Uninvolved he could hug Jeff Kenny's daughter and kiss Jeff Kenny's mother. We are the uninvolved, he thought, we are the obsessed. But in his mind's eye all he saw was the rattlesnake in that frozen moment of time when its head had turned and its body had coiled to spring at him.

Rose stood between Virginia Kenny and Murray Forde in the middle of the graceful drawing room at 234 Upper Canyon Circle—an iron filing caught between two emotional magnets. She felt very out of place in her scruffy jeans and old sweater, but there was something right and proper about that; it suited her symbolically to be out of place in this dreadful situation which her honesty had created.

The honesty was all she now had to cling to. She had even abandoned her bright new car forever, outside in the carport. On the driver's seat she had placed a strong brown envelope containing the cash left over after its purchase. She intended to go home by cab.

She had told them everything that she knew, quickly and simply, confining herself carefully to facts and omitting any hint of guesswork. It had been a short speech, much shorter than she'd expected, because basically she didn't know very much. The two people had watched her with very differing expressions: Murray had even exploded into exclamations of rage; Virginia remained calm, withdrawn, but in some odd way her face had grown rigid and pinched, showing her age. Rose had realized with a pang that this was the same face she had seen in Scotty's on that other disastrous night. But why not? Why shouldn't the destruction of this second Jeff Kenny produce the same look of anguish as his rebirth?

"I'm sorry," she said, not for the first time. "I'm terribly sorry, but . . . I've been thinking and thinking all afternoon—I don't see that there was anything else I could have done."

"No," said Virginia evenly, but in a shadow of her usual voice, "there . . . there really wasn't anything else you could have done."

Murray found coherent words for the first time. "You . . . you're quite sure?" Rose made a gesture, and he added quickly,

"Oh Jesus, of course you're sure; it's as bad for you as it is for Virginia, you . . ." He looked around the quiet room a trifle wildly. Rose finished the sentence for him: "I loved him. Yes, I think I did."

Virginia Kenny made a small sound which might have been a stifled sob and turned away from them swiftly, leaning on her piano; above it, just over her bent head, hung the portrait of Cass which her son . . . which *he* had so cunningly "recognized" on that first night. She looked up at it as if assimilating all that this gambit implied.

"What a bastard!" said Murray, a kind of admiration, Rose noticed, finding its way into his voice. "What a clever bastard!"

She sighed. "Oh yes, he was clever all right."

"Well, he won't feel so clever when he walks back into this house and comes face to face with the police." He moved quickly across the room towards the telephone.

Without turning, Virginia Kenny said, "No, Murray."

"But . . ."

"*No!*" She abandoned the examination of her husband's portrait and looked over her shoulder at the big exasperated man behind her; her face was as hard as her voice.

Murray exploded again: "For God's sake, Virginia, the guy's a criminal, he was after your money."

"That had occurred to me."

The acid sarcasm might have discouraged a lesser man than Murray Forde. "But he worked on this thing, he planned it all cold-bloodedly. How come he knew so much about Jeff? How come he . . .?"

"They were prisoners-of-war together, that's obvious."

Rose was fascinated by this defense of him, it could hardly be called anything else, coming from another woman he had victimized. Murray was obviously infuriated by it. "And what about Jeff's medallion? How come he got his hands on that?"

Virginia Kenny nodded. Rose was remembering how she had pulled that medallion from under his shirt, in the private room at Scotty's, remembering how, at the sight of it, this woman had slid from her chair in a dead faint. Virginia nodded again. "Yes, there are . . . there are a lot of questions he's going to have to answer." She looked up at the angry man. "But *we're* going to ask them, not the police."

"Don't be a fool, Virginia! He won't answer *us,* he'll . . ."

"Not the police!"

"He's taken us all for a ride once, and he'll do it again. What's the matter with you? Can't you understand the kind of man we're up against."

"Better than you, maybe."

"It's our duty as citizens . . ."

"Nonsense, Murray! And stop shouting, you'll wake Chris."

"No he won't, I'm here." The clear young voice made them all turn, startled: adults caught at their games. She came in from the shadowy hall, barefooted, wearing her pajamas.

Angrily, Virginia said, "How long have you been out there?"

"I heard it all, if that's what you mean." The once-untidy hair was nowadays held back with a ribbon or, for more practical purposes, a shoelace. This, plus the absence of the once-ubiquitous sunglasses, left the amazing eyes unscreened in any way. They passed over her suddenly aged grandmother, over apoplectic Murray, and settled on Rose, who felt a desire to flinch before their blazing brilliance and their unmistakable contempt.

"Golly," she said, "how stupid can you get!"

"Chris, go back to bed, I'll talk to you later."

She ignored her grandmother absolutely. "You say you loved him, why couldn't you keep quiet like me? *I* knew he was a phony ages and ages ago."

There was, there had to be, a stunned silence. Virginia managed to say, "You . . . knew!"

"Of course. I searched his room the second day he was here."

"You . . . ?"

"Everybody searches everybody's room, don't they? I know you search mine."

Virginia said, "Chris, I never . . ."

"When you found that silly book Lorene lent me, with all the positions in it."

Silence.

"I searched his room and there they were, hidden away inside a rolled-up pair of socks. I hide things in socks too."

"What . . . what was hidden?"

"His second pair of contact lenses, of course. Brown ones. I didn't know you could get them colored." She looked back at Rose. "All adults are dumb, I guess, but you . . ." She shook her head. "You take the prize!"

Virginia decided it was high time for decisive action: she moved forward from the piano. "Don't be rude, Chris. Rose acted the only honest way she could."

Perhaps they had none of them appreciated the rage that was in the small girl; she evaded her grandmother with ease and shouted, "Honest! Why do you all talk such a load of crap? What difference does it make if he isn't my real father as long as we all loved him?"

Virginia looked helplessly at Murray, who turned on the enraged child.

"You keep away from me, you old crumb! You wouldn't even know a rattler if you *stepped* on one!" She vaulted nimbly over a large sofa, thus putting it between her and the forces of the adult world. Leaning on the back of it, she shouted, "Why do you always have to destroy things? As soon as you get hold of anything nice, anything good, you can't wait until you've killed it stone-dead. And don't talk to me about honest, you don't know honest from shit, not one of you.

"Okay, I'm going." This last to forestall Virginia, who was just opening her mouth to speak.

They watched her trail away across the hall, stumbling once over her pajamas, which had come down a little during the acrobatics. They watched her in silence as she went slowly upstairs to darkness.

The silence lasted a long time. Virginia had turned once more to the piano, studying the keyboard, lost in her own thoughts. Murray said haltingly, "You don't think . . . She *can't* have known."

Not turning, Virginia sighed. "Oh yes, she knew. If she said so, it's the truth."

Murray looked longing at the telephone, then at Rose. He felt that some sort of apology was called for, and since Virginia seemed disinclined to make it . . . "I'm sorry. The kid's upset. I guess she . . . liked him a lot."

Virginia spoke to the keyboard. "We all liked him a lot. Even you, Murray." She reached out with one finger and struck middle C, as if this center of all harmony might bring harmony back into the room, into their lives.

He had no idea, later, where he drove after leaving the empty house up in the hills. Twisting roads led him down onto Sunset, and some time later he was passing one of the gates to Bel Air. He was dimly aware of U.C.L.A. buildings, of a good deal of traffic in Westwood, and then it seemed that he was somewhere in Culver City, heading south.

His thoughts were similarly directionless, and wherever they wandered they led him back to one point, just as the Ferrari was now leading him back to Coldwater Canyon. This one point was very simple: he was trapped. Trapped by that emotionless and formidable sand-colored man, trapped by his own thoroughness and cunning, which had made him into Jeff Kenny, and trapped by Kenny himself, who had never for one instant been the man he imagined him to be.

There was no point in driving aimlessly around like this, no point in thinking, seeking to find a way out—no way out existed; he had been beaten at his own game. All that he had to do now was to collect two hundred and fifty thousand dollars by midday tomorrow, the first of four payments, put the money in a document case and deliver it to the sand-colored man in the bar at the Beverly Hilton.

Why hadn't he brought a couple of those pills with him; his head was splitting in half; it felt as though a demon wearing an iron glove was gripping the back of his neck from the seat behind him. He was seized by alternate fevers of raging fury and aching helplessness.

Lost in this limbo, he did not immediately recognize the figure that suddenly materialized in the beam of the headlights halfway up the canyon, peering anxiously, and then, as the car passed under a streetlamp and was clearly visible, signaling him frantically to stop. Chris, wearing jeans and a windbreaker.

He jerked himself back to the immediate present and its problems, desperately trying to recapture his Jeff Kenny persona as he braked to a standstill, opened the passenger door and called out, in suitable surprise he hoped, "Hi! What the hell do you think you're up to, you should be in bed?"

Joanne Christina didn't reply; she turned to the bushes beside the road and heaved out of them a suitcase—one of his own suitcases—which she flung into the back seat before tumbling in beside him and gasping, "Drive! Don't go home!" Her desperate urgency communicated itself to him right away. "What are you talking about?"

As they drove on up the canyon towards Mulholland, Joanne Christina told him what she was talking about.

In her elegant drawing room at Number 234 Upper Canyon Circle, Virginia Kenny had turned at last from her silent scrutiny of the keyboard. Rose had sat down on the arm of a chair and was knocking back the vast brandy which Murray had thrust at her; tentatively he offered one to Virginia, but she shook her head. It seemed to her that at this moment she needed very much to be herself, wholly herself; all the trouble of her entire life had possibly been caused by not being herself, but perhaps this could be said of anyone; it *had* been said, in better words than she could form. "What was it, in Shakespeare? 'To thine own self be true . . .'"

She looked at Rose, ignoring Murray, who was staring at her as if she'd taken leave of her senses.

"'To thine own self be true, and it must follow as the night the day thou cans't not then be false to any man.'"

Virginia nodded. "In a way, a way she probably didn't understand and a way I don't think I understand myself, Chris was right."

Round-eyed, Murray gasped, "Don't tell me *you* knew he wasn't Jeff!"

"I knew nothing." Only Rose had noticed the very faint emphasis she had placed on the word "knew," but then, only Rose would understand it. Virginia searched her mind, and in all honesty, even in the honesty of Joanne Christina, she could find no knowledge of the fact that he hadn't been her son . . . But?

"But in a way what happened was my fault . . . No, please, Murray, let me say this, it's very important to me to say this." She pressed fine, long fingers to her forehead, as if they might draw from it the thoughts she so badly needed to express. "I wanted him back too much. I never would believe that he was dead. I wanted him back for selfish reasons, and in a way . . . in a way, I was asking for what I got."

Murray could contain himself no longer. "This is plain stupid, Virginia, blaming yourself because . . ."

"For Christ's sake, Murray, let me get it out, let me get it all out now, while I can." There was anguish in this which silenced him.

"I *am* blaming myself because my reasons were selfish, don't you see that? I was . . . I was guilty, and I wanted to wipe out the guilt—we all want to wipe out our guilt." She could see from their faces that this meant nothing to them; she forced herself to explain, without knowing why the explanation was so vital to her. "I spoiled him when he was a boy; I gave him everything he wanted, everything that didn't matter, but I . . . I held back love. I loved his father too much, there was none left for Jeff. And so . . ." She sighed deeply, spreading her beautiful hands. "I was responsible for what he became—for the things he did later."

She glanced at Rose. "Murray already knows that he wasn't always a good boy. No, no—I must say exactly what I mean; he was bad, he could be"—it cost her a great effort, but she managed to say it—"evil."

Rose could see that Murray, loyal and loving Murray, was about to burst out again. To prevent him, she said gently, "I understand. But you *were* true to yourself."

Virginia shook her head. "I was true to what suited me."

Rose thought, Aren't we all? but did not say it. She hadn't quite realized the depth of the older woman's honesty.

Virginia said, "I have to tell you this, you'll see why in a moment. Jeff was selfish, self-centered, he had too much money, he'd do anything for kicks. I suppose the . . . the drug scene was inevitable. There was this party. A girl died."

Murray exclaimed under his breath, and she gave him a quick look. "You didn't know? I was never sure. That's the horror of it, you're never sure who knows what. Jeff killed her, there's no doubt of that. Not intentionally. He was . . . freaked-out." She used the expression with enormous distaste. "He paid a lot of money to certain people who . . . covered up for him."

She turned, again leaning on the piano as if unable to let them see her face now that she had come to the crux. "I never blamed him—it was so much my fault. I suppose that's why I wouldn't believe that he was dead, why I wanted him back. I wanted to make everything all right between us, I wanted to give him the love I'd never given him before. And when he *came* back, like that, back from the dead, with no memory of all those appalling things he'd done, no memory of the person he'd been . . ." She did not have to finish the sentence; it had obviously seemed like the answer to a prayer. "And yet," she said, "I was afraid. I was terrified that he'd remember everything; go back to being . . . what he was."

She looked around at them; it was the face of an old woman. She said, "Sometimes I think God answers our prayers just to show us how selfish we really are." She pushed herself away from the piano and moved towards Rose. "I'm saying something despicable—do you know what it is?"

Rose nodded. "You're glad it wasn't your son who came back—you're glad he was . . . an impostor."

Virginia put both hands to her cheeks and held them tightly. "My God, what does that make me? But it's true. When you came in here and told us that . . . incredible story, I . . . I should have burst into tears, I should have felt my heart breaking inside me, but I didn't. I felt . . . I only felt an appalling sense of relief."

Rose glanced away abruptly. The older woman put out a hand, hesitated, and then touched the young face gently, turning it back so that she could see it, so that their eyes must meet. "I'm sorry," she said. "I'm deeply sorry you loved him. Don't blame yourself, he was . . . lovable. Unlike my son."

After a moment she looked at Murray. "Now do you see why we won't call the police? And I hope, I dare to hope, that we'll none of us ever mention this to anyone else."

Quietly, almost unbelievingly, Murray said, "Let him get away with it!"

"Yes."

"But people will think . . ."

"People will think what I tell them—that Jeff is coming to Europe with us."

The big man's head jerked up, eyes wide. Virginia Kenny smiled. "Oh yes, Murray, Chris and I will be leaving with you on Thursday."

He had parked the Ferrari at the exact spot on Mulholland where he had so often parked his old pickup while he spied on 234 Upper Canyon Circle far below. Chris studied his face in the reflected cloud-glow of the city's billion lights. She said, "I had to hurry, I just packed a few things I knew you'd need, like your razor and your headache pills, your nice leather coat, some pants, shirts. I think I remembered shoes."

He nodded, withdrawn, distant, his face grim.

He didn't blame Rose for what she'd done. That was the kind of girl she was; that was why she'd been the right girl for his plan; and in a sense he was glad that he *hadn't* seen her when she had so unfortunately seen him, staring, without contact lenses, at the house where he'd lived as a child.

Some memory of Fran and young Joseph had drawn him back there, and he'd wondered why. Had they drawn him back for Rose to see him? That was a wry thought. It was wry, too, that in gazing at the ramshackle house with loathing, he had known (perhaps at the very moment of Rose's seeing him) a pang of regret for his lost youth. And all the time, unknown, unknowing and apart, the sand-colored man had been quietly going about his own business. There had to be more than coincidence in that collection of circumstances. Perhaps one day in the future it would all be plain to him, the whole pattern. Somehow he doubted it.

On consideration, it was a good thing for all of them that he hadn't caught sight of Rose at her moment of seeing him without his contact lenses; for if he *had* seen her, he might have been driven to silence her, and how cruel, as well as disastrously unnecessary, that would have been in view of what the sand-colored man was about to produce out of the conjuror's hat!

He turned his head and looked at the small girl beside him. "They're not putting the police on to me?"

"Uh-huh. She said no and she meant no."

"I wonder why not."

"She'd look such a clunk," replied Chris practically, hitting on a truth, but in her innocence on only part of a truth. "What will you do, where will you go?"

He shrugged, studying the smooth, almost beautiful face. It was no good feeling pangs now; long ago he had accepted the fact that this child and Rose meant something special to him, something he had never before known; he wasn't the first man to sacrifice love on the altar of expediency, and to suffer contortions of the stomach, too late, for having done so. He had wept for his youth sixteen years later; perhaps it would be sixteen years before he could weep for what he had done here. Right now, all that he could say, in a voice which was not quite steady, was, "You're a great girl, Chris. Some man's going to be lucky."

She glanced away. "What I'd like best would be to come with you, but . . ." He recognized in the phrasing of this the same acceptance of realities as he felt himself. No passionate and childish cry of "Take me with you!" from this child. He took her small, soft unformed hand. "We had some good times."

"Oh yes."

He knew that she was thinking in particular of the desert, their day of the rattlesnake. He remembered now that as he had stood in that sun-blasted ravine awaiting his moment to strike, it had come to him that he was actually balancing all that he was, and all that he'd become, against the possibility of the snake twisting on him like a whiplash to fasten its fangs into his unprotected leg above the boot; it had seemed to him that he was asking Providence a question by means of the snake, a question to which he'd received no answer. Now it occurred to him that he'd been wrong; an answer had been given in the shape of Rose and the sand-colored man. He was sorry that he'd had to kill the snake.

Chris said, "Here—it's money."

He looked at the brown envelope which she was holding out

to him. "Rose left her car behind; you know, the one you gave her, the VW. This was on the seat."

He smiled, shaking his head. Oh, Rose, Rose! He hoped that in the end Virginia would force her to retrieve the little car. As for the brown envelope, he knew exactly how much it contained. "Thanks. Just what I need." (It was a pity he couldn't make one last visit to the Jeff Kenny bank account, but no doubt it was closed to him already.)

"Maybe," she said, "maybe we'll meet again one day. I mean, people do. Sometimes."

"Sometimes."

Their eyes met, bright blue eyes and bright grey eyes, both so aware of life's fallibility. "Sometimes" was as near as either of them could honestly get to certainty.

He let the car coast quietly down the canyon, bringing it to a silent stop a little beyond the entrance to Upper Canyon Circle. They looked at each other again, a long and searching look; then Chris got out of the car; then she turned back to him. "I forgot to ask. Was it you, with a beard, who followed me that day down at Malibu?"

"Yes."

"I thought so."

"Chris, why did you search my room? Didn't you trust me?"

"I never trust anybody."

"Not a bad idea."

"What I mean is, trusting people has nothing to do with loving them or anything. I loved you just as much, more, when I knew you were a phony."

Again they exchanged a long look of understanding.

"Goodbye, Chris."

" 'Bye. And good luck."

He released the brake and the car slid away down the hill. Chris waved to him before disappearing into darkness. She had already noticed that there were far too many lighted windows in the house for this time of night; the reception committee was lined up in there, waiting for him, waiting for the answers to all those complicated and unnecessary adult questions which they had planned to ask.

Caught between the implacable authority of the house and the aching void left by the departing car, she felt suddenly unable to move. Now that he had gone, the reality of his going struck her with full force, and a black tide of loss welled up inside her, threatening to explode into tears. Standing alone on the shadowy drive, she fought this tide down inch by inch, exerting every scrap of her already considerable will. That she finally won this battle was the ultimate proof of how much she had grown up during the past few weeks. After all, tears would have completely ruined the confrontation that awaited her. With tears, she would simply be a little girl come home at last out of the night; without tears, she would be Joanne Christina Kenny —and she couldn't wait to see the expression on their faces when the door opened and she walked into their little trap. Alone.

In the brown envelope he found $1,745. In his pocket he had $120 and a few cents. Total, $1,865.

He smiled, realizing that he now possessed almost exactly the same amount of money he'd had on the day he returned from Denver to embark on the final stage of his Jeff Kenny impersonation. Ten dollars' difference. Call it the price of experience, a very small price to pay. After all, only an infinitesimal twist of chance had saved him from having to stand trial as a fraud and possibly a murderer; but then, only an infinitesimal twist of chance had decreed that of all the men in the world, it should be Jeff Kenny that he physically resembled, and that Jeff Kenny should be, of all the men in the world, the *wrong* man to resemble.

How dumb he'd been! Poor ruined Holly had warned him in words of one syllable, and he'd ignored her, just as he'd ignored a dozen other warnings; it had taken that loathsome flicker of film on the wall of a deserted house to prove to him that not only was failure a foregone conclusion, but also a blessed release from the terrible prison of Kenny's past.

Rose hadn't betrayed him; true to the end, she'd saved his bacon—and so, in a way, had that sand-colored bastard who would be waiting for him at midday in the bar of the Beverly Hilton.

He derived a very subtle satisfaction from the look on Clifford's face when he walked into the bar at twelve exactly, as planned, but not, as planned, carrying the document case containing his first payment of a quarter of a million dollars. Watching the pale eyes as they narrowed and widened again, watching the sudden rigidity of the featureless beige face, he experienced a moment of total triumph which was as satisfying as anything he'd ever known. This was not the only man who could topple a carefully built construction of faultless plans and immaculate preparations, who could trample an overruling obsession into the dust.

In a tight little voice that only just contained his rage and (oh yes, no doubt about it) his fear, Clifford managed to say, "Where is it?"

"Where's what?" He took off his sunglasses.

The effect was even more spectacular than he'd expected. At the sight of those cold grey eyes which were so very definitely not the eyes of Jeff Kenny, whatever the rest of the face might imply, the sand-colored man let out an instinctive gasp of pure astonishment; one pale hand flew to his chest, revealing that the shock had induced a satisfactory and perhaps quite violent reaction from his heart.

He stood up, enjoying all this, and added, "So you can junk your little strongbox of tricks, Mr. Adams, Ackenbacker or Asshole, it's no good to you now."

"Who . . . who the hell are you?"

"Let's just say I'm not your old friend Jeff Kenny. He's dead."

He drove away from the hotel, away from Los Angeles, heading southeast but not yet sure where he wanted to go. For the first time in ten years he felt free, because for the first time in ten years a dead weight of obsession had been lifted from his mind.

Later, driving through the desert, he remembered the medallion which still hung around his neck; he'd meant to ask the child to give it to her grandmother but was glad now that he hadn't done so; everything it represented was best forgotten.

He took it off and flung it with all his strength out into the desert. Somebody might find it, or it might lie there until the dust of time covered it—a golden eye staring into the golden eye of the sun, a peace offering to the rattlesnakes.

218

About the Author

Philip Loraine is a pseudonym. Under his real name, this writer has produced a number of other novels, film scripts, etc. In fact, shooting has recently finished on his screenplay based on the Loraine novel *WIL One to Curtis*. The movie, as yet untitled, will be released in the fall. He is now at work on an adaptation for the screen of yet another Loraine novel, *Photographs Have Been Sent to Your Wife*.

He has spent most of the last eighteen years visiting or living in some two dozen countries (including five years in California). He finds that the more he travels the less he knows where he would finally like to settle down, but he readily admits that in the end living out of a suitcase becomes a bore.

Apart (obviously) from travel, he likes writing, the sun, painting, when he has time, and music of all kinds. He feels that his *dislikes* are, in common with anyone else's, not really very important; however, the older he gets the more he is inclined to agree with the poet—that while most prospects really do tend to please, man, by and large, really does tend to be vile.